Johnny Montana

JOHNNY MONTANA

A WESTERN STORY

MICHAEL ZIMMER

FIVE STAR
A part of Gale, Cengage Learning

Detroit • New York • San Francisco • New Haven, Conn • Waterville, Maine • London

Set in 11 pt. Plantin.

LIBRARY OF CONGRESS CATALOGING-IN-PUBLICATION DATA

Zimmer, Michael, 1955–.
Johnny Montana : a western story / by Michael Zimmer. — 1st ed.
p. cm.
ISBN-13: 978-1-59414-831-6 (alk. paper)
ISBN-10: 1-59414-831-7 (alk. paper)
1. Gold miners—Fiction. I. Title.
PS3576.I467J64 2010
813′.54—dc22 2010003742

First Edition. First Printing: May 2010.
Published in 2010 in conjunction with Golden West Literary Agency.

Printed in the United States of America
1 2 3 4 5 6 7 14 13 12 11 10

Johnny Montana

Chapter One

"Someone's coming, Johnny."

In the cavern-like darkness of the dug-out above Redhawk Creek, John Owens paused in his search for winter gloves. The warning had come from outside, spoken softly, yet with an urgency that made his scalp crawl. Leaving his packs where they lay, Johnny edged toward the dug-out's low door. It was brighter outside, but not by much. A few stars glittered in the east, while to the southwest the purpling light of sunset silhouetted the tall pines across the cañon. To the west, the snowy crown of the Ruby Range shone with a faint, crimson glow.

Several yards in front of the dug-out, the supper fire crackled pleasantly. Its flames had grown small while the men relaxed with their pipes before turning in for the night. Russ Bailey sat alone beside the low blaze, solid, broad-shouldered, his round cheeks above a full beard catching the light from the fire like a pair of polished apples. Russ had been staring drowsily into the flames when Johnny ducked inside the dug-out for his gloves. Now his head was up, his eyes fixed alertly on the edge of the small flat where Andy Tabor was staring into the gulch below.

The little piece of flat ground was theirs, part of the claim they'd staked out last spring when they'd first come to the Redhawk Mining District of southwestern Montana. From it, they could see the lights of Ruby City to the west, a rough-hewn mining community built on the south side of the gulch, half a mile downcañon from the dug-out. It was Andy who'd voiced the warning that had brought Johnny to the dug-out's door. Andy was looking down the path that sloped off through the sage to their claim on the banks of the Redhawk, directly under them.

Johnny hung back in the shadows of the dug-out. His revolver, a .44 Remington-Beals, resided in a plain California holster hung on a peg just inside the door; his heavy Hawken rifle leaned against the jamb beneath it. Both guns were loaded and capped, ready to fire, although he left them where they were. Times had turned perilous along the Redhawk Gulch in recent weeks, but they still had friends scattered up and down the creek, and it could be one of them who had come for a visit. Or it might be Del Kirkham, the fourth partner working the claim registered under the title of Bailey, Tabor, Owens, and Kirkham.

Del had hiked down to Ruby City before supper for a drink and to catch up on the latest news. It was the news Del might be returning with that had everyone so jumpy. Six days ago, a party of Illinois prospectors—eight men and a twelve-year-old boy—had set out for Salt Lake City in a wagon pulled by four horses. The fruit of their summer's labor, nearly $16,000 in gold, had been locked inside a sturdy oak box bolted to the center of the wagon bed. The boy had driven the team with the men crowded in back, their rifles at the ready.

Leaving Montana wasn't all that ill-advised, considering the lateness of the season and the autumn snows already clogging the higher passes, but it was a more recent, two-legged threat that had the local prospectors on edge. Over the last six weeks, nearly two dozen men had attempted to leave the Redhawk district, bound for either Salt Lake City to the south or Fort Benton to the northeast. So far, not one of them had made it. Those who came back did so with empty pockets and soul-withering tales of bandits prowling the roads like jackals. The ones who didn't come back were eventually found by search parties and buried where they'd been gunned down. Word coming into the gulch had been as clear as its source was nebulous: try to escape and you'll be caught; resist and you'll be killed.

The wagon party had intended to meet that challenge with force. Their plan was to travel as far as Monida Pass by wagon, then cross over into Idaho on snowshoes, using the horses to carry their gold and supplies.

"Who's there?" Andy Tabor called sharply into the cañon's shadows.

Johnny slid his fingers warily around the Hawken's cool, octagon barrel. At twenty-four, he was the youngest member of the group, but he was no greenhorn. Slim, sinewy, strong as a mule, he had a lean, angular face and gray eyes that could darken in a flash when angered. His dark brown hair was long and slightly wavy, falling past his collar in back, although he'd avoided the full-bearded look of his partners and tried to shave a couple of times a week when he could.

From the gulch, a distant voice rose like smoke. "It's me."

Johnny let his hand fall away from the Hawken, but he didn't feel any less uneasy as he walked out to stand beside Russ at the fire. Andy drifted back as well, his visage grim under the drooping brim of his hat, his work-scarred hands thrust into the pockets of his canvas overalls. A few minutes later, Del hove into view, puffing and red-faced from his long climb up from Ruby City—Del, lanky and bald and sharp-featured, his too-thin lips struggling to cover a bucktooth even as he gasped for breath.

"What's the news?" Andy asked, before Del could fully recover.

" 'Bout what we . . . expected," Del puffed. "Wagon party's back . . . shot to hell. Only three men came in with it . . . and two horses."

"What about the boy?" Russ asked.

"Ain't no word on the boy, especial," Del said, sniffing and rubbing his nose with the back of his hand. "Was Mugher and Smith and that old coot, Harrison, that come back, but all of 'em's bloodied up. They say the bandits hit 'em hard about halfway between Twin Bridges and Beaverhead Rock. Said they came outta them willows there with their guns blazin'. Didn't give 'em no kind of chance to surrender."

"They murdered them all?" Russ asked.

"Must've, 'cept for them three I mentioned. I didn't hang around to catch the particulars."

"That's a new twist," Andy said. In the past, accosted miners had been given an opportunity to surrender first.

"Maybe Brett Cutter got word of their intent," Del said. "Was some of his boys in town tonight when I left."

"Who?" Johnny demanded.

"That Chickasaw half-breed, Shirt Jackson, was one. Charlie Ryder and Sam Hulse was a couple others I saw. Frank McCarty says Otis Call is around somewheres, too."

"Those are all Cutter's men, all right," Russ said bleakly. He looked at Andy, then Johnny. "I'd lay you odds it was them that hit the wagon party."

It was said, and more and more openly of late, that Brett Cutter was the man behind most of the lawlessness plaguing southwestern Montana that year, and that, through a firm hand and unerring marksmanship, he'd managed to bring organization of a sort to some of the worst hardcases in the territory. In safe company, this criminal element was often called Cutter's Cut-throats, although smart men avoided the term among strangers.

Cutter apparently controlled these outlaw crews from a roadhouse along the Ruby Range cut-off that had once bypassed the longer, easier route through Twin Bridges. Few travelers used the cut-off any more or stopped at the stone trading post called Lost Spring, because of the harassment they'd received there from Cutter's hard-bitten crew.

"Did they get the gold?" Andy asked after a short silence.

"Yeah, they got it," Del replied, his voice rising. "What the hell do you think?" He looked away, and Johnny saw that he was trembling. "Them boys control the roads," Del added. "You couldn't squeeze a mouse outta this territory without Brett Cutter knowin' about it."

Johnny glanced at Andy. "I think I'll mosey on down to Ruby, see what folks are saying."

"You go ahead," Del sneered. "You go ask Warshirt Jackson what happened out there on the Beaverhead, then see if you've still got your scalp left when he walks away."

"Easy, Del," Russ said. "Johnny just wants some more information. We've gotta know what's going on if we want to get out of here with our own gold."

Del flashed Russ a wild-eyed look. "We ain't gonna get out of here, Russ. Ain't you figured that out yet? We ain't gettin' out unless they haul our dead bodies out in the spring. That's the only way we're leavin' Montana. The only way."

Johnny returned to the dug-out without comment. He already had on his wool coat and hat, but he wanted his pistol, too. There was a time when he might have walked Ruby City's broad, single street unarmed, but those days were gone now.

While Russ stayed by the fire to try to calm down Del, Andy wandered over to the dug-out with Johnny. "Whatever you learn in town, maybe you ought to keep it just between you and me and Russ," Andy said quietly. "I think Del's about reached the end of his rope."

Johnny buckled on his gun belt. A small, hard-leather pouch just behind the holster carried a dozen extra linen cartridges and a small tin of caps. A Bowie knife in a plain sheath and another small pouch containing his fire-making gear—flint and steel, a wad of shredded juniper bark, and a small brass box of char cloth—rode handily on his left hip. Pulling the hem of his coat out to cover the Remington-Beals' grips, he said: "We could burrow in for the winter, if we had to. It'd be rough going, but there are plenty who'll do it."

"You're wanting to stay?" Andy asked, surprised.

"I'm just saying it could be done."

"We're short on supplies right now, and prices are already going up. Five pounds of flour will set you back twenty bucks today. By Christmas, that same five pounds will fetch fifty dollars. We'd spend half our summer's diggin's just to eat, and still be bone and gristle by spring."

"My vote is to get out as soon as we can. Truth is, I'm bone-weary tired of that pick and shovel. If I never wrap my fingers around either one again, I'll be happy."

Andy offered a rare smile. "That's how I feel. We came out here to make our fortunes, and we've come close enough to it to suit me. Let's get, before Cutter's men come callin' late some night. I got a hankering to live like a man again, instead of underground like a damn' gopher."

At the fire, Del's voice rose with sharp finality, and he stalked off into the night.

Russ came over to the dug-out with a heavy expression. "That boy's scared clean down to his socks," he said. "If something doesn't break soon, I'm fearful Del will."

"Maybe Johnny will turn up something," Andy said.

"I hope so," Russ replied. "Del's got a wife back East, as fine a woman as you'd ever want to meet. I'd hate to take that boy home to her as a half-wit."

"I'd better go," Johnny said, slipping past Russ. "I'll be back in a couple of hours."

"Watch yourself!" Andy called. "Folks'll be touchy tonight."

But Johnny already knew that. As he stepped off the little flat and began his descent toward Redhawk Creek, his fingers went to the holster at his side, gliding down the smooth leather to touch the cold muzzle of his pistol, extending about a half inch below the sheath's open toe. When he'd come to Montana in the spring, he'd only carried five rounds in the Remington-Beals' cylinder, so that he could rest the hammer on an empty chamber as a safety precaution. It wasn't until the night of the wagon party's departure that he loaded the sixth chamber, then lowered the hammer to a shallow notch he'd hacksawed between a couple of capped nipples. Some claimed it was more dangerous that way, but Johnny had decided the risk was worth it. Just in case hell came a-calling.

Chapter Two

It was colder away from the fire, and Johnny pulled the collar of his coat up around his ears. Save for some crusty patches of snow under the larger clumps of sagebrush, the cañon side was bare, but across the gulch, among the tall pines on the north-facing slope where the sun seldom reached, the snow was already a foot deep. In Ruby City, some of the old-timers were predicting there would be five times that much snow by the end of January.

The prospects of being snowed in for the winter brought a knot of apprehension to Johnny's chest. It wasn't the frigid temperatures that worried him. He'd grown up in Minnesota and knew how to deal with sub-zero weather. Rather, it was the isolation of the gulch, their vulnerability in it if Cutter ever sent a crew up here after them.

At the bottom of the gulch, Johnny paused before the dark heaps of gravel and half-frozen earth they'd wrestled from the stream's channel over the summer. It was a fine mess they'd created, but a profitable one. Over the past five months, the four partners had gleaned nearly $48,000 in dust and small, pea-size nuggets from the stream's bed. That was almost $12,000 apiece, more money than Johnny could have earned in a decade 'skinning mules. He was rich by most standards, but his newly acquired fortune wouldn't amount to a tinker's dam if they didn't find a way to get out of Montana alive.

Johnny turned to look downstream, where the flickering lights of other campfires marked claims that were little different from his own. Probably three-quarters of Ruby City's population had headed for warmer climates with the first blustery snowfall. A lot of prospectors had abandoned their claims, too. But others had hung on to take advantage of the creek's shallow waters and uncrowded banks before the real rush began next summer.

Redhawk Creek had its source up high in the Tobacco Root Mountains to the east, where no one Johnny knew of had ever gone. But they would. Over the summer, and in the last three months in particular, several hundred prospectors had taken almost $1,000,000 worth of gold from the lower Redhawk. Give it another season, and Johnny figured there wouldn't be an inch of bank remaining that hadn't been turned with a shovel or gouged with a pick.

He started up the south side of the cañon, picking his way carefully along the dark trail until he reached the narrow, winding road. After that, it took only a few minutes to hike the rest of the way into town.

Ruby City sat on the shoulder of a hill about a mile into the gulch. From the top of the road at the east end of town, a man could look west and make out a good portion of the Ruby valley in the distance, yet not be able to see the lower end of the street because of the crest of the hill and the quick bends of the gulch.

Nothing in Ruby City was squared with anything else. Even the street ran on a slant, so that the buildings on the north, or creek side, were anywhere from three to ten feet lower than the buildings directly across from them. Steps between businesses, even those standing next door to one another, were often a necessity rather than a convenience. In Ruby City, a man was always climbing or descending, even if all he did was step to the edge of the boardwalk to spit.

Johnny was startled by the size of the crowd he found on the street in front of Halstead's Saloon. Judging from the number of campfires he'd seen in the gulch, he'd assumed most of the prospectors were staying close to their claims in the wake of the wagon party's return. Now it looked like many of the camps had sent one or two representatives into town. Quite a few of them were carrying torches that cast a yellow, pulsating light over the mob.

Cautiously Johnny edged into the crowd. He saw a lot of familiar faces, but no one he knew well. Most of the men appeared fairly worked up, but, as he listened to the ebb and flow of conversation, he began to detect an undercurrent of fear, the first traces of panic. Apparently several more of Cutter's men had shown up at dusk, the whole lot of them hunkered down now in Halstead's, drinking whiskey. On top of that was the news that one of the wagon party's survivors had died since being brought in, raising the number of casualties to seven.

There was a gentle prod at Johnny's elbow, and he turned to find old man McCarty standing at his side. Frank McCarty ran the town's livery, and had been one of the first businessmen to settle in the gulch.

"Hello, Johnny," Frank said. "Come to see the show?"

"Frank," Johnny said, then nodded toward the crowd. "They look mad as hornets. What do you think they'll do?"

"Not a damn' thing," the hostler replied scornfully. "They don't have a leader, and without that, it's just a bunch of rabble shouting threats. It won't go anywhere unless someone takes the reins." He gave Johnny a furtive look. "You could do it."

"Me?" Johnny laughed dismissively. "I don't even know most of these men. Besides, I'm a pick and shovel man."

"You might not know them, but they know you. They've all heard of Johnny Montana."

Johnny winced. "That's just Russ Bailey's blowing, Frank. It doesn't mean anything."

"Russ gave you that name after you saved their hides from the Sioux."

"All I did was talk to those Indians," Johnny said. "Gave 'em some trinkets. They weren't looking for trouble."

Frank snorted. "Like they weren't looking for trouble last summer when they killed all those settlers in Minnesota." He was talking about the Uprising of 1862, and the seven hundred whites—men, women, and children—who had been butchered by Little Crow and his followers.

"Those were Santees," Johnny said. "It was Yanktons we met on the James River."

"It doesn't matter whether they were Yanktons, Santees, or Eskimos. The boys all know what you did, and they admire you for it."

"Well, I still ain't leading a mob," Johnny said. "I didn't come into town tonight to get myself shot."

"What did you come in for?"

"I don't rightly know," Johnny admitted after a pause. "I guess I was hoping for some fresh idea that'd get us out of here alive, but now they're saying Cutter's sent even more men into town."

"Dave Worthy and Little Tate Orr," Frank confirmed. "That makes six, with Shirt Jackson, Charlie Ryder, Sam Hulse, and Otis Call."

Johnny whistled softly. "That's a lot of meanness to turn loose on one town. You figure Brett Cutter's got something up his sleeve?"

"Yeah, I do. I surely do."

Johnny gave the hostler a surprised look. That wasn't the answer he'd expected. "What do you reckon he's got in mind?"

"I wouldn't know, but I've never seen six Cut-throats in Ruby City at the same time before. There's got to be a reason for it." He gave Johnny a searching look, as if trying to make up his mind about something. Then he said: "Why don't you come with me? I have something to show you."

"What is it?" Johnny asked, but Frank only shook his head.

"Come on. It won't take long."

They walked back up the street to McCarty's livery. Inside, Frank latched the door securely, then lit a lantern. "This way," he said, moving down the broad central aisle. At thc rear of the stable he hung the lantern on a hook driven into an upright post, then swept a hand toward the stalls on either side of it.

Johnny looked inside. A horse stood hip-shot in each one, their muzzles almost brushing the wood-chip bedding. One was a short, muscular bay, the other a taller, leaner sorrel, its hip bones jutting sharply. Both looked trail-worn and gaunt, although he noticed that their hoofs were in good shape and recently shod, their coats brushed.

"Horses," he said, glancing at Frank curiously. "What about them?"

"I think I've got us a way out of Montana, Johnny, if you're game."

Chapter Three

Johnny remembered the first time he'd met Frank McCarty, last spring just after he, Russ, Andy, and Del had arrived in Redhawk Gulch. The livery had still been under construction then, but some of the corrals out back had been completed. At the time, Frank was doing business out of a small wall tent.

Although the four partners had intended to keep their horses through the summer, the effort of managing livestock without adequate graze nearby soon proved deterring. It was Del who'd suggested they sell them, and, after a couple of weeks, the others had reluctantly agreed. Keeping their tack, they'd led the horses into town, where Frank had paid them a fair price for four saddle mounts and a trio of pack animals.

Over the summer, Johnny had kept in touch with the older man, stopping by in the evenings once or twice a week to chew the fat and look over the new stock that funneled steadily through McCarty's pens. As the months passed, his respect for the silver-haired liveryman had grown. Frank had been knocking around the West for a good many years by then. He'd come out with Kearney in 1846 as a teamster, and he'd been one of the first to reach California in '49, after gold was discovered at Sutter's Mill. He was in Colorado in '58 as well, but, except for his first year in California, Frank had never done any panning. He'd learned early on that the real money was in supplying the miners with something they needed. He'd settled on a livery because horses were normally scarce in a mining community, where their care took too much time away from a claim, and because plenty of merchants were already selling beans and shovels and whiskey.

Frank's corrals were empty now, and had been for some weeks. The winter's exodus had begun with the first light snow in mid-September, and had maintained a steady tempo ever since. Only the diehards and those with better-paying claims—like Johnny's—had tarried. Right now, there probably weren't a dozen horses left in Ruby City, and half of those belonged to Cut-throats.

Frank stood across the aisle, holding what looked like a small, thick blanket in his hands. "Is it starting to sink in yet?" he asked.

"Maybe, but tell me anyway."

Frank nodded toward the dozing horses. "These are from the wagon party's hitch. They had four going out, but only these two came back. They look run-down, but they aren't. They're just tired after their long haul back to Ruby."

"You considering making a run for it, Frank?"

The older man looked suddenly embarrassed. "Naw, my bones are too creaky to be bucking the high country at this time of year. You could do it, though. On these two horses right here."

Johnny glanced at the nearest stall, where the bay hadn't moved since they'd arrived. "How do you figure that?"

Frank swung what Johnny had mistaken for a blanket over a nearby gate. Stretched out, he saw that it was a kind of homemade pack saddle, with shallow pockets sewn down each side.

"Sam Hulse and Charlie Ryder were in here earlier tonight," Frank said. "They were checking to see how many horses I had, and they weren't too subtle about it, either. But all I've got are these two, and they look half dead." His eyes seemed to light up. "That's why this can work, Johnny. Cutter won't expect anyone to try to slip out of the gulch on a couple of worn-out nags like these."

"Frank," Johnny said uncertainly, "I'm not sure I don't agree with 'em."

"And that'll be our edge. Listen, you boys have dug up a good little chunk of gold this summer, and everybody knows it, thanks to Del."

"Del?"

"Del drinks too much, Johnny. He thinks he's sly, but he ain't. He's let it slip that you boys are sitting on almost fifty thousand dollars worth of dust up there."

Johnny swore softly. "That damn' fool."

"Yeah, he is. Especially when everyone knows Cutter has spies in all the local camps. If I've heard about your gold, you can bet Brett Cutter has, too, and that he'll send some men up here to check it out."

The hairs across the back of Johnny's neck stirred. "You figure that's why there're so many Cut-throats in town tonight?"

"I couldn't say, but I'll tell you this. You boys aren't the only ones who've had a prosperous summer. There's been a few other claims that panned out big."

"But they didn't have Del Kirkham shooting off his mouth about it."

"Listen, Johnny, I've made a nice little nest egg myself this year. Eight thousand dollars in dust and coin, all of it profit."

Johnny glanced at the blanket pack. "Is that what this is for?"

"Gold's hard to carry on a horse. It wants to settle toward the bottom of your panniers, and that makes a heavy load that rides too low. It'll wear your horse out before you've gone a hundred miles, but this will distribute the weight more evenly." He held up one end to point out a fist-size hole cut in the material; a slot had been added to the other end. From this new angle, Johnny could see that it wasn't really a blanket at all, but heavy leather covered with blanket material.

"I patterned it after a *mochila,*" Frank explained. "The hole fits over the saddle horn and the slot goes over the cantle, so that you can use it on a regular saddle instead of a sawbuck. There're six pockets sewn horizontally in two columns along each side. Each pocket has a flap that closes securely when it's buckled. I've reinforced all the corners and double-stitched the seams. It ought to handle a hundred thousand dollars worth of dust and nuggets without a problem."

"What are you asking me to do, Frank?"

"I asking you to get our gold out of Montana. Yours, mine, Russ's, Andy's, Del's. I want you to take it to Salt Lake City and deposit it in a bank. Salt Lake's the closest thing to civilization that we have out here right now. If you can get it that far, it'll be ours to keep." He paused for a moment, as if in thought, then said: "Folks keep riding out of here like they have a God-given right to use the roads, but they don't. Rights don't happen because you think they ought to. You have to demand them, fight for them. And safety in numbers is an illusion. The fact is, Brett Cutter controls this part of Montana, especially its roads. You're going to have to avoid those roads, Johnny. You're going to have to slip out of here like a mule deer sneaking around a hunter. It's the only way."

Johnny remembered the last mule deer he'd shot for meat, up in the hills above Ruby City. It had tried that same trick, slipping around behind him to escape detection. But Johnny had been expecting it, and he had doubled back just in time to make his shot. Still, it had been close; had he hesitated only a couple of more minutes, the big muley would have gotten away. It made him wonder if Cutter's men were hunters, too—or just killers.

"Will you do it?" Frank asked.

"Hell, man, you're trusting me with your life's savings," Johnny said tautly.

"Part of it, yeah."

"You know there's no guarantee I'll make it."

"I'm not asking for a guarantee, Johnny. I'm asking if you'll try. Because if you don't, I'm afraid we'll all be broke by spring, and maybe dead, too."

"I could lose it all, Frank. Your gold, mine, Russ's, the others'. . . ."

Frank waited patiently, without speaking.

"I don't even know the route. I came out here through Dakota Territory from Saint Paul. I've never been south of Dolsen's trading post."

Frank continued his silence.

"Dammit." Johnny shook his head in defeat. "All right, if you're fool enough to trust me with your gold, then I reckon I'm just damn' fool enough to give it a try."

"Now you're talking," Frank said, smiling broadly.

Johnny's expression remained somber. "Wait until midnight, then sneak these horses out the back way and circle them around to the east," he instructed. "Come into our camp from the ridge. You figure you can find it in the dark?"

"I'll find it."

"Good. I'm going to go talk to the others. I'm pretty sure Russ and Andy will throw in with us, but I don't know what Del will say."

"Del's a loose cannon. I say the fewer that come in, the lighter the load for the pack horse and the better your odds of making it to Salt Lake City."

"Maybe, but Del's a partner, too. I won't sneak around behind his back, no matter what I might think of him." He headed for the livery's door. "Midnight, Frank," he called softly, "and don't let anyone see you."

"I'll be there," Frank promised.

Chapter Four

A shot rang out from the street just as Johnny exited the livery's side door. Hugging the shadows close to the wall, he moved to the front of the alley where he could see the mob in front of Halstead's. A second shot was fired into the air just as Johnny reached the corner, arching sparks from the muzzle blast over the crowd like cheap fireworks.

Johnny studied the crowd thoughtfully. It had shrunk noticeably in the time he'd been in the livery with Frank. Only a hard-core knot of protesters remained, but the pulse of their anger seemed erratic, surging out in too many directions at once. Then the front door to Halstead's swung open and a tall man in a bear-hide coat stepped onto the boardwalk. The crowd turned instantly silent as the tall man strode to the edge of the boardwalk. In addition to the shaggy coat, he wore a broad-brimmed hat with a domed crown, checked trousers tucked into stovepipe boots, and a pair of revolvers belted around his waist. In the flickering torchlight, the man's skin glistened like polished coal, and Johnny knew this had to be Otis Call, one of Brett Cutter's two lieutenants.

It was rare for a black man to rise in rank above whites, even in the West, where prejudice didn't seem to burn quite so fiercely as it did back East. Johnny figured it spoke highly of Call's skills, either as a leader of men or for his ruthlessness as a bandit, to achieve such a high position within the outlaw gang.

"I'm getting tired of this foolishness," Call said suddenly, his voice booming. "I've been trying to enjoy a drink with my friends, but all I hear is you boys crying for our blood. I say, if you want it, then come and get it, and start with me."

Johnny arched a brow. Call's words were bold, flung into the faces of nearly two score of angry men. Yet the outlaw lieutenant stood there almost casually, his thumbs hooked behind the buckle of his gun belt. There were a few dark mutterings from the rear of the crowd, but they were quickly silenced when Call bellowed: "What's that? What's that I hear?"

"We . . . we was wonderin' . . . ," a voice began hesitantly.

"Well, there's your trouble," Call jeered. "Wondering is best left to those who know how to do it properly. Can you do it properly, boy?"

A hush greeted Call's question, deep and, in its way, decisive.

"I figured as much," the black man said. "I figured as much an hour ago, when nobody came in to fetch us for that bloodletting." His voice rose in sarcasm. "I figured as much when all I heard out here was talk. Big talk, squirting out of little men like the trots. You!" He stabbed a finger at an individual standing near the front of the crowd. "What's your name?"

Johnny didn't hear the answer.

"Bill, or Billy?" Call didn't wait for an answer. "You're wearing a gun, Billy. Know how to use it?"

Again, Johnny was unable to pick up Bill's low reply; whatever it was, it made Call laugh mockingly.

"I've got you pegged as a blow-hard, Billy boy. Am I right?"

"No," came the faint reply.

"No? You sure?"

"Damn you," Bill said, clearly this time.

The crowd went rock still, waiting for Call's response.

Without rush, the black man moved his hand to the butt of his right-side revolver. "I believe those are fighting words, Billy. I believe you've just called me out."

Even from half a block away, Johnny could see the color drain from the white man's face. "Look, I . . . I ain't callin' nobody out. I just came into town to see what all the ruckus was about."

"Billy," Call said easily, "I'm thinking this ruckus is about finished. Pull your hogleg, boy."

"I ain't drawin' on you!" Bill glanced around wildly for help, but a gap had opened up around him until he stood alone in its center. "Sweet Jesus, boys, are you gonna let him do this to me?" he demanded shrilly.

"The real question is, are you gonna let me do it?" Call interjected.

"I ain't fightin' you," Bill said, shaking his head. He raised both hands level with his shoulders. "I just . . . I ain't gonna do it."

"You want to die, Billy boy?" Call roared.

"No, sir, I don't."

Call cocked his head slightly to one side, as if he wasn't sure he'd heard correctly. "What did you call me? Did you just call me sir?"

Bill nodded. "Yes, sir, I did."

"Yes, sir," Call repeated, as if replaying the word in his mind. "My, that does have a nice ring to it, doesn't it?"

"Yes, sir, I expect it does."

Call was silent a moment, staring at the unmoving white man. Bill kept his hands raised, while the gap around him continued to edge outward. Finally Call nodded. "All right, Billy boy, you get to live tonight. But you go on home now, you hear? All of you, git on home before I get my dander up for real."

Almost immediately, the crowd began to break apart. There were a few murmurs of discontent, but no loud protests. Johnny could hardly believe what he'd just witnessed—forty hard-fisted prospectors backed down by a single outlaw. Although he considered slipping away himself, something stopped him, and he paused in the darkness next to the livery's wall. Then, even before the crowd had completely dispersed, Otis Call turned and looked right at him.

Johnny's blood went cold. He knew there was no way Call could see him in such unbroken shadow, yet there was no denying the direction of the black man's gaze, the intensity of his stare. Call was looking directly at him, as if he could see in the dark, could peer not just into Johnny's eyes, but into his soul. For nearly a full minute, Johnny couldn't move. He could barely breathe. Then the moment passed and Call turned away, disappearing into the saloon.

Drawing a ragged breath, Johnny pushed clear of the livery's wall. He stared at the saloon for a long time, but the big double doors remained closed. After a time, Johnny turned away with the rest of the crowd, allowing it to pull him back into the gulch.

CHAPTER FIVE

"It's risky," Russ said.

"It's risky as hell," Andy contended angrily. "You'll be on your own out there, all alone."

"That might be for the best," Johnny said as he rummaged through his packs inside the dug-out.

"One mistake, Johnny," Russ said soberly. "That's all you're gonna get. Did Frank mention that?"

"Frank didn't have to mention it, Russ. I already know it'll be dangerous, but I also think it can be done. Besides, I doubt if it'll be any more dangerous than staying here. Cutter's men aren't going to be happy when they find out I've made a run for it."

"Do you even know the way?" Russ asked.

"Mormons have been shipping produce up here for a couple of years. There'll be a road to follow, and, once I get over Monida Pass, it'll be a straight shot into Salt Lake City."

"What if they come over Monida after you?" Andy asked.

Johnny's hands slowed unconsciously. "I doubt if they'd follow me all the way to Salt Lake," he finally replied, although the idea that they might hadn't occurred to him until that moment.

"We don't know what they'll do," Del piped up. "Nobody does." He sounded frayed, his eyes darting like a cornered rodent's. "What we ought to do is buy our way out."

"You can't deal with killers," Andy said. "Why should they let you go free when all they have to do is bust a cap on you and take what they want?"

"They might not take nothin' if we gave 'em something better," Del returned.

"What have you got that's more valuable to them than your gold?" Andy asked derisively.

"It was just an idea, Andy," Russ said gently.

"Well, it's a damn' dumb one," Andy replied.

"Johnny skatin' outta here with all our gold is what's dumb," Del countered. "What's to stop him from just going on, takin' it all, and never lookin' back?"

"Rein it in, Del," Andy said sharply.

"Come on, you two," Russ chided. "We've got problems enough without you two jumping down one another's throats."

"All right, let's take a vote," Andy said. "McCarty won't do it, he's too old, but any of the rest of us can go. Me, I'm voting for Johnny. He's got more experience out here than the rest of us."

"I'll back that," Russ said. "Del, what about you?"

"You wouldn't vote for me, Russ? After all the years we've known one another?"

"You're a good friend, Del, and our wives like one another, and that's important. But no, I'm voting for Johnny."

"Well then, the hell with you, and the hell with Johnny Montana, too. I ain't givin' him my gold. Not unless I'm two foot behind him with a loaded scatter-gun."

"Then it's settled," Johnny said tautly. "I'll take my gold and Russ's, Andy's, and Frank's. Del can keep his."

"You damn' right I'm keeping mine," Del spat, then stalked outside. Looking exasperated, Russ followed him.

When they were alone, Andy said: "I hate that little pasty-faced bastard. I didn't used to, but I do now."

"He's just scared," Johnny said, returning to his packing. He wouldn't take much with him. A small tin of salve for injuries to him or the horses, a change of clothing, some jerky, rice, dried fruit, and coffee, with a little tin billy to prepare it all in, plus all the ammunition he had for his rifle and pistol—about forty rounds each. He planned to run if discovered, and fight only if cornered.

"How much food are you taking?" Andy asked, eyeing the little cloth bag of rice Johnny was shoving into his bags.

"Maybe a week's worth."

"They say it's a week to Salt Lake City. That's on a good horse and in the summer, when the roads are dry."

"I'll pick up some more grub at Fort Hall. That's about halfway. Truth to tell, I'm more worried about Cutter and his men than I am about food."

"McCarty's idea is a good one. Stay off the roads and ridge tops as much as possible. Russ and I will continue to work the claim like normal. Hell, they might not even discover you're gone until you're too far south to catch."

"Del could be a problem," Johnny said. He briefly related the information Frank McCarty had shared with him, about Del's loose talk regarding the gold they'd taken from Redhawk that summer.

"That son-of-a-bitch," Andy said softly. "He'll get us all killed yet."

"Keep him out of town for a few days if you can." Johnny closed the flaps on his saddlebags, then pushed to his feet. "If I make it, I'll wait for you in Salt Lake City."

"What else you gonna need, Johnny?"

"I was thinking I could use that big ol' greatcoat of yours. It's probably the warmest coat in the gulch, and I'll want to do without a fire as much as possible."

"It's yours. What else?"

"Russ's gloves. The wolf-hide ones with the hair still on."

"Sure, Russ'll let you borrow those."

They made a quick list of the gear they could pool so that Johnny would have the best of what they owned. He'd use his own saddle, but borrow Andy's rig to carry the gold pannier Frank had made, and it was agreed that, if he got the chance, he should try to purchase better mounts. Russ returned after several minutes with the news that Del hadn't softened his position.

"It ain't nothin' personal," Russ added apologetically to Johnny. "I doubt if he'd trust me any more."

"Well, that says a mouthful," Andy said cynically. "A man who doesn't trust his own partner ain't much of a man, in my book."

"I'd like to borrow your gloves, Russ," Johnny said quietly, stepping between the two partners. "Do you mind?"

"Not a bit," Russ said, but he was looking at Andy without any more give in him. Russ Bailey was an easy-going man, but he had his limits, like everyone.

They spent another twenty minutes putting together the rest of Johnny's outfit, then snuffed the candle and headed for the door. Johnny took the Hawken with him. He wanted to clean it thoroughly, then reload it with a fresh charge, but when they exited the dug-out, they found the camp abandoned. Del was nowhere in sight.

Chapter Six

Andy swore loudly. "He's gone in to make a deal with the Cutthroats, boys. I'd bet you anything."

"Naw, Del wouldn't do that," Russ protested, but his tone betrayed his doubt.

"Grab your pistol, Russ," Johnny said, leaning his Hawken against the dug-out's front wall.

"I'm goin', too," Andy snarled.

"No, you stay put," Johnny said. "If Del is trying to make a deal with Cutter's men, the fat's going to be in the fire for sure. I'll grab Frank's ponies and get back up here as quick as I can. You have my gear outside ready to go. If I've gotta make a run for it, we won't have much time."

Johnny set a brisk pace down the dark path to Redhawk Creek, then back up the far slope to the road. Russ scrambled up behind him, puffing loudly.

"I don't . . . think he'd . . . do it," Russ panted, standing in the middle of the road with his hands on his knees.

Johnny didn't reply, but he thought the odds were pretty good that, if he was panicked enough, Del Kirkham would squeal like a stuck pig. The question, he supposed, was if Del would have enough courage to approach a room full of Cutthroats without first stopping off somewhere for a couple of drinks.

There had been as many as a dozen saloons in Ruby City at the height of the summer, most of them housed in tents. Only four remained now, log structures with sturdy roofs to withstand the heavy winter snows. If the Cut-throats were still holed up in Halstead's, Johnny intended to set Russ out front while he searched the other establishments—The Bucket Saloon, The Elkhorn, and The Great Western.

It was a different scene that greeted Johnny in Ruby City this time. The mob was gone, the torches doused, and hardly a light shone. The Elkhorn and Great Western were closed, but The Bucket was still open, as was Halstead's across the street.

Glancing at the saddled horses in front of Halstead's, Russ said: "It ain't right that we got to go up against these kinds of people. Where's the damn' law?"

"The law's back East, Russ," Johnny reminded him. "It'll sit out the early years, then show up about the same time the doctors and lawyers do."

That was something Frank McCarty had explained to him last summer, describing the various stages of a community as it grew from a rough-barked camp into a *bona fide* town with an honest chance for a future. Johnny had never thought of it quite so analytically before, but he was young; Frank had seen it happen several times, both in California and Colorado. It would happen in Idaho and Montana, too, he asserted, and he'd urged Johnny to watch for it, to observe how it arrived so tentatively, barely a shadow in the corner at first, then gradually stretching and pushing, like a chick emerging from its egg. "Civilization is a hell of a thing to behold," Frank had said, "and kind of awe-inspiring, too, if you don't get trampled by it."

Russ, though, was shaking his head. "I should've waited," he contended. "I should've waited until it was safe for the doctors and lawyers, then come out."

"Why don't you go stand in front of Halstead's, in case Del shows up?" Johnny suggested. "I'll take a peek inside The Bucket. If he's there, I'll wave you over."

"If one of Cutter's men pokes his head out that door, I'm gonna piss my britches," Russ said, so seriously that Johnny laughed.

"No you won't," he assured the older man. He watched Russ walk down the street to Halstead's, then headed for The Bucket.

The Bucket was a cramped, low-ceilinged room with a short bar across the back, a trio of tables staggered toward the front. There were no house games here, no dance-hall girls or rag-tag orchestra. There were just the tables where men could sit and talk and play a little poker, a bar that wouldn't accommodate more than twenty men, a cast-iron stove in the middle of the room, emitting a comfortable warmth. A pair of hurricane lamps on the walls battled feebly against the artificial gloaming.

There were half a dozen men inside The Bucket that night. Four of them shared a table in the shadows to the left of the front door; a fifth stood alone at the bar with a beer. The sixth was the barkeep, folded over the counter, looking bored. Del was nowhere to be seen, but something about the four men at the table caught Johnny's attention. Giving them a closer look, he recognized Arnie Waters and a short, stocky man known around the gulch as Stumpy Reems. It was Stumpy who called him over.

Johnny shook his head. "I'm looking for Del Kirkham. Have you seen him?"

"Not today."

One of the men Johnny didn't know growled something unintelligible, but Stumpy just grinned. "*Aw,* Johnny's all right. They call him Johnny Montana. Johnny, this is Bart. . . ."

"Shut up, Stumpy!" the burly stranger said.

Stumpy's grin faded. "Johnny's a good man," he said evenly. "He's well-respected in the gulch. He could be a big help to us."

Arnie Waters stood and walked over, carrying his beer. When

he was close enough that he wouldn't be overheard, he said: "We're talking about forming a committee, Johnny, maybe cleanin' up some of the riff-raff that's blown into the gulch recently."

"A vigilance committee?"

"We'd likely come up with a better name, but, yeah, in a nutshell."

It was tempting, Johnny reflected. He didn't relish the long, lonely journey ahead, the empty miles filled with nothing but snow and ice and wind. But he didn't know if he wanted to hang around waiting for some kind of home-grown justice to take shape, either. With a band of Cut-throats already in town and Del's loose talk about their gold, Johnny wasn't sure he had that kind of time any more.

Before he could reply, a shot echoed along the street. Arnie cursed and pushed Johnny out of the way, then slammed the door shut.

"Gawd dammit!" the burly stranger hollered, clawing for his revolver. The other two, Stumpy and a red-headed man with a droopy mustache, kicked their chairs across the room in their haste to get clear of the table. At the bar, the man drinking alone looked around, bleary-eyed, but didn't move. The bartender shouted: "Take it outside, boys! I don't want this place wrecked again!"

Another shot sounded from the street, followed by a strangled cry, and Johnny flung open the door and ran outside. In the middle of the street, Russ was climbing awkwardly to his feet. His hat was gone and his hair had fallen forward over his eyes. The front of his shirt was slick with blood and he was limping badly as he hobbled toward The Bucket.

In front of Halstead's, a skinny, bearded man Johnny had never seen before was standing with his knees slightly bent, his stomach curved in as if someone had taken a swing at his gut and he'd sucked it in to escape the blow. He was clutching a pistol in his right hand but the muzzle was swaying wildly. He was so drunk he looked like he could fall down at any moment, yet, with an alcoholic's determination to fit a key in a lock, he continued to try to capture Russ in the revolver's sights.

Palming the Remington-Beals, Johnny snapped off a shot that smacked into the wall of Halstead's Saloon, less than a foot from the gunman's shoulder.

"Hey!" the skinny tough shouted, incensed that someone was shooting back.

Then Halstead's door swung open and a second gunman appeared. Johnny had never seen this man before, either, but he had a fair idea who he was. Dusky-skinned, tall, his long, raven-colored hair falling below his shoulders in back—an Indian, but dressed in the trousers, boots, shirt, and vest of a white man, and wearing a low-crowned brown hat. It was the mixed-blood Chickasaw, Warshirt Jackson, more commonly called Shirt. Stepping alongside the first gunman, Shirt drew one of a pair of revolvers holstered at his waist. At the same time, Johnny heard the thump of boots on the wooden walk behind him. Arnie appeared at his side; Stumpy came up on Johnny's other shoulder.

"Here's our chance to get two of 'em," Stumpy said grimly, just as Russ reached the boardwalk and collapsed across its steps.

Holstering his revolver, Johnny hurried to his partner's side. On the street, an uneasy truce had developed between the two factions, but Johnny knew it wouldn't last long. The men coming to Russ's aid had momentarily stalled the two Cut-throats, but, as soon as the outlaws realized their opposition was nothing more than a handful of poorly armed prospectors, they'd start the ball rolling again.

Arnie understood that as well. "We'd better get him inside, Johnny," he hissed. "All hell's fixin' to break loose here."

Johnny eased Russ onto his back, cushioning the older man's

head with his knee. A ragged cry caught in his throat at the sight of so much blood.

"I'm hit bad, Johnny," Russ gasped. "I'm dead for sure."

"Naw, you ain't dead," Johnny lied, forcing his eyes away from the bullet hole in Russ's chest.

"The hell I ain't. Listen, boy, get my share of the gold outta here. Get it back to my wife, in Wisconsin. Town called. . . ." He arched his back off the boardwalk as a spasm of pain shot through him.

"I will," Johnny promised, tightly grasping his friend's shoulder.

"Town called Milwaukee, couple o' days north of . . . of Chicago. You know where Chicago is?"

"I know where Milwaukee is," Johnny assured him. "I'll see that she gets it."

"You've been a good friend, Johnny. You tell my wife . . . you tell her. . . ."

That was it. Russ's hand fell away, his head lolled, and his body sagged. Johnny sensed someone moving beside him. "We're out of time, hoss," Arnie said gently.

Johnny looked up. Across the street, a half dozen men were standing on the boardwalk in front of Halstead's. Shirt Jackson and the gunman who'd killed Russ still had their pistols drawn, but the rest seemed content to watch. A few of them were holding beers. The tall black man, Otis Call, was standing next to Shirt, the two men conferring quietly.

"Come on," Arnie said. "We'll take care of Russ for you."

Johnny pushed to his feet with a grunt, as if sucker punched. Behind him, Stumpy said: "That son-of-a-bitch."

Peering out of Halstead's door like a frightened child hiding behind his mother's skirt was Del Kirkham. He was unarmed and hatless, and in the saloon's bright light his bald head gleamed like bone.

Arnie began crowding Johnny toward The Bucket's door. "Let's go, hoss," he urged. "You can't do anything about it now."

The two men backed toward the door, where Stumpy stood firmly to one side. "There's a back door to the left of the bar," Arnie told Johnny out of the side of his mouth. "As soon as you get inside, make a run for it. There's a path behind the saloon that'll drop you straight down to the creek. You can work your way back upcañon from there. Find Andy and get the hell outta here. The Cut-throats are onto you now."

"Thanks," Johnny said tautly. Then Shirt Jackson and the tough who'd shot Russ started down the steps to the street, and Stumpy said—"Git!"—and shoved him into the saloon. By the time Johnny reached the back door, the shooting out front had already begun.

Chapter Seven

Standing beside the big pot-bellied stove at the rear of Halstead's, Otis Call regarded the bald-headed prospector at the bar curiously. Del Kirkham had come through the saloon's back door over an hour ago, wide-eyed and trembling and ready to sell out his partners for his own safe passage out of Montana. There was nothing about the heavily perspiring tin-pan that Otis had found to his liking, but he supposed even a back-stabbing skunk had its uses.

At Otis's side, the big Atlantic & Pacific stove popped and crackled pleasantly. A coffee pot sat on the warming tray bolted to its side, its contents as bitter as a stem of mountain sage. Otis didn't mind the taste, and he welcomed the warmth. He held a cup in his hand now, the milk-white china contrasting sharply with the blackness of his fingers. Although he continued to stare at Del, his thoughts began drifting in other directions.

An uneasiness had begun to form within him over the past couple of hours. It wasn't the crowd of tin-pans and their feeble attempt at lynch law earlier that evening that bothered him. In his years riding with Brett Cutter, he'd learned to read men quickly, and, while he had respected the mob's instability, he hadn't been intimidated by it. That was why he'd been able to back it down so easily.

Buffaloing a mob was a skill Otis had learned from Cutter years before, shortly after he and a lanky ex-seaman named Tom Tucker had thrown in with Brett to work the lower slopes of the Sierra Nevadas in California. It had been a sunny spring day when the three bandits stopped a Sacramento-bound stagecoach filled with miners flush from the digs above Placerville. They hadn't anticipated the number of men the stage company was willing to cram inside its coaches, or stack on top, where they clung to the baggage racks like dusty, bearded monkeys. Nor had Otis been prepared for how well-armed the miners were. The sight of so many men bristling with guns of every shape and caliber had just about sucked the spine right out of him. But Brett had seen something Otis hadn't caught onto yet, and he'd thrown down on the whole bunch with a sawed-off shotgun, cool as a bucket of ice. And damn if the miners hadn't nearly fallen all over one another in their efforts to follow Brett's instructions.

Their luck on that, their first job together, had stunned Otis. Between the company box and what dust and nuggets they'd taken off the miners, they'd netted close to $100,000, divvying it out at $30,000 apiece to Otis and Tuck, and $40,000 to Brett, who'd already assumed the position of leader. They'd been rich men for a while, but managed to fritter it away in less than a year. High living was an addiction Otis understood now, and he vowed that, if he ever got his hands on that kind of money again, he'd live smarter and retire early.

Coming to Montana Territory had been Brett's idea, pitched to them last winter at their base in San Diego. He'd baited the plan with talk of the riches to be had, then snapped the trigger with the dream of one last big haul that would make them all as rich as kings. It had sounded pretty good at the time—trunks filled with gold, a life of incredible luxury somewhere south of the border—but Otis knew it wasn't going to pan out that way. They'd grown too big over the summer. Brett's greed had swelled their ranks with too many others, now vying for their share of the proceeds. Unless something dramatic happened,

Otis figured they'd be lucky to leave Montana with $5,000 apiece.

A rifle boomed from outside, the report rolling down the street like summer thunder. At the bar, Del Kirkham swiveled toward the closed front doors with widened eyes. Dave Worthy tossed his cards on the table and stood up. Opening one of the doors, he peered cautiously outside. Then, drawing his revolver, Dave slipped through the door into the night. The saloon turned silent as they listened to the sounds from outside. A couple of minutes later, two more shots rang out, muted by distance.

"That's gotta be Shirt or Little Tate," Charlie Ryder said.

"Maybe," Otis replied noncommittally. After the exchange of gunfire with the prospectors from The Bucket Saloon, Otis had sent Shirt Jackson, Little Tate Orr, and Sam Hulse out to see what they could find. He was especially curious about the man Russ Bailey had struggled so valiantly to reach, before collapsing on The Bucket's steps. Kirkham had insisted it was one of his partners, Johnny Montana, but Otis wanted more than just a name. The memory of those minutes immediately after backing down the mob in front of Halstead's shifted to the forefront of his thoughts. He couldn't have said why he'd stopped to stare into the shadows next to McCarty's livery. Nor could he explain how he'd known someone was there, watching with a cougar's silent intensity. Yet he had, and the moment had marked him in a way he couldn't explain.

Twenty minutes passed before Dave Worthy returned. "They're coming back," he announced as he slipped inside.

Otis nodded but didn't break his silence. Five minutes later, Shirt, Little Tate, and Sam Hulse trooped into the saloon. Shirt and Sam went to the bar, crowding in so close on either side of Kirkham that they jostled his drink, but Little Tate came over to Otis.

"Looks like that sniveling shit was tellin' us the truth," Little

Tate said quietly, meaning Kirkham. "We didn't learn nothin' at The Bucket, so we waited outside McCarty's. Was me 'n' Sam out front and Shirt in back, but the old geezer slipped his horses out a side door. We didn't even spot him until he had them ponies in a flat-out run."

"I heard shooting."

"Someone took a pot shot at us with a rifle just before McCarty made his break. Might've been one of them boys from The Bucket. I couldn't say. Soon as me 'n' Sam took cover, McCarty lit outta there like a scalded duck. Shirt snuck around and managed to get off a couple of rounds at the rifleman, but didn't hit anything."

"So McCarty escaped with the horses?"

"Uhn-huh."

"And you didn't follow him?"

"He was mounted, Otis. We was on foot. We could go after 'im now, if you wanted us to, but we wouldn't find 'im."

"It doesn't matter," Otis said. "We know where he's heading." He was quiet a moment, studying Kirkham. Sam and Shirt were still crowding him, and the prospector's bald head was shiny with perspiration. Otis waited a couple of minutes to let him stew, then called him over.

"What did you say your name was?" Otis asked.

"Del Kirkham."

"Where are you from, Del?"

Kirkham licked nervously at his lips, his bucktooth flashing briefly into view. "Place in Wisconsin called Milwaukee."

"Never heard of it," Otis said.

"It's just a small town . . . a port on Lake Michigan. Got a. . . ."

"That's all right," Otis interrupted. "I wasn't planning to visit the place. Do you want to go back?"

Del's head bobbed rapidly. "I sure do."

"My man informs me you were telling the truth, and that McCarty did slip away with his horses."

"I tolt you he would."

"Where'd he go, Del?"

"Reckon he went up to my claim, remember? The dug-out 'crost the gulch. Johnny's gonna ride 'em to Salt Lake City with the gold."

"And your gold? Your twelve thousand dollars?"

Kirkham's knees nearly buckled. "I . . . ah . . . I stashed it out in the sage."

"So it's safely hidden?"

Kirkham nodded cautiously. "Uhn-huh. I hid it real good. Ain't nobody gonna find it."

"All right, here's the deal I want to make you, Mister Kirkham." Otis stared intently into Del's face to emphasize his sincerity. "Go find your gold and get out of Redhawk Gulch tonight. Do it right now, and don't tell anyone. Not even your partners. Understand?"

"Yeah, sure, I understand." Kirkham replied, hope creeping into his voice. "Sure, I'll be gone by first light, you'll see."

"No, I want you out of the gulch before that. I want you on your way within the hour. Can you do that?"

"Yeah, I can do that."

"One last question, Del. Johnny Montana. Who is he?"

"Johnny? Why, he ain't nobody."

"How'd he get the Montana moniker?"

"That was Russ's doin', on account of Johnny pulling our butts outta a sling with some Sioux, back on the James River in Dakota Territory."

Otis raised a brow questioningly. "He has experience with the Sioux?"

"Naw, Johnny's just a muleskinner. Was, at least, back in Saint Cloud. He lost his outfit when the company sold its wagons to the Union Army for the war. He come out here with us 'cause he wants to buy his own rig when he goes back to Minnesota. Says he don't ever want to work for another man again." Del grinned confidentially. "I guess workin' for someone else is gonna look pretty good to him after tonight, huh?"

Otis's friendly countenance disappeared. "He made a poor choice in partners, I'll say that about him."

"Huh?"

"Go on, Del, before I change my mind."

Kirkham's face paled, and he hurried to the door. Dave Worthy was still standing there. He grinned maliciously as the prospector approached, but pulled the door open politely. Del nodded and started to thank him, but Dave took a half-step forward and said—"Git!"—in a loudly menacing tone, and Del sprinted out the door as if he'd been stung with a bullwhip.

Dave and Charlie laughed as Dave shut the door. Then, as one entity, they turned to Otis.

"We'll give him a couple of minutes to find his gold," Otis said quietly.

"What about the liveryman?" Little Tate asked.

"McCarty will be at the dug-out when Kirkham gets there. If we time it right, we ought to catch all four of them there together, their gold already sacked up." He glanced at the barkeep. "You've been more than helpful tonight, Asa. I'll be sure to let Cutter know about your co-operation."

The bartender nodded fearfully, but Otis knew he wouldn't talk. Not that there was much to hide any more. Tossing a $20 gold piece onto the bar, he said: "Add that to what Cutter's already paid you." Then he turned away from the warmth of the big stove and snapped: "Let's ride!"

Chapter Eight

"It was Sam Hulse who shot Russ," Frank McCarty announced, fiddling with one of the buckles on his custom-made pack saddle. "He's a mean little bastard, like runts sometimes are."

Johnny was on his knees beside the fire. Sweat dripped from the end of his nose from his long run up the cañon. Nearby, Frank and Andy were readying the horses Frank had brought up from the livery. Frank's actions were quick and deliberate, without waste, but Andy was as unco-ordinated as a drunkard, still reeling, Johnny knew, from the shock of Del's betrayal and Russ's death.

"Who were the others?" Johnny asked hoarsely, dipping a dented tin mug into the water bucket.

"Oh, they were all there," Frank said. "Dave Worthy, Little Tate Orr, Shirt Jackson, Charlie Ryder, Otis Call. Call's the leader, but Shirt and Sam are the ones you have to watch out for. They both piss pure rattlesnake venom."

"You figure they'll come after us?"

Frank shot him a surprised look. "Johnny, I figure they're already on their way."

"Son-of-a-bitch," Johnny said softly.

"What'll they do to Del?" Andy asked.

"Shut up about Del," Johnny snapped, throwing his cup into the bucket violently enough to splash water over the rim. "I'll strangle that bastard if I ever see him again."

After a moment's silence, Frank said: "Del will come back

here if the Cut-throats don't shoot him. He'll want his gold, and, as sick as it might sound, he'll want forgiveness, the sorry cur. Cutter's men won't let him keep his gold, and I doubt he'll find any absolution in Redhawk after what he did tonight."

"They won't let him live," Johnny predicted. "You can't wiggle out of a den of vipers like that without getting bit."

"Maybe you ought to take his gold, too," Andy suggested. "At least that way. . . ."

"No!" Johnny pushed to his feet. His calves still trembled from the hard climb back from town. He'd run almost all the way, stumbling into camp only minutes before Frank showed up with the horses. "Del's not a partner any more. If he survives, he can keep his share of what we've already dug, but that's it. Whether we come back in the spring or sell our claim to someone else, Del ain't a part of it any more."

Frank nodded agreement. "That'd hold up in a miner's court," he said.

Andy shrugged and stepped away from the sorrel. "She's ready."

"So's this one," Frank said, lowering the stirrup on the bay.

Johnny hobbled over to the dug-out to retrieve his rifle. Checking the cap on the Hawken, he was surprised to find it freshly sealed with bear grease.

"I cleaned it while I was waiting," Andy explained, then came quickly around the fire as if remembering something else. Picking up a holstered revolver from a stump beside the dug-out's door, he handed it to Johnny. "I cleaned this, too. All six chambers are loaded."

"You'd best hang onto that," Johnny said. "You might need it."

"Not as much as you will. Go on and take it. It's a Forty-Four and shoots the same size ball as your Remington."

Johnny nodded his thanks and slid the Colt into one of the

deep pockets on Andy's greatcoat, strapped across the pommel of his saddle. He'd thread it onto his belt later, when things slowed down.

"I think you're set," Frank said, handing Johnny the reins to the bay gelding. "Don't try to outrun 'em. Stay in the hills and out of sight as much as possible."

"I will," Johnny promised, but his hopes had dimmed. Sneaking out of Montana had seemed like a good idea when he thought it could be done without drawing attention to himself. That opportunity had been blown all to hell now, thanks to Del and the gunfight outside Halstead's.

There was a sound from down below, like splashing in the creek, followed by a short, startled yelp. Johnny stepped into the saddle and Frank handed him the sorrel's lead rope. "Godspeed, son."

"Thanks, Frank."

"Get out of here, Johnny," Andy said tersely. He was crouched at the edge of the flat, peering into the gulch. "Someone's coming up the trail."

Johnny slipped his rifle through a broad leather loop fastened to his saddle horn, where it would ride handily across his thighs. "I'll see you in Salt Lake City, boys," he called softly, then slapped the bay's ribs with his heels.

He rode around the far side of the dug-out with the sorrel in tow, then kicked the bay up the slope toward the top of the ridge. In the east, a gibbous moon was just peeking over the crest of the Tobacco Root Mountains. Its light would have been welcome under different circumstances, but Johnny knew it could work against him tonight.

He hauled up briefly on top, with a clear view to the west and north, where the low, rolling mountains were capped with snow. To the south, his view was blocked by the high, stony escarpment of the gulch's south wall. Below him, the lights of

Ruby City looked almost close enough to touch.

A game trail followed the ridge top and Johnny swung onto it, lifting his horses into a trot as they wound through the clumpy junipers. The air seemed colder up here, the breeze stiffer, but maybe that was a consequence of the moment; everything seemed sharper tonight—his vision, his hearing, even his sense of smell.

Johnny might have enjoyed these heightened sensations if his world hadn't turned so abruptly topsy-turvy. He'd suppered that night on beans and side pork, sharing his thoughts with Russ and Andy on whether or not they ought to move their sluice box higher up the hill in anticipation of next spring's run-off. Now Russ was dead and Del probably soon would be, and no telling what would happen to Andy and Frank.

No telling what would happen to him, either, in the next few hours or days. He was fleeing in the middle of the night with a fortune in gold and half a dozen stone-hearted killers on his trail. That didn't bode well for any man, let alone a Minnesota muleskinner.

Then a rifle bellowed from behind him and Johnny yanked the bay to a jarring halt. After a few seconds, he heard the lighter bark of Andy's brass-mounted Kentucky caplock, and his hand twitched on the reins. He had to resist the urge to ride back as a flurry of revolver fire crackled through the gulch, but breathed easier a couple of minutes later when he heard a second report from Andy's squirrel rifle, this one coming from farther upcañon.

As the sound of gunfire faded, a nugget of anger stirred in Johnny's breast. Squaring his shoulders, he tapped the bay's ribs with his stirrups. "Come on, horse," he said to the stocky gelding. "We've got our own job to do."

Chapter Nine

Allison Purcell paused at the edge of the pines to throw a haunted look over her shoulder, then led her long-legged jack deeper into the trees. She was thankful that, save for its small, rust-colored muzzle, the mule was as black as a crow's beak. With dawn coming on, a lighter color might have stood out among the dark trunks of the conifers, but black would all but vanish.

After securing the mule to a tree, Allie returned to the edge of the forest. Below her lay the Bannack road to Van Dolsen's trading post on the Beaverhead River. The shallow wagon ruts followed the curve of the hill for a good three-quarters of a mile before peeling off to snake past other hills similar to her own—rounded mounds no more than a couple of hundred feet tall, with grassy shoulders, jagged outcroppings of crumbling red rocks, and small, dense pine forests.

When no one appeared along the road after several minutes, Allie began to relax. Still, she knew what lay ahead, just as she knew what her fate would be if captured, and despite her relief at having made it this far without detection, tears brimmed at the corners of her eyes. Stubbornly she wiped them away. She'd made her decision to stay last summer, when Alton deserted her and their Grasshopper Creek claim for an auburn-haired strumpet named Lola, and she vowed she wouldn't bend now, no matter how frightening and unexpected her situation had become.

Returning to the mule's side, Allie patted the long black neck affectionately. She wished there was time to allow the mule to graze for a few hours, but she felt too agitated to risk it, too vulnerable to let the jack roam. Surely Tuck and his men had discovered her secret by now. He would know and, with his men, he would follow. Sadly she knew that for Tom Tucker, it wouldn't be the gold he came after.

Allie Purcell was tall for a woman, framed slim and willowy, with sandy blonde hair worn in a loose ponytail down her back. Her hands were callused and brown as walnut hulls after the summer working along the exposed banks of Grasshopper Creek, prying gravel from the stream's bed only to wash it slowly back into the current—a futile effort, it had seemed in its earliest days, and no doubt a contributor to Alton's decision to run off with his harlot.

Before the Cut-throats showed up, Allie often wondered if Alton would have stayed if he'd known they were so close to finding gold. With the Cut-throats' arrival, she'd soon discovered that what Alton might or might not have done was hardly important any more.

Coming to Montana to look for gold had been his idea. Allie had been content with their home in Davenport, taking pride in her garden and the foods she put up every fall to feed herself and her husband through the winter. But Alton had been born with a restless soul. He wanted more out of life than a dead-end job firing kilns at the local brickyard, and Allie, ever the dutiful housewife, had hid her own fear and grief behind a façade of support as she watched him sell their home and larger pieces of furniture, then pack their meager belongings into the small Studebaker Brothers wagon that had brought them to Montana.

What a fool she'd been, she chided herself, pressing her forehead to the cool leather of her saddle. An absolute ninny, and she vowed—never again.

The mule shifted, whickering softly of its exhaustion. Allie's heart suffered for the aging jack. Even now, she could hear the muted pop of his joints every time he shifted his weight. She knew the leggy animal would never survive the arduous journey ahead. Somewhere along the way, Allie would have to replace him with a better mount, abandoning him as Alton had abandoned her.

Six months ago, that thought might have distressed her, but it didn't any more. She didn't enjoy the animal's sufferings, but there was no doubt in her mind that she'd ride him until he dropped dead if she had to, sacrificing the mule's life for her own. Allie had learned a bitter lesson that summer. One her mother had never taught her, that perhaps she'd never had to learn herself. And that was that life was hard at best, and often brutal, and in the end—her fingers tightened on the soft stirrup leather of her saddle—in the end, there was only one person a woman could truly count on.

Red-eyed and tight-lipped, Allie pulled the long, double-barreled shotgun from her saddle and walked back to the edge of the timber, where she would sit for a while and watch her back trail. If she saw nothing alarming in the next thirty minutes, she would rethink her decision not to unsaddle the black and let it graze. Until then, she would wait, and watch.

Chapter Ten

The sun hadn't yet made its appearance above the cañon's rim when Johnny stepped into the bay's saddle. Far off in the dim gray light, he could make out the leafless cottonwoods lining the banks of the Ruby River. In the frosty air along the dry creek that led to the river, the sound of the horses' hoofs seemed as loud as breaking glass.

Johnny had threaded Andy's Colt onto his belt that morning while the horses grazed and rested. He carried it butt forward on his left hip, where it could easily be reached by either hand. The Remington-Beals still rode on his right, both revolvers fully loaded and capped. But it wasn't a pistol he wanted now. It was the Hawken, with its thumb-size ball capable of dropping an elk at two hundred yards. Sliding the heavy rifle from its loop on his saddle horn, Johnny butted it to his thigh, keeping his right hand firmly around the wrist, close to the hammer.

There was no surprise when he rounded a bend in the trail and spied a trio of horsemen, sitting their mounts fifty yards ahead. He'd spotted them earlier with the aid of a brass telescope carried in his shooting bag. Although he hadn't been able to identify them in the hazy, early morning light, he was pretty sure they didn't belong to Otis Call's bunch. At the same time, he had little doubt that these men were Cut-throats, either out looking for him, or just looking.

They must have heard him approaching, for they were already fanned out and waiting. The nearest one sat a sturdy-looking roan Appaloosa in the middle of the dry streambed. A second man was positioned about ten feet behind him and slightly to his left, on top of the low bank. The third rider had spurred his horse about sixty feet up the east side of the cañon's wall, halting it where the slope began its sharp, upward tilt. All three were sitting their mounts casually, although Johnny noticed they had their rifles in their hands, ready to swing into action.

Most men would've stopped when they spotted the three horsemen, but Johnny didn't. The cañon behind him, where he'd ducked just before the moon set last night, was boxed. There was only one way out, and that was straight ahead.

He held the bay to a steady walk and had covered maybe a third of the distance between him and the Cut-throats when the man on the Appaloosa, a hulking figure with long, reddish-blond hair, straightened suddenly and waved him back.

"Hey, stop!" Longhair called.

Johnny continued on as if he hadn't heard, managing to clip off another forty paces before the man on the cañon's wall, a wiry-looking individual, wearing a Mexican sombrero, stirred threateningly. Pulling the bay to a stop, Johnny offered a pleasant, " 'Mornin'."

Longhair scowled. "Who the hell are you?" he demanded.

Johnny breathed a sigh of relief. From the simple directness of the question, he knew that word of his flight from Redhawk Gulch hadn't yet drifted this far. "Who are you?" he countered, buying time.

Longhair's scowl deepened as he exchanged a glance with the man behind him, who Johnny had already dubbed Shy Boy. But Johnny was more interested in Sombrero, sitting his seal brown mare high up on the cañon's wall. Of the three, this was the one who worried him most.

"Whatcha got in them there packs?" Sombrero asked in an accent that sounded more like South Carolina than Sonora.

Sliding his thumb over the Hawken's hammer, Johnny said: "Gold."

That perked up all three men.

"Gold, ya say?" Sombrero echoed.

"We've got a tax on gold out here," Longhair added, smirking. "Not to mention a toll to pass through the Ruby and Beaverhead valleys. Likely you've been back in the hills a spell, and hadn't heard about it."

"No, I've heard," Johnny replied, tightening his grip on the bay's reins. "Why don't you boys turn those nags around and tell Cutter you didn't see anyone? There's no point in dying for someone else's riches."

Silence greeted Johnny's statement. Longhair and Shy Boy exchanged wary looks; Sombrero straightened in his saddle, easing a hand back along the rifle that rested across his saddlebows.

"Who are you?" Sombrero repeated, his voice echoing faintly upcañon.

"Friend, I'm a man with a wall at my back and a Fifty-Three-caliber Hawken rifle that's loaded for bear. You ever seen what a big-bore Hawken can do to a bear?"

"Oh, I don't doubt it'd punch a fair-sized hole," Sombrero allowed. "I was just wonderin' whether you had what it'll take to pull the trigger, that being a single-shot rifle and all."

Johnny wrapped his reins around the horn of his saddle. With his left hand, he made a motion toward the Colt. "There's one way to find out."

The broad, curled brim of Sombrero's hat tilted upward. "By God, let's do it," he said hoarsely, and Johnny lifted the Hawken even as Sombrero started to raise his own rifle.

Johnny was faster by a hair, and he was a good shot. He found Sombrero in his sights and squeezed the trigger without hesitation. With the rifle's roar, Sombrero was twisted violently from his saddle. Letting the Hawken drop, Johnny drove his heels into the bay's ribs. The gelding jumped, then leveled off into a run.

Longhair was just shouldering his own rifle when Johnny snapped off his first round from the Remington-Beals. The ball smacked into the dirt under the Appaloosa's nose, but the spotted horse stood firm. Longhair began firing, not once and then reloading, as Johnny had expected, but several times in rapid succession. But Longhair was rattled, and his shots were going wild. A couple of them kicked up chunks of sod close to the bay, but the rest went high, well over Johnny's head.

With Johnny racing toward him and firing both pistols now, Shy Boy quickly lost his nerve. He wheeled his mount and fled downcañon. Sombrero's seal-brown mare ran at his side, its empty stirrups flapping.

With Shy Boy out of the fight, Johnny focused his attention on Longhair. Although Longhair continued to return fire, his aim grew wilder. Johnny was able to close within twenty yards of Longhair's position before one of his bullets smashed into a boulder at Johnny's side. The bay squealed and bucked sideways at the sudden bite of shattered stone across its flank. Johnny dropped his Colt and grabbed for the reins, half out of his seat before he could pull the bay to a stop.

Hooting victoriously, Longhair took careful aim. With Johnny barely hanging onto the saddle, Longhair thought he had him dead to rights. He almost did, but, rather than try to regain his seat, Johnny allowed his legs to go slack, falling deliberately from the saddle just as Longhair pulled the trigger.

Johnny hit the half-frozen ground under the bay hard, nearly jolting the Remington-Beals from his grasp. Seeing him fall, Longhair lowered his rifle. He was still grinning when Johnny fired from under the bay's stomach. The gelding jumped and kicked at the muzzle blast that raked its belly, then lunged clear of the trail. Downcañon, Longhair got a funny look on his face. Then he slowly tipped off the near side of his horse, making no sound as he fell, other than the solid thud of his body striking the earth.

Chapter Eleven

Johnny climbed to his feet, the Remington-Beals gripped vise-like in his right hand. Far below, he could see Shy Boy just approaching the mouth of the cañon at a fast gallop, Sombrero's seal brown running at his side. Johnny's gaze shifted to the base of the cañon wall where the third bandit had rolled. Checking the Remington-Beals and finding that it still had two loaded chambers, he cautiously approached the body.

Sombrero lay on his face with his arms stretched above his head. A hole in the middle of his back, where the Hawken's ball had exited, convinced Johnny there was no need to check for a pulse. He walked back to where Longhair had fallen, still clutching the Appaloosa's reins. Longhair's eyes were open, but rolled back in his head, already glazed in death. Taking a deep, steadying breath, Johnny holstered the Remington-Beals.

The Appaloosa stood at the end of its reins, its head high, nostrils distended. Johnny knew only someone's careful training prevented the animal from bolting. Speaking calmly and in a conversational tone, he edged forward. The Appaloosa bobbed its head and nickered questioningly, but made no effort to break away. Gently Johnny eased the reins free of Longhair's fingers.

The Appaloosa impressed him. It was a short-coupled gelding with a broad, deep chest and well-defined muscles—a conformation that promised good wind and endurance. The head was small but attractive, the eyes intelligent. It was only when Johnny turned the horse broadside that he noticed the fresh spur marks along the ribs, the hair scraped away as neatly as if peeled with a razor, the flesh pink and tender-looking. Glancing at the sharp-roweled Mexican spurs on Longhair's boots, Johnny said: "You son-of-a-bitch. I was starting to feel sorry for you."

He led the Appaloosa to a nearby juniper and tied it there with a lead rope from its halter, then went back to catch his own mount. The sorrel was grazing peacefully on the other side of the streambed, and Johnny left it there.

With the horses secured and both pistols and the Hawken reloaded, Johnny returned to Longhair's side to take a look at his rifle. He already had an idea of what he'd find. Word of the new repeating firearms coming out of the war back East had made interesting fodder for campfire conversations for a couple of years now, and Johnny had a working knowledge of both of the new lever-action long guns gradually making their way into civilian hands—Christian Spencer's .56 carbine and Oliver Winchester's .44 Henry.

The Spencer loaded through a channel in the butt, the Henry via a tube under its barrel, as this one did. It was said a fully loaded Henry carried fourteen rounds in its magazine; fifteen, if a man wanted to keep a cartridge chambered. Those numbers put Johnny's single-shot, muzzle-loading Hawken into a whole new perspective. Turning the Henry over in his hands, he whistled appreciatively at its sleek lines, eyeing the oblong lever under the wrist curiously. The receiver gleamed like pure brass and the walnut stock was richly polished. The rifle was, if not new, then close to it.

Johnny glanced at the body sprawled at his feet. Longhair was a lot younger than he'd originally thought. Maybe no more than nineteen or twenty. He had broad, sloping shoulders and the start of a pot gut that probably would have stretched into a sizable belly had he lived. His skin was soft and doughy, the fingers without calluses, and he wore a ring on his right hand that contained a polished black stone set with the letter *L* in silver.

There was a cartridge belt buckled around Longhair's waist. That was another first for Johnny, although he was quick to see its advantage in carrying the Henry's stubby metallic cartridges. A pair of New Model Remington revolvers, similar to his own older Remington-Beals, were holstered on the belt as well, their matching ivory grips spotted with dirt.

Hefting the rifle experimentally in his hands, Johnny felt a sudden, unexpected anger for what he was about to do. He knew he'd be a fool to pass up the opportunity Longhair had presented him, no matter how much it galled him to rob from the dead.

Johnny quickly stripped the cartridge belt from the dead man's waist, bringing the two new Remingtons in their carved leather holsters—both of them .44s, like his own—with it. Then he hurried away, as if afraid of getting something unsavory on his clothes.

He took the weapons to the bay and tucked the pistols inside his saddlebags to deal with later. The cartridge belt, he strapped around his waist. Then he unbuckled the scabbard from the Appaloosa's saddle and rigged it to his own. Retrieving the tin of salve from his saddlebags, he doctored the spur gouges along the Appaloosa's sides, then tied the stirrups together over the seat so that they wouldn't bounce against the wounds and irritate them further. Although the injuries looked bad, Johnny knew that they weren't, and that they would heal quickly.

He fetched the sorrel, then tied the Appaloosa's lead rope to the pack mare's tail where it would be easy to slash with his Bowie knife if he needed to make a quick escape. Satisfied with the arrangement, he swung astride the bay. It was full daylight now, and he was eager to push on. As he rode down the cañon's trail, he glanced back only once at the bodies he was leaving behind. He doubted if he was ten miles out of Redhawk yet, and, all of a sudden, Salt Lake City seemed a long way away.

Chapter Twelve

It was mid-morning when the three outlaws came in sight of the Lost Spring roadhouse. Riding slightly in advance of his two trail companions, Otis Call eyed the low stone structure with a feeling of trepidation. The roadhouse sat in the middle of a grove of gnarled cottonwoods, their limbs bare at this late date. A small creek ran through the trees on its way to the Ruby River, several miles to the north, and on the far side of what passed for the road—the Ruby Range cut-off—was an abandoned blacksmith shop and livery.

At one time, the Lost Spring roadhouse had been a place of likely prospects, but that had come to a jarring halt last July when Otis, Brett, Tom Tucker, and a handful of others had moved in with an impunity that surprised even Otis, who'd thought nothing Cutter did could shock him any more.

Otis and Tuck had feared retaliation from one of the nearby mining camps, but Brett had scoffed, insisting Montana was too young yet, its government too embryonic, to bother them this season.

"Give it another year or two," he'd predicted calmly, while the frightened proprietor and his leathery-skinned wife looked on in helpless terror. "They'll come after us with hangman's nooses then, but I expect the governor and his cabinet are too busy scrambling for their own claims this summer to worry about someone else's troubles."

It hadn't hurt, Otis supposed, that Montana wasn't officially a territory yet, and wouldn't be for several more months, when it finally broke its last tie to Idaho.

With no one to stop them, Brett had given the Lost Spring proprietor $100 for the land, buildings, and all the merchandise they had on hand—almost $2,000 worth of trade goods—then had him sign the property over with a quitclaim deed. For the proprietor and his wife, facing a hail of bullets as the alternative, the deal was too good to pass up, and they were soon skedaddling back East, taking only their oxen and a small wagon with some personal possessions.

The others had laughed, but their treatment of the elderly couple had bothered Otis. It still did.

It was odd the way his feelings toward Brett had eroded over the last few months. They'd been partners for going on eight years, and friends for most of that time, but something had changed recently. Nowadays, Otis dreaded these periodic visits to Cutter's Lost Spring headquarters, and, more and more, he was starting to resent the man, too. He couldn't have said what had caused the split, but it was obvious to everyone that the easy camaraderie between the two had disappeared.

Tom Tucker was a different matter. Otis had never cared much for the lanky killer and his unpredictable peculiarities—especially with women. To Otis's way of thinking, Tuck wasn't quite right in the head, for all that he was a reliable partner in any kind of robbery, a crack shot, and skilled at handling men. Still, Tuck was an odd one, and recently Brett was starting to act too much like him to make Otis comfortable.

He wasn't looking forward to telling Brett about last night, although he knew Little Tate Orr's death wasn't going to mean nearly as much to Brett as Johnny Montana's escape with over $40,000 in gold. Brett was going to be furious, and Otis was dreading the cold, quiet rage. When that happened, only violence and revenge could temper the outlaw leader's ferocity.

No one greeted them as they rode up, but Otis knew their arrival hadn't gone unnoticed. Swinging down at the hitch rail in front of the roadhouse, he looped his reins over the rack, then glanced at Dave Worthy and Charlie Ryder, sitting their horses some yards away. "You boys forget how to get off a horse?"

"We was thinkin' maybe we'd. . . ."

"No," Otis said bluntly, without giving Charlie a chance to finish. "I want you two with me, in case Brett gets snarly."

"Brett's always snarly," Dave countered. "Besides, he's your friend."

"Brett Cutter doesn't have any friends," Otis replied, feeling a strange sense of loss at his words.

Charlie and Dave exchanged glum looks, then dismounted. Otis led them inside, stepping clear of the door as soon as he entered so that he wouldn't be silhouetted by the outside light. Charlie and Dave did the same, moving in the opposite direction after Dave kicked the door shut.

Like always, Otis glanced first at the small iron safe sitting in the middle of the room. The safe contained all of the loot they'd taken from the Ruby and Beaverhead valleys over the past few weeks. Then he raised his eyes to seek out the Cut-throats' leader.

Brett Cutter was standing on the business side of the plank counter that ran across the rear of the room. A clay jug of Kentucky bourbon sat at his elbow, and he held a dented tin mug in his hand. Brett was a large man. Not as tall or as broad through the shoulders as Otis, but thick through the chest and gut. He was clean-shaven and wore his silver hair short under a broad-brimmed military hat. His eyes were green, set deeply in a creviced face, his hands large and fight-scarred. A red silk bandanna around his neck stood out like a fresh wound in the poor light.

Bud Dixon was standing at the counter with Brett, slumped

over the planks with his own tin cup. At the long table beside the kitchen door, Harry Spindell and Poke Hardesty were eating some of Poke's cooking. As the rich aroma of venison stew reached Otis's nostrils, he inhaled deeply. "Poke," he said, "I hope you've got some of that good grub left. I'm hungry enough to eat my saddle."

"They's some in back," the grizzled old-timer answered, dribbling a little gravy down his stubbled chin when he looked up. "Hep yerself."

"I will in a minute," Otis promised, then turned to Cutter. "Hello, Brett."

"Otis," Brett returned charily. His gaze flitted briefly to Charlie and Dave, then came back to Otis. "Tell it."

"We didn't get it."

Cutter's expression remained unchanged. "What happened?"

Briefly Otis related the previous night's events, keeping the story simple and straightforward, eliminating what didn't directly add to the explanation. When he finished, Cutter's voice remained eerily calm, his hand steady as he raised his cup. He drank deeply of the bourbon, then lowered the cup and wiped his lips with the back of his hand. Finally he said: "If it was anyone else but you, Otis . . . anyone . . . I'd kill the son-of-a-bitch right here."

"You're getting too caught up in this, Brett," Otis replied, hooking a thumb behind his belt, close to his Colt. "I'm not happy about it, either, but Shirt and Sam are tracking Montana now. They'll catch him."

Cutter was staring at Charlie and Dave, scowling. "Where's Little Tate?" he asked suddenly.

Otis sighed and crossed the room to the counter. "Gimme a drink," he said.

"You figure you'll need one?" Brett asked coolly.

"Uhn-huh. Better pour yourself another, while you're at it."

Otis told Brett everything—the mob's reaction to the wagon party's return and how Del Kirkham had come into Halstead's later that evening to cut a deal for his own safety. He told him about Sam's gunning down the prospector called Bailey, and McCarty's flight with the two horses. Brett smiled icily when Otis related how Del had come forward at the dug-out with his hands raised, as trusting as an idiot seeing old friends, just before Shirt shot him down.

"We should've caught the others, too," Otis acknowledged, "but that old liveryman, McCarty, let out a yell before anyone could get off a shot, and him and Andy Tabor hightailed it into the darkness."

"You didn't follow them?"

"Little Tate followed them," Otis reminded him.

Brett made a dismissing gesture with his hand. "So the kid . . . what did you call him?"

"Johnny Montana."

"So this Johnny Montana got away with the gold?"

"Everything except what we took off Kirkham. Between the three remaining partners and whatever McCarty had, I figure Montana's running loose with around forty thousand dollars in his packs."

Brett's knuckles whitened on his tin cup as he walked to a small window in the back wall, staring out past the trees to the north. "You have confidence in Jackson and Hulse?" he asked.

"Shirt Jackson in particular. He's part Indian."

Brett's voice cooled. "That's a flaw in your character, Otis . . . your willingness to allow popular opinion to cloud your judgment. Jackson is Indian, *ergo,* his tracking skills must be exceptional, his eyesight keen as a hawk's, his stealth the equal of any cougar's."

"I didn't say that," Otis protested.

"You implied it." Brett glanced at Bud Dixon. "Who did

Harley Lamont ride out with this morning?"

Bud looked startled by the question. "Why, Prairie Richards and Lloyd, I think. They were going to nose around the hills north of here."

Brett returned to the counter. "Harley is coming in on a lathered horse. Prairie's mare is at his side, without Prairie. That portends bad news, in my opinion."

Bud straightened and set his drink aside. Poke and Harry had quit eating and were watching Brett guardedly. "You want me to go take a look?" Bud asked, but Cutter shook his head.

"Harley knows the way to my door. If there's news. . . ." He let his words trail off, but his knuckles remained white on his cup, like nuggets of milk quartz. "Who killed Little Tate?" he asked.

Otis gave him a quizzical look. "Andy Tabor. He got off a lucky shot with a squirrel rifle."

"What do you know about Montana?"

"Not that much. He's young, but they say he's savvy. He got the Montana moniker last summer after he pulled a wagon train of settlers out of a tight spot with the Sioux."

Brett cocked a brow. "Then he's not a kid."

"I just caught a glimpse of him," Otis admitted. "He looked young, but it was pretty dark." Once again, the image of the young man he'd spotted briefly on the boardwalk outside The Bucket Saloon flashed through Otis's mind, and he almost said something. Then the memory of the man he hadn't seen, but had sensed in the shadows beside McCarty's livery returned, and he shut his mouth. They would meet again, somewhere down the road, their futures as entwined as wind and rain. But Brett didn't need to know that yet.

The clatter of hoofs came around the front of the roadhouse, and Harley Lamont hollered: "Whoa, ya damn' idjit!"

Bud Dixon walked to the door and flung it open just as

Harley Lamont stumbled up the steps, his eyes as wide as saucers. His horse stood, spraddle-legged and trembling, in the yard behind him, its muzzle nearly brushing the ground. Harley came to a sudden stop when he saw Brett.

"*Aw,* hell," Harley breathed, shaking his head as if he felt like bawling. "He's dead, Brett. Lloyd's dead." He stood stockstill a moment, then swallowed audibly. "Brett, did you hear me? Your brother Lloyd's been killed."

Chapter Thirteen

It turned warm as the day progressed, almost in mockery of the season. By noon, Johnny had shed his coat to ride along in his shirt sleeves, tipping his hat back to take advantage of the sun's warmth on his face. The breeze out of the south felt almost balmy after the frosty temperatures of the past few weeks, although Johnny didn't trust it. Frank McCarty had warned him last summer of southerly zephyrs, especially late in the year.

"A warm wind out of the south ain't necessarily your friend," Frank had often remarked. "You might think I'm joshing you, but I ain't. If you find yourself enjoying a southerly breeze too much, you'd better start keeping an eye peeled to the north. You're apt to look up one day and find a blizzard rolling down on you."

Their first storm of the season had happened that way, Johnny recalled, although it had been some less than a blizzard. Still, it was good advice. It was November now, and past time, he reasoned, for a big storm.

Up ahead, he could just make out the group of squatty log dwellings that was Twin Bridges. He was approaching the town from the north, having circled wide around it that afternoon for fear Brett Cutter had men staked out along the Ruby Valley road. Johnny's original intent had been to ford the Jefferson River somewhere below town, but he'd discovered the waters there—the combined flows of the Ruby, Beaverhead, and Big

Hole Rivers—were too deep after the recent melt from earlier storms. Short of returning to the upper Ruby and losing everything he'd gained over the past twenty-odd hours, his only option seemed to be Twin Bridges.

Johnny was still riding the bay, with the Henry rifle booted under his right leg and the Hawken balanced across his saddle. He'd taken time that afternoon to replace his older Remington-Beals and Andy's rattly Colt with Longhair's ivory-handled New Models, belting them around his waist in their fancy, floral-carved holsters. While his horses grazed on the rich, summer-cured grasses, Johnny had discovered that the pouch on Longhair's cartridge belt, where most men carried a few extra linen cartridges, contained two fully loaded cylinders for the Remingtons, sitting side-by-side and already capped.

The extra cylinders would make reloading twice as fast as replacing a pistol's empty chambers with linen cartridges, then ramming the ball down tightly against the powder and capping the nipples. They offered the kind of speed a freighter or prospector seldom needed, but which a man on the run might.

Twin Bridges' main street ran north and south along the right bank of the Beaverhead, just above its junction with the Big Hole, where it became the Jefferson, itself one of the three forks of the Missouri. The Utah road that would take Johnny over Monida Pass teed off from the main artery near the center of town, running west for nearly half a mile to by-pass the numerous sloughs. After that, it curved south toward Dolsen's trading post at the upper end of the Beaverhead Valley. Dolsen's would be the last outpost Johnny passed before Fort Hall, on the far-off Snake River of Idaho Territory.

Twin Bridges was more of a community than a mining camp, and its future seemed quite a bit more assured than Ruby City's. Johnny, Russ, Andy, and Del had passed through the town twice last spring, and Johnny could remember a restaurant, a large general store, and at least two liveries with blacksmith shops. There had also been several saloons, the more opulent of them being the New Yorker, at the head of the Utah road. The four partners had stopped at the New Yorker briefly on their way to Redhawk Gulch, marveling at the large selection of whiskies displayed along its ornate backbar.

As the saloon came into view now, Johnny's gut tightened. A pair of heavily armed men were lounging under the verandah. Both wore their hats low against the afternoon sun. Although he tried not to look at them, his scalp was crawling as he approached the corner that would put him on the Utah road. He kept the bay to a shuffling jog, resisting the urge to kick it into a run.

One of the men, wearing a black and white steer-hide vest with the hair still on, was sitting on a bench beside the front door. The other leaned against a lathed post with his heel propped against it, a yellow bandanna the color of freshly shucked corn knotted around his neck. Both men were watching him closely, but it wasn't until he was almost to the corner that Bandanna shouted: "Hey, come over here!"

The sorrel's lead rope was wrapped lightly around the bay's saddle horn, and Johnny casually loosened it and tossed it over the pack mare's neck. At this point, there was nothing he could do about the Appaloosa, still tethered to the sorrel's tail.

"Dammit, I'm talkin' to you, boy. Get over here!" Bandanna called.

Then the man in the cowhide vest leaped to his feet, tossing his beer mug into the street. "Watch out, Joe Bill!" Vest called, reaching for a pistol. "He's got Lloyd's horse!"

Johnny swore and slammed his heels into the bay's ribs. The horse snorted and lunged into a rough, protesting canter. Palming his right-hand gun, Johnny snapped off a round that streaked across the street like a homing pigeon. The man called Joe Bill howled and grabbed his thigh with both hands, pitching off the New Yorker's steps into the hard mud.

Dropping to a crouch behind one of the verandah's posts, Vest swiftly returned fire, but Johnny was already around the corner, the bay's gait smoothing out as the first bridge came into sight. Then a third gunman scrabbled up the bank next to the bridge with a rifle in hand. Johnny leveled his Remington and fired twice. Both bullets raked at the muddy earth just in front of the third Cut-throat's feet, and the man quickly dived back into the tall grass beside the road.

Twisting in his saddle, Johnny saw the sorrel and Appaloosa running effortlessly less than a dozen yards behind him. Vest was still firing from the New Yorker's boardwalk, but, at this range, he wasn't even coming close. Johnny squeezed off a shot for luck, then fired a couple of rounds into the grass beside the bridge abutment, where the third bandit hid and where a saddled, line-back dun was struggling frantically against the sapling where it was tied. Then the bay was pounding across the bridge. Johnny yelled and looked back. No one was in sight—not even Vest—but the dun had pulled loose and was racing after the sorrel and Appaloosa. Straightening in his saddle, Johnny whooped the shrill war cry of a Sioux. It didn't occur to him until he was a couple of miles down the road that the extra horse might come in handy, and then not until the sorrel started weaving erratically from side to side, blood streaming down its coppery flank.

Chapter Fourteen

Otis yawned as he reached for his boots and pulled them on. He was sitting on his blankets under the sloping trunk of a cottonwood, with an unobstructed view of the flat plain to the north, where Poke Hardesty and Harry Spindell were returning with their grisly cargo.

Until that moment, Otis had entertained some hope that Harley Lamont had been mistaken when he claimed Brett's little brother had been killed; he knew now it had been a false hope. Lloyd Cutter was dead, and, although Brett had taken the news with uncustomary composure, Otis figured that was about to come to an abrupt and bloody end.

Shoving to his feet, he strapped on his gun belt, then draped the gray wool blanket over his shoulder like a serape. He considered Lloyd's death a small loss to the outfit. Otis had never liked or trusted the kid. Not since their first meeting five months ago in San Diego, where he and Brett and Tuck met the ship that brought Lloyd around the Horn from the East Coast. Brett was a smart man. He was cruel and maybe a little bit of a coward, but he was as cunning as a fox and a natural leader.

Lloyd wasn't even close to being the man his brother was. Almost twenty years Brett's junior, Lloyd was weak and easily intimidated. He was twice as mean, though, and he was arrogant, which was what had probably gotten him killed. Standing up to a two-gun man charging in on horseback, rather than diving for cover and returning fire from behind a rock, was just plain dumb, as far as Otis was concerned.

Turning away from the plain, Otis headed for the roadhouse where Brett was waiting on the porch with Bud Dixon. Dave Worthy and Charlie Ryder were nowhere in sight. Neither was Harley Lamont, and Otis smiled thinly. *Smart men,* he thought.

Brett's visage darkened as Otis approached. "By damn, I do hate to interfere with a man's nap. Especially for something as piddling as burying kin."

"I was up all night getting here," Otis reminded him, tossing his blanket over the porch railing. "Up all day yesterday, too. Besides, Lloyd isn't my kin." He gave that a moment to sink in, then added: "Who I've been thinking about is Little Tate and Prairie Richards."

"The hell with Tate and Richards."

"I liked Little Tate," Otis said stubbornly. "He was dependable. The only foolish thing I ever saw him do was try to follow that tin-pan into the sage last night."

"This ain't a business for fools," Brett replied with a sneer.

"This outfit's too big," Otis said bluntly, ignoring Cutter's attempt to bait him. "We've got too many men and way too many fools. Little Tate wasn't one of them, but Harley Lamont is."

"Harley Lamont ain't gonna be a problem much longer," Brett growled.

"Don't do anything rash. We're too close to finishing this job to risk a mutiny now."

"This job is about done," Brett said. "As soon as. . . ." He shut up as Poke and Harry rode around the front of the roadhouse. Following the direction of his gaze, Otis saw Lloyd's long, reddish-blond hair swaying loosely beside the stirrup of the horse he was strapped across.

"Harley!" Brett shouted. "Harley, get your ass out here. Now!"

Harley's head popped out from behind the blacksmith shop,

reminding Otis of a boy who knew he was in trouble and about to get a switching for it. Harley came around the small log structure carrying a bottle of whiskey, then paused and reluctantly handed it to someone still behind the building. Otis's smile returned. So that was where Dave and Charlie were hiding.

Brett's expression looked hard as stone as he stared at his brother's body. "I sent Lloyd out there to keep him away from trouble, and he rides straight into the path of a cold-blooded killer. Has God forsaken this land, Otis, that He'd allow something like this to happen to one so young? Twenty. That's all Lloyd was, just twenty years old and as sweet a lad as ever to tread the Earth."

Otis didn't reply. He knew it would be useless to remind Brett that it had been Lloyd who had led the attack on the wagon party, Lloyd who had gunned down the kid handling the lines, even when everyone else begged him not to. Otis had been running cross-grain to the law most of his life and had killed his share of men, but he'd never popped a cap on a kid, or known anyone to brag about it afterward if they had, like Lloyd had.

"Yes, sir?" Harley said, stopping some distance away. He was hatless, his face and hands dirty from digging in the soil.

"Did you finish those graves?"

"Yes, sir. Six feet down and square as a box at the corners."

"What about the other one?" Otis asked.

Harley gave him an uncomfortable look. "It ain't so deep," he admitted, "but I doubt if ol' Prairie'll mind. Shoot, me 'n' him's buried more'n one body over the years, and never put 'im more than a foot or so under. Just enough to hide the corpse from a posse or keep the smell down, if we was camped nearby."

"How deep?" Otis repeated impatiently.

Harley shrugged. "Coupla feet's all, but that'll be. . . ."

Brett cursed and stepped off the porch, and Harley quickly shut up. Brett went to the pack horse where his brother was lashed. "Bring a shovel," he snapped over his shoulder to Harley. "And get those two lazy friends of yours over here to help."

When Brett had moved out of earshot, Bud Dixon pushed away from the front wall of the roadhouse where he'd been leaning. "That old man is getting frayed around the edges," he said to Otis.

"It's his brother we're burying," Otis reminded him.

"Sure, today, but Brett's been slipping closer to the edge for a couple of weeks now. You haven't been around, Call. I have."

Otis turned slowly to face the younger man, his dark eyes menacing. "Meaning what?"

"Pull in your horns, pard. I ain't out to castrate the old boy, but I've seen this happen before. Brett's gotten greedy. He wants it all, every damn' nugget we've collected, and I think knowin' he ain't gonna get it is drivin' him a little crazy."

"We're pulling out soon. Brett's greed won't matter once we get out of Montana."

"A lot of the boys are thinkin' we ought to pull out now, before the mountain passes close for good."

Otis studied the snowy crown of the Ruby Range to the west. Their original plan had been to make as big a haul as possible in that window of time when the first snows of winter cut off wagon and stage traffic over the higher elevations, but they could still get out on horseback. By Otis's reckoning, they were already pushing their luck. Still, it aggravated him to hear Dixon voicing similar concerns. Moving away, he said: "You let me and Brett and Tuck worry about the gold and the weather. Don't forget you wouldn't have a share of it if not for us."

"Oh, I ain't forgettin'," Bud returned mildly. "Just don't you forget that it's been me 'n' Jack McGrew that the old man's been confiding in lately."

Otis kept walking, but he knew there was truth in Dixon's words. Neither he nor Tuck were really privy to Cutter's plans any more. Not like they had been in years past, like Dixon and McGrew, who Brett kept close to him here at Lost Spring, were now.

They buried Lloyd under the cottonwoods behind the roadhouse, covering the turned soil afterward with stones hauled up from the creek. Poke Hardesty drove a crude wooden cross into the ground at the head of the grave, then set Lloyd's hat on top of it. Brett spoke a few words of remembrance that didn't make much sense to anyone other than himself, then they all shuffled over to Prairie Richards's shallow trough, some yards away. Poke and Harry Spindell had laid him out in a blanket, but Brett told Harley Lamont to cover the grave; Poke and Harry had covered Lloyd's.

"Me?" Harley sounded perturbed. "Hell, Brett, I dug them holes. Let someone else. . . ."

"You do it," Brett said curtly.

"Well, hell," Harley murmured, yanking a shovel from Poke's hands. He was halfway around the grave when the blast from Brett's six-shooter cracked like lightning through the trees. Harley plunged into the grave on top of Prairie, quivered once, then lay still. No one spoke or looked surprised.

"Poke," Brett said, his demeanor calmer now than it had been all day. "Would you finish the job?"

"Sure, Brett." Poke paused, staring at the corpse.

"Go ahead and rifle the pockets. You and Harry can keep what you find."

Poke grinned and Harry hurried forward to assist him.

Returning the smoking revolver to its holster, Brett said: "Gentlemen, our time in Montana has come to an end."

Bud, Charlie, and Dave grinned hugely.

"We have but one final task to accomplish," Brett continued.

"I want the murderer of my little brother, Johnny Montana."

"Hell, he's probably already been got," Dave Worthy said cheerfully. "Sam and Shirt are on his trail now, and Jack McGrew and his boys are out there to cut him off if he gets past Twin Bridges. Ain't no point worrying about Montana, Brett. He's as good as dead, if he ain't already."

Brett looked at Otis. "Do you agree, old friend?"

Otis hesitated, then shook his head. "I doubt it. We've got three dead already, not counting Harley, and Montana hasn't been out twenty-four hours yet." He met Cutter's gaze evenly. "This one's different, Brett. He won't be easy to run down."

Cutter nodded as if he'd already come to the same conclusion. "I don't think he's dead yet, either, but I don't agree that he's different. He's just been lucky, but that's going to change damn' fast." He raised his voice, as if speaking to a hundred men. "We're pulling out. Otis, take your men to Twin Bridges and pick up Bonner, Ewing, and Hodson. Send someone out to bring in Dover and Miles as well. Meanwhile, I'll go west along the cut-off and rendezvous with McGrew and his outfit. We'll split the gold at Dolsen's trading post . . . after Montana's killed."

"After?" Charlie Ryder echoed.

"After," Brett repeated, his voice turning cold. "Hear this, all of you, then pass it on to the others. That gold won't be divvied out until Montana's dead. Not to anyone, but there'll be an extra five thousand dollars to the man who kills him." He paused briefly, then added: "Five thousand in gold to the man who brings me the head and hide of Johnny Montana."

Chapter Fifteen

It was Tom Tucker's eyes she hated most. Always so cold and empty and unrelentingly direct. Like tiny hands pawing at her, making her want to crawl into a hole to hide.

They stared at her now, bright with triumph, and she screamed and rolled away, kicking at her blankets, swinging her fists wildly. Laughing, he tugged at her bedroll, spilling her onto the pine needles that carpeted the forest floor. She tried to scramble away, but he grabbed her ankle and yanked her back, ripping her dress. Then more hands landed on her, gliding up her legs like so many snakes. She screamed again, flailing desperately, and opened her eyes. . . .

For a long moment, Allison Purcell didn't move. She didn't even twitch as she stared uncomprehendingly at the evergreen ceiling overhead. Then she drew in a long, shuddering breath and rolled onto her side. Several yards away, the black mule watched her curiously.

Pushing to her hands and knees, Allie crawled to where her blanket lay tangled up at the base of a pine several feet away. The shotgun her father had given her last spring leaned against its trunk, and she pulled it into her arms as if cradling a baby. It was her only protector now, all that stood between her and the men who surely followed.

After a while, she got to her feet and moved to the edge of the trees, where she had a clear view of the Bannack road. She hadn't meant to fall asleep, but she'd been so tired. All those days of frantic digging, forever worrying that her secret would be discovered and that Tucker and his men would find out about her gold, had taken its toll. Nor was it the first time she'd had this particular dream. It had originally assaulted her sleep more than a month ago, shortly after Tuck and his men arrived in Bannack. They'd stayed only a day and a night on that first visit, and the townfolk had hoped they were gone for good when they pulled out the next morning, but most had known they'd be back.

Allie could still remember the look of dread on the faces of the town's people on the day Tuck's gang had ridden out of town. Twenty-four hours later, three men had been found dead along the road to Dolsen's trading post, gunned down on their way out of the territory. It wasn't long afterward that she first heard the term Cutter's Cut-throats, but, by then, she didn't need to be told that Tuck and his crew were part of a larger gang.

Over the weeks, tales of violence continued to filter into Bannack. Some of the citizens had trouble believing the viciousness of the attacks, but not Allie. By that time, Tuck had learned of the woman who lived alone along Grasshopper Creek, gamely working the claim her husband had filed in the spring. He'd been down to see her several times, but the visit she recalled most vividly was his first.

Quite a few of Bannack's male population had come calling on her in the weeks following Alton's desertion. Most had just wanted to make sure she was all right. Some bore gifts of venison or coarse camp bread. A few had asked permission to court her, requests she'd firmly denied. Still, having men show up at her claim hadn't been unusual, and never anything to fear . . . until the day Tuck showed up.

Allie had known from the moment she saw him, sitting his horse atop a rise fifty yards away, that this one was different.

Tuck hadn't come to inquire after her welfare or beg conversation. He wanted something more.

She supposed a smart woman would have fled immediately, but there'd been her claim to think of, the gold she'd struck just days before Tuck's arrival, a shallow pocket no bigger around than her hat and less than six inches deep, but the sandy gravel had been woven throughout with fine, bright yellow swirls. A fortune waiting to be plucked.

She'd discovered the gold under the big, flat stone where she'd knelt throughout the summer to do her laundry, less than thirty feet from the rocker box she'd labored at like an ox all these months. She'd glanced down late one afternoon to search for a dropped sliver of soap, and spied a single, pinhead-size fleck of gold instead. The sun's light had caught it just right. A feeling of disbelief had fogged her mind for days afterward as she carefully sifted the tiny flakes from the gravel with tweezers and deposited them, one at a time, into small leather pokes, six altogether, more than enough to take her home to Davenport.

The gold and what it promised for the future—her future—was why she'd stayed, risking Tuck's advances, living day and night with the knowledge that, sooner or later, he wouldn't allow her to drive him off with a cold shoulder or a curt response.

Allie knew that day had been drawing steadily nearer. Winter wouldn't hold off much longer, and soon Tuck and the rest of the Cut-throats would abandon Montana the way Alton had abandoned her. And she'd known, with absolute certainty, that if Tuck didn't take her with him—and that was her worse fear—then he would certainly never leave the territory without knowing her . . . using her.

Perhaps even sharing her.

Allie shivered and her gaze swept the Bannack road from east to west, but the distant trace was empty. If anyone had passed this way while she slept, they'd left no sign that could be seen from here.

She made her way back into the darkness of the trees. The mule whickered as she approached, and she felt a pang of guilt for leaving him there all day on such a short lead, without food or water. She murmured an apology as she stroked the animal's thin neck. "I should have picketed you on grass," she said, "and taken you down to water."

But even as the words left her lips, Allie knew she wouldn't have done it. Better a starving mule, she reasoned, than a black-hided flag wandering the side of the hill to signal Tuck and his men.

She tightened the cinch on her old Dragoon saddle, then mounted and adjusted her skirts around her ankles, as much for protection against the dropping, late-afternoon temperatures as for modesty's sake. She carried the shotgun across the saddle with both barrels charged, their nipples capped. She would have liked a pistol in addition to the shotgun, but Alton had taken that, and Allie hadn't dared purchase a new one for fear of betraying the secret lying hidden beneath her laundry rock.

She left the small forest and made her way down to Rattlesnake Creek, where she watered the mule and slaked her own thirst. Then she remounted and reined downstream. She stayed off the road to avoid leaving tracks, but paralleled it for guidance. It was another twenty miles to Dolsen's trading post, and she wanted to be well past that and on her way toward Monida Pass before first light. Once she made it that far, if she was careful and not spotted, she thought she would be safe. Tuck would never believe a woman would challenge the high spine of the Rockies alone. Not at this late date and on an ancient mule. He'd figure she turned north toward Twin Bridges or one of the mining camps east of there—Virginia City or Adobe Town or Ruby City—and he'd go to those places first to look for her.

The thought that he might not, or that she might leave some trace his trackers could find, lingered in her mind, despite her efforts not to dwell on it. Monida Pass was her best hope. She would not speculate on the alternatives.

Chapter Sixteen

It was after midnight when Otis Call, Charlie Ryder, and Dave Worthy rode into Twin Bridges. The town was dark save for the lights of the New Yorker. Otis guided his horse in that direction. As he drew closer, he recognized Sam Hulse's grulla and Warshirt Jackson's pinto hitched out front. Riding to the next rail, the three men dismounted and wearily climbed the steps to the saloon.

The New Yorker was a long, narrow building with a high ceiling. The bar ran down the right-hand side of the room; tables and chairs were scattered along the left. Although only a couple of lamps were lit, there was enough illumination to glint off the rows of expensive whiskey bottles along the backbar.

Berthed in the deeper recesses on the sober side of the bar stood a stocky man wearing a full-length white apron, his hair slicked down and parted in the middle. On the business side were Shirt, Sam, and Chris Ewing in his black and white steerhide vest. Hank Bonner was slumped in a chair at one of the tables midway down the room, one foot resting on a neighboring chair, where he was idly rolling his spur back and forth across the seat. At the far end of the room, Joe Bill Hodson sat on the floor with a bottle of whiskey at his side, a blood-stained bandage wrapped around his thigh outside his trousers; sweat glistened on Joe Bill's face, and his lips were drawn into a grimace as he watched Otis cross the room. There were no other customers.

"Whiskey," Otis said, propping his elbows on the bar; he jerked his head toward Dave and Charlie. "For them, too."

"Howdy, boys," Sam said loudly, offering a lop-sided grin that told Otis the normally dependable gunman was already well into his cups.

Turning to Shirt, Otis said: "Did you get him?"

The half-breed Chickasaw shook his head, but his eyes were still on the bartender. When the barkeep finished pouring for Otis, Dave, and Charlie, Shirt slammed his glass down on top of the polished mahogany, causing the barkeep to flinch. "How about another one, bardog?" Shirt asked, his dark eyes glittering. "Or are you still refusing to serve redskins?"

"N-No," the bartender stammered, quickly stepping forward. Otis watched as the long-necked bottle rattled against the rim of Shirt's glass.

"Damn, Shirt, you've got that boy half scared you're going to scalp him," Otis observed.

"The night ain't over yet," was Shirt's terse reply.

"He ain't scalpin' no white man," said a voice from behind them, and the bartender scurried back into the shadows.

Otis didn't have to turn around to know who'd spoken. Mostly he got along well with the men who rode for Cutter. Part of that, he knew, was because of his standing with Brett, but he'd proved himself over the summer, too, busting knuckles on some of the meanest of the bunch so that the rest of them knew he could back up any order he gave. Still, there were a few men in the outfit who refused to dampen their prejudices. Hank Bonner was one of them. He was a New Jersey boy, but his intolerance toward Negroes, Indians, and Chinese ran deep. Otis had seen Hank's kind of poison before, and knew it had a tendency to fester up at the worse times.

Leaning against the bar, Otis regarded Bonner thoughtfully. "What happened to your partner, Hank?"

"He got shot."

"Joe Bill caught a bullet," Sam Hulse added obliviously, flashing his toothy grin as he glanced toward the rear of the room. "Ol' Joe zigged when he should've zagged."

Otis didn't bother asking who'd shot him. He knew Shirt and Sam wouldn't be in Twin Bridges if Montana wasn't nearby. "How bad is it?"

"It gouged a pretty big hole in his leg, but didn't break any bones," Chris Ewing said. "Damn' town ain't got a sawbones. Me and Hank had to patch it ourselves."

"Can he ride?"

There was a long pause, then Joe Bill hollered: "Hell, no, I can't ride! It feels like I got a red hot poker jabbed into my leg."

Otis turned back to his drink, the nettling feeling that had been dogging him ever since staring into the shadows of McCarty's livery rearing its head once more. *This ain't gonna turn out good,* he thought morosely.

"He's still out there," Shirt said, as if reading Otis's mind. "He picked up a four- or five-hour lead last night. He'll lengthen it tonight."

"He was riding Lloyd's horse," Chris added tentatively.

"He killed Lloyd. Prairie Richards, too," Dave Worthy said.

"Damn," Chris murmured. "I'll bet the old man's going loco for sure now."

"He's offering five thousand dollars to whoever brings in Johnny Montana's head and hide," Dave said.

Hank pushed to his feet, kicking a chair out of the way as he came to the bar. "You bullshittin' us, Worthy? What the hell's Cutter expect us to do, skin the bastard?"

"I'm telling it straight up," Dave insisted. "The old man wants the hide off Montana's back and shoulders. Says he's gonna tan it, then braid it into a quirt in memory of his brother. He didn't say what he wanted the head for, but some of the boys are speculating that he's gonna mount it on his saddle horn. Was a Mex down in Monterey did that a few years ago with a horse thief he'd hung."

Glaring at Otis, Hank said: "By God, he's your partner, Call. What are you gonna do about this?"

"Not a damn' thing," Otis replied calmly. "It's none of my business, for openers, and, for a kicker, Montana's carrying better than forty thousand dollars worth of gold with him. Brett can have his head and hide. I want the gold."

Ewing whistled. "Forty thousand. Damn."

"All right," Hank allowed grudgingly. "We need to run this kid down, but I ain't choppin' off his head."

"Brett wants it so that one of us can identify him," Dave explained. "Me 'n' Sam, Shirt, Otis, 'n' Charlie, we're the only ones who've seen him so far."

Shirt looked up but didn't say anything, and Otis figured he'd probably spotted Harley Lamont's tracks in the cañon where Lloyd and Prairie had been killed. But Shirt didn't say anything, for which Otis was grateful. This job was becoming complicated enough without trying to explain why Brett had gunned down one of his own men.

"We're pulling out," Otis said abruptly, changing the drift of the conversation. "All of us," he added, his glance taking in Chris and Hank. "Brett's already gone ahead to find McGrew and his outfit. You boys are to pick up Dover and Miles off the Deer Lodge road, then come on down to the Beaverhead Rock. Brett'll be waiting for us there. He wants to squeeze Montana between us, if someone doesn't tree him first. Once we're done with that, we'll head south and pick up Tuck and his boys in Bannack. Then we'll get our asses over Monida Pass before the heavy snows shut it down completely."

Hank's eyes narrowed. "What about the gold, Call? When are we gonna split that?"

"Somewhere down south, I'd guess."

"At the Beaverhead Rock?"

Otis picked up his drink, downing it in one fiery swallow. Then he slapped the glass back on the bar and turned to face Hank. He voice was still raw from the liquor's burn when he said: "Saddle your horse, Bonner. You, too, Ewing."

Hank didn't budge. "It's a fair question, Call."

"We'll split the gold when Brett says we split it," Otis replied coolly. "That's not something you need to worry about."

"But I am worryin' about it, and I'll let you in on a little secret. I ain't keen on you and Tuck and Cutter getting too close to Monida Pass without us divvying up that gold. I don't trust you."

"Son-of-a-bitch," Otis breathed, stepping away from the bar. His fingers brushed the butt of his Colt.

Hank slid his hands around the grips of his pistol. Then Chris Ewing said: "Dammit, Hank, there's no call for this. Not this close to the end."

"Stay outta it, Chris."

"Call's always treated us square, Hank. Besides, he'll kill you if you draw against him." After a pause, Chris added: "You know he will."

Chuckling, Shirt said: "If he don't, I'll do it."

"Come on, Hank," Chris urged. "Let's get our horses. I'm sick of these mountains. I want to see California again."

Bonner's shoulders slumped, and his hand fell away from his revolver. "The hell with you, Otis Call. We'll finish this later."

"Sure," Otis replied mildly, but he kept a wary eye on Hank and Chris as the two men exited the saloon. When the door finally closed behind them, he tossed six-bits on the bar for their drinks, then walked back to where Joe Bill was watching him with pain-teared eyes.

"You ain't leavin' me behind, are you, Otis?"

"If you can't sit a horse, you're no good to us any more, Joe Bill. You know how it works."

The tears in Joe Bill's eyes began to trickle down his sunburnished cheeks. "You know what they're gonna do to me, soon as you boys is down the road a piece."

Otis knew. Likely the townfolk wouldn't even take time to form a proper noose, but just take him out back and hang him with a lariat—assuming the bartender didn't shoot him first.

"It's a raw deal, Joe Bill, but we've got to ride. They say the snow's already knee-deep on a horse going over Monida."

"Shit," Joe Bill said softly, turning his head away.

Otis reached down to shake Joe Bill's hand and wish him luck, but the injured man wouldn't look at him. Otis couldn't blame him. Turning away, he walked over to where Dave, Charlie, Sam, and Shirt waited at the bar. "Let's ride," he said brusquely, and the men silently fell in behind him. They were almost out the door when Joe Bill called after them.

"Good bye, boys, and God bless you! Pray for my soul at the next church you pass."

Chapter Seventeen

They discovered the dead horse at dawn, lying on its side in a shallow depression well off the road. Johnny Montana had abandoned the sorrel in the alders along the Beaverhead River, but Shirt spotted it as they rode past. Although there was a bullet wound in the sorrel's flank, it was the slit throat that told Otis the horse had only been wounded in yesterday's dash through Twin Bridges. The wound was serious enough that the sorrel wouldn't have recovered, though, so Montana had cut the mare's throat to put it out of its misery.

"Well, he's down a horse now," Dave said, but Shirt quickly set him straight.

"He's got Lloyd's Appaloosa and Joe Bill's line-back dun. He's better mounted now than he was when he left Redhawk Gulch."

Otis glanced at the men around him. It was just the five of them again—Shirt and Sam and Charlie and Dave. He'd sent Chris Ewing and Hank Bonner down the Deer Lodge road to pick up Fred Dover and Ed Miles, where the two were holed up in a little flat-roofed trapper's shack, watching the Deer Lodge and Big Hole routes in case some prospector tried to escape the valley in that direction.

Otis took a last look at the dead horse. It impressed him that Montana had taken time to do right by it. He wasn't sure he would've done the same, and the thought bothered him.

Pulling his buckskin around, he said: "Let's spread out and

find some tracks."

It was slow-going through the alders. The ground was low and damp and white with frost, the clumps of slim, arrow-straight alders creating a patternless maze for them to wander through. After half an hour, Shirt forced his pinto through some brush to Otis's side. "I don't think he came this way," Shirt said.

"Back to the river?" Otis asked.

"Maybe," Shirt replied distractedly.

They reined in that direction, and, when they reached the river, Otis spotted Dave and Charlie almost a mile upstream, leaning from their saddles to study the ground as they rode along. Shirt turned downstream just as Sam Hulse rode out of the brush. Five minutes later, Shirt motioned them forward.

"Call 'em in," Otis told Sam grimly, kicking his horse after Shirt. Sam drew his revolver and fired a couple of rounds into the air, and, upstream, Dave and Charlie wheeled their mounts and galloped back.

Riding alongside Shirt, Otis studied the river. With the aid of the bright morning sunshine, he could just make out a few shallow indentations that led into the water.

"He went north," Shirt said, "staying in the water."

"North?"

"Not far. Just enough to throw us off for a while."

"I'll be damned," Otis said with grudging approval.

They followed along for another hundred yards before they found where he'd splashed out on the west bank. Coming to the main road, Dave swore softly at the sight of their own prints overlaying Johnny's, made in the gray half light just before dawn. They forced their horses up the low bench above the river to the hard plain above. Here, the trail was fainter, the flat grassland empty. Far to the south, Otis could just make out the hump of Beaverhead Rock, where Brett was supposed to be waiting. Pulling his buckskin to a stop, he studied the distant, snow-capped mountains that hid Monida Pass from their view.

"What do you see?" Charlie asked

Otis shook his head in admiration. "He's going to slip around them, behind the Beaverhead Rock."

"Naw," Dave said. "Jack'll cut him off if he tries that."

"Jack's down low, watching the alders. Nobody's going to expect Montana to ride out in the open like this."

"Well, he'd be a damn' fool to do that," Charlie said, frowning. "If he don't dodge back into cover somewhere between here and the Beaverhead, he'll be a sitting duck."

But Shirt and Sam knew what Otis was talking about, and Sam suddenly laughed. "That's right, Charlie. A man'd have to be plumb crazy to do that. Which is why Jack ain't gonna send no one out there to watch." He looked at Otis, and his expression sobered. "That boy's makin' for Monida, and, if Brett and Jack are still down in the alders waiting for him to try to sneak past, there ain't gonna be a soul between him and Idaho unless Tuck's got someone at Dolsen's."

"Let's ride," Otis said grimly. He kicked his horse into a run, and the others strung out behind him. It was a long ride to Dolsen's trading post, but there wasn't a man among them who doubted that Johnny Montana would be there before them.

Chapter Eighteen

Tom Tucker came charging out of the cabin like a stung bull, his face livid, jaw clenched. He glared at Jake Haws, who was sitting his horse at the edge of the clearing with a smirking grin.

"Wipe it off, by God, or I'll wipe it off for you," Tucker threatened.

"Hell, Tuck, don't take it so personal," Jake said. "Some gals just don't appreciate being sparked."

"This gal ain't got a choice in the matter," Tuck growled, walking to his horse and stepping into the saddle.

In the trees behind the cabin, Chico Sanchez rose from where he'd been breaking apart a pile of manure with a stick. Tuck spurred his jug-headed roan over. "Whatcha got?"

"A couple of nights ago, about dusk," Chico replied, nudging an apple out of the heap with his toe.

"Where'd she get a horse?" Tuck asked, scowling.

"No horse," Chico said, tossing his stick away. "Is a mule."

Coming up behind them, Jake said: "I'll bet it's old man Thompson's mule." He glanced at Chico. "Remember that tall black he kept picketed above his claim? We didn't see it yesterday, and commented on it."

"*Sí,* I remember, but that mule is old . . . its teeth bad. Ver' skinny, too. She will not get far, riding that mule."

"Now, wait a minute," Jake cautioned. "We ain't chasin' after no gal just because one of us has got a soft spot in his head for her. We got a job to do right here."

Before Tuck could reply, Chico said: "Come over here. I show you something." He led them to the edge of Grasshopper Creek and nodded to a flat rock about the size of a washtub, sitting just off the bank. Tuck remembered the stone well. The first time he'd seen the woman, she'd been kneeling on it, doing her laundry. Now the stone was tipped to one side, the gravel scooped out from beneath it. "What the hell?" he muttered, puzzled.

"I'll be damned," Jake said. "She found herself a little cache of gold."

"I think so, too," Chico agreed. "She found gold. Now she runs."

Jake laughed. "Well, bless her heart. All that digging finally panned out for her."

"Shut up," Tuck snapped. He was staring at the rocker box upstream, the heaps of overturned earth surrounding it.

"Hell, Tuck, let her go," Jake said. "You know she couldn't have found too much. Even a pure pocket wouldn't have yielded more than a few thousand dollars, and she sure didn't find no pure pocket in a streambed. That kind of gold comes outta quartz, if you find it at all."

Tuck stiffened. "No, by God, that gold is ours, not hers."

"You want for me to find her?" Chico asked.

"Yeah, I want that gold," Tuck said, then glanced at Jake. "You hightail it back to camp and gather up whatever supplies we've got left. This could take a few days." A smile crossed his face. "As a matter of fact, I'd pretty well guarantee it's gonna take a few days, once I catch that bitch."

A veil dropped over Jake's face, but Tuck didn't care. Chico was already riding through the timber behind the woman's cabin, looking for sign. Tuck spurred after him. They picked up her trail easily enough, and, by mid-afternoon, Chico announced that they'd closed some of the gap.

"At night, she is forced to go slow through these trees," he explained. "If she continues this way, to travel by night, that will be a help for us."

"She ain't none too bright," Tuck said. "Maybe she'll get lost."

Chico looked doubtful. "She does not travel like one who is lost," he said, his brows furrowing above his deep black eyes and olive-hued cheeks.

Chico Sanchez was a Spaniard, his blood pure all the way back to Castile. In fact, being mistaken for a Mexican—a *mestizo,* with its alleged taint of Indian blood—was the only thing Tuck had ever seen Chico get really angry about.

Tuck had never questioned Chico about the circumstances that brought him to North America, riding under a name some might have deemed offensive. It was enough that he considered Chico second only to Warshirt Jackson in his ability to follow a trail, a skill Tuck figured would come in handy in the days ahead.

The sun was still a couple of hours above the horizon when they climbed the bare shoulder of a hill and entered its cap of tall pines. Thirty yards into the trees, Chico pointed to a spot on the ground in front of them. "She stopped here. Maybe yesterday."

Tuck scowled. He saw no sign of a fire or any of the other amenities that made a camp comfortable. There was only a patch of bare earth under a pine where the woman's mule had stood, a flattened spot some yards away where she'd laid.

They rode through the trees and came out on the far side, where Chico halted once more. Dismounting, he ran his fingers lightly over the grass, as if he could feel the mule's passage in the slim, tawny blades. "I think she is even closer now. Maybe twenty-four hours, maybe less. That is good, no?"

Tuck nodded hungrily. "Yeah, that's real good."

She was not the first, this blonde from Bannack with the tall, willowy form. By now he'd accepted that she probably wouldn't be his last. It was just something that happened from time to time, something he had to accept. There was never any telling what might set it off. A look, perhaps—a glint of the eye or a set to the shoulder? He'd quit trying to analyze it years ago, fearing that a deeper understanding might actually make it worse.

He'd felt it this time on his first visit to the woman's cabin. He'd gone there thinking he'd have a little fun with her, a grass widow with no man around. He could leave some coins afterward to shut her up. But when he'd seen her kneeling over the creek doing her laundry, he'd known. That old feeling was like a hard kick to the gut, taking away his breath, and he'd known then that it was going to happen again.

Tuck had killed his first woman when he was sixteen, plunging a knife into her stomach so many times he'd nearly cut her in half—although for the life of him, he couldn't remember why. Nor could he really remember the other women he'd killed. There'd been a lot of them, he knew that. Sometimes, in his dreams, their faces would swim before him like hazy apparitions—not fearful so much as confused, as if they also wondered why he'd done it.

Perhaps someday the face of this woman from Bannack would also haunt his dreams. It was a certainty she would have to die. She'd sealed her own fate by running, which was no fault of his, whether she saw it that way or not. He would weep when she was gone, as he always did, but there would be a certain amount of pleasure in the killing, too, and, for some reason he didn't understand, a temporary release of a peculiar tightness within himself that was like a cleansing of his soul.

He always felt kind of holy after a killing, reborn.

"Tuck?"

He looked down. Chico was standing beside his horse, watching.

"What?" Tuck growled.

Chico pointed east, toward the Bannack road. Following the direction of his gaze, Tuck saw Jake Haws leading a pack horse along the road at an easy jog. The pack horse carried their personal gear, plus a tent and some pots for cooking. But it wasn't Jake who caught Tuck's eye. It was the horseman loping toward him from the direction of Dolsen's trading post. Straightening in his saddle, he said: "Ain't that Poke Hardesty?"

"*Sí,* but what does he do here? Was he not at Lost Spring with Brett?"

"Yeah, he was," Tuck replied, gathering his reins. "Let's get down there, Chico. Something's stirring."

Chapter Nineteen

Johnny kept the Henry rifle booted as he approached Van Dolsen's post. It was midmorning, and he'd been in the saddle for the biggest part of the last thirty-six hours. He was exhausted, yet felt taut as a bowstring.

Dolsen's trading post was a simple affair. The main building was made of logs, and sat on the left side of the road, facing west. There was a fenced-in pasture to the southeast encompassing several acres, and to the right of the road, a blacksmith shop, smokehouse, and a couple of one-room shacks for summer help, although they looked deserted now. The whole complex set a couple of hundred yards east of the Beaverhead, above its flood plain.

It was still too warm for that time of year, but the winds had been gusting steadily out of the south since early yesterday morning, and Johnny could sense a change approaching. Something dark and ominous, just over the horizon. Monida Pass lay directly ahead now, its snowy flanks taunting him with the question: Was the trail over the top still open? Or had he waited too long and backed himself into a corner?

Keeping a wary eye on Dolsen's post, Johnny looped the Appaloosa's reins over the hitch rail, then casually pulled the bay, with its cargo of gold, alongside. He'd switched horses last night, after losing the sorrel. As heavy as the gold was, it still weighed less than he did with his saddle and gear and guns, and the Appaloosa was a much stronger horse. He hadn't tried to catch the dun that had followed him out of Twin Bridges, but now the horse walked up docilely, allowing Johnny to secure it on the other side of the bay, flanking the smaller horse and keeping its oddly-shaped panniers partially concealed.

Returning to the Appaloosa's side, Johnny surreptitiously slipped Andy's Colt from the near-side saddlebag and tucked it inside his jacket, sliding the barrel and cylinder down the sleeve of his left arm in a sort of makeshift shoulder rig. Keeping his arm against his side, Johnny entered the trading post and went immediately to the far end of the counter, where he could put his back to the wall.

There were four men inside. One stood at the far end of the counter; two others were seated at a table in the corner of the room closest to the front door. All three had the rough-barked look of Cut-throats—well-armed and dressed for hard riding, rather than mucking in the dirt. A lean young man with a full black beard stood behind the counter, his expression neutral, his hands in plain sight. Resting both elbows on the counter, Johnny let his right hand slip inside his jacket to touch the Colt.

"What can I do for you?" the man behind the counter asked.

"Are you Dolsen?"

"I am, though most folks call me Van."

"Got any coffee, Van?"

"In back," Dolsen said pointedly, then waited while Johnny mulled that over.

"Maybe I'll have the coffee later," Johnny said, his gaze flitting briefly to the Cut-throat at the opposite end of the counter. "What have you got up front?"

"Whiskey. It'll warm your toes but burn your belly." He plucked a bottle off the shelf behind him. "But I don't have to go in back to get it."

"Yeah, whiskey sounds good," Johnny agreed.

Dolsen set a tin cup on the counter, then splashed in a generous amount of liquor. "This one's on the house," he said, then met Johnny's eyes as he recorked the bottle. "You the one they call Montana?"

"I've heard the name. I was born Owens."

"Heard of you."

"Shut up, Dolsen," said the man down the counter.

"Oh, don't mind me, Bud. I just like to talk. It gets lonesome up here when the stagecoaches quit rolling."

"See that you're still here next summer to meet those coaches," Bud advised. "A man who talks too much can sometimes come to an untimely end."

Johnny wrapped his fingers around the Colt's grips, keeping his elbows on the counter, his shoulders hunched, as if he was cold. Leaving the whiskey untouched, he said: "I noticed four horses in that holding pen out back, Van. Any of them for sale?"

"I couldn't say. They ain't my nags."

At the table, a heavily bearded man got to his feet. "That's a mighty fine-looking Appaloosa you're riding. I knew a man up north had one looked a lot like it."

Johnny swung partway around, gauging distances and cover. "I'm just looking for a drink, friend, and maybe some information about Monida Pass. I'm not looking for trouble."

"Didn't say you was," the bearded man replied. "I was just commenting on your horse."

Bud turned to face Johnny. His elbow was also on the counter, handy to make a quick dive for the pistol canted, butt forward, across his belt buckle. "Horse thieves aren't looked upon too kindly in these parts, stranger. You got a bill of sale for that Appaloosa?"

"There's another man in back," Dolsen said.

"I'd already figured as much," Johnny acknowledged.

"You're gonna regret that big mouth of yours, Dolsen," the man standing beside the window snarled.

Van's expression didn't change. "I'd regret it more if ol' Cam back there bushwhacked young Montana and I didn't do anything. . . ."

That was as far as he got before hell broke loose. Bud and the man beside the window both went for their guns in the same instant, but Johnny had already drawn his Colt, even though no one in the room realized it. Pushing away from the counter, he snapped off a shot before any of the others could clear leather. Bud took the bullet square in the chest and stumbled backward with a surprised look on his face. Turning his Colt on the man beside the window, Johnny rocked him into the wall with a .44 to the neck. Johnny fired twice at the man who'd remained seated, but the Cut-throat was already diving to the floor, pulling the table over with him.

Then the man Dolsen had called Cam burst out of the back room with a pistol in each hand, blazing wildly. Johnny dropped to the floor and swiftly crabbed behind the shelter of a thirty gallon barrel containing an assortment of picks and shovels. Cam's bullets burrowed into the wall above him. Johnny fired twice more, then dropped the empty Colt and palmed his strong-side Remington. Cam zinged a shot off the wooden barrel's steel band, and Johnny ducked lower. Then a shotgun roared, deafening in the cramped confines of the trading post, followed by a sudden, ringing silence.

Figuring that if the shotgun's blast had been meant for him, he'd already be dead, Johnny cautiously raised his head. Across the room, the Cut-throat who had dived behind the overturned table was taking aim at Dolsen. Shouting a warning, Johnny fired three times as fast as he could cock the hammer and pull the trigger. All three bullets struck the outlaw in the torso, and he crumpled to the floor.

At the counter, Dolsen was standing in plain sight with a shotgun in his hands. Suddenly setting it aside, he scooped up the whiskey bottle beside Johnny's cup and drank deeply, his Adam's apple bobbing six or seven times.

Johnny peered over the bar, then turned abruptly away from the carnage Dolsen's scatter-gun had done to Cam's head and right shoulder. Bud was also obviously dead, and Johnny walked past him to check on the other two. Then he holstered the Remington and yanked the door open to create a draft that would suck the thick powder smoke outside. Returning to the bar, he said: "I'm obliged for your help, Van."

"I reckon it was time somebody lent a hand," Dolsen replied shakily. "These birds should've been run out of the territory weeks ago."

"When the others show up, you tell 'em I did this. Tell 'em I slipped in the back way and gunned down all four men before they even knew I was here. If you don't, if Cutter thinks you had a hand in this, he'll kill you in a heartbeat."

"He might anyway, but I'll tell him."

Johnny retrieved his Colt and shoved it behind his belt.

After a pause, Dolsen said: "You know they have a reward out for you, don't you?"

Johnny stopped. "No, I didn't."

"That man at the bar was Bud Dixon, one of Brett Cutter's right-hand men. He rode in here last night with Harry Spindell, then sent a man to Bannack to bring in Tom Tucker and his boys. Dixon said Cutter's gathering the rest of his gang right now. I don't think they realize you're this far south, but they will."

"They must want me pretty bad."

"That Appaloosa you're riding belonged to Brett Cutter's little brother, Lloyd."

Johnny swore softly. "So it's personal now."

"It is for Cutter. He's offering an extra five thousand dollars to the man who brings you in." Dolsen hesitated, then added almost apologetically: "Not all of you. Just your head and some of your skin. They say Cutter wants to tan your hide for a quirt and . . . well, that he wants to bleach the flesh off your head and mount your skull on his saddle horn."

Dread gripped Johnny's heart, squeezing it tightly. "I guess it's true, what they say about Cutter not being quite right in the head?"

"I don't see how he could be," Van agreed, his words so low Johnny barely heard them.

CHAPTER TWENTY

Monida Pass was open. At least that was Van's opinion.

"I ain't been over it myself, mind you, but I don't think we've had enough snow to close it completely."

"It's a risk I'll have to take," Johnny said. "I can't backtrack now." He was standing at the Appaloosa's side, rubbing fresh salve on the wounds Lloyd had carved there with his spurs. Although the gouge marks looked tender, the salve was already helping, and there had never been any evidence of blood or raw flesh—just bare skin where the hair had been scraped away. Rough treatment for any animal, but not enough to injure tissue.

"I guess if I was smart, I'd switch these horses for some of those in your holding pen," Johnny said.

"You're welcome to 'em, although I doubt if there's an animal there that's equal to this Appaloosa and dun. Them little bitty scars on your Appy's ribs won't slow him down any."

"No, they won't." Johnny lowered the stirrup, then put the salve away. He eyed Dolsen thoughtfully for a moment. "I reckon you saved my life in there. I'm obliged."

"I was more than glad to do it," Van replied. "When you get to Salt Lake City, send some law up here. Hell, send the Army. I'd like to see the whole bunch thrown in a hole somewhere until they're all withered and toothless."

"I'll do that," Johnny promised, stepping into his saddle.

"Good luck, Montana!" Dolsen called as Johnny reined away.

With a wave, Johnny urged the Appaloosa into an easy, ground-eating lope. The bay followed obediently on a lead rope, the dun trailing after them without urging. Following the Utah road, Johnny soon passed its junction with the Bannack cut-off that came in from the west. His own route continued south, along the Beaverhead River.

The winds grew stronger as the day progressed, tinged now with a sharpness pared off the snowy fields ahead. The weather was starting to worry Johnny. He kept glancing over his shoulder to the northwest, but the skies there remained clear. Not even a cloud marred the deep, crisp blue, but Frank McCarty's warning continued to echo in his mind: *A warm wind out of the south ain't necessarily your friend, Johnny.*

He camped that night on a piece of high ground halfway up a broad, beautiful valley surrounded by snow-covered mountains. With no wood for a fire, he suppered on jerked deer and dried apples, then crawled into his blankets. Although exhausted, he couldn't sleep. Not immediately. He lay awake listening to the wind moaning through the rabbitbrush, watching the stars glittering in the heavens. Eventually he dozed, but it was a broken slumber, filled with twitching muscles and disturbing dreams, and he awoke the next morning feeling more wrung out than when he'd gone to bed.

He was in the saddle by first light, but took it slow until the sun came up and melted the ice in the road. The wind had died overnight to barely a whisper, and, when he looked to the northwest, he wasn't surprised to see a thick blue haze spread across the horizon.

"I reckon Frank was right," he said, speaking more to himself than his horse. "I just hope we make it over the top before that thing hits."

It was cooler without the southerly breezes, and Johnny kept his greatcoat on all morning. Toward noon, the hills began to close in, the road crowding close to the river where the land was flatter and easier to navigate with wagons. Pulling up to rest the horses before entering the steeper hills to the south, Johnny took his spyglass and the Henry and climbed a nearby ridge to where a large, flat-topped boulder offered a clear view of his back trail.

The temperature was dropping more rapidly than the rise in altitude could account for, and his breath fogged the air in front of the telescope. To the north, the haze had darkened noticeably, but it wasn't the approaching storm he was looking for. It was pursuit. From here, he could see almost all the way to the bottom of the long, broad valley, yet the road remained puzzlingly empty.

He closed the telescope, frowning. Surely by now, Cutter knew he'd slipped past them at the Beaverhead Rock and was making his run for Monida. According to Dolsen, Bud Dixon had sent a man to Bannack to fetch the rest of Cutter's crew two days ago. So where were they? What held them back?

He let the horses graze for an hour, then mounted and pushed on. He began to come across patches of old snow almost immediately, and the brown earth around him seemed to shrink like the spring melt in reverse. Within another hour he'd crossed the snow line, the land white and frozen on both sides of the road. Barely five miles into the hills, he pulled the Appaloosa to a sudden stop. His blood turned cold as he stared at the single, iron-shod track at the tip of a crusted snowdrift angling into the road in front of him. He lifted his eyes to the looming hills but saw nothing out of the ordinary. Shucking the Henry, he dismounted and knelt beside the track, running his finger lightly along its rim. There were no leaves or other débris inside the indentation, no softening of its edges by yesterday's melt. A few hours old, he decided, but no more than that.

Rising, Johnny looked ahead to where the road rounded a

bend a quarter of a mile away. Was this why Cutter wasn't pushing him from behind? Had the bandit leader already sent a man ahead to pick him off before he reached the pass?

Johnny eased back along the Appaloosa, his gaze never leaving the surrounding hills, but nothing stirred in that frozen landscape; not even a hawk smudged the pale blue of the sky. Standing beside his horse, he watched for nearly twenty minutes without seeing anything. He knew he couldn't stay there forever. He had no proof that whoever was ahead of him was a Cut-throat. The track could just as easily have been made by another prospector trying to escape Cutter's many nooses.

Hooking a toe in the stirrup, Johnny stepped into the saddle. He paused there a few minutes, listening to the silence, then heeled the Appaloosa forward.

The long, low snowdrifts fingering into the road became more frequent as the road climbed, like the whitened claws of some long-dead beast sprawled across the mountainside. Johnny dodged them when he could, as the rider ahead of him seemed to be doing, but now and again the bay or the dun would cut across a drift, adding its own tracks to the frozen trail. Johnny didn't like it, but he knew it wouldn't make much difference in the long run. Soon, the entire road would be blanketed with white.

He half expected to catch up with whoever was in front of him before sundown, but, as the light faded, the tracks remained at least an hour ahead, the rider pushing his mount hard, as if expecting pursuit. By now, Johnny had given up his fear that he was following a Cut-throat. There was no need for a sniper to climb this high.

Abandoning the chase, he dismounted and loosened the cinches on his horses. There was a little grass growing between the wagon ruts and along the road where the snow had melted back, and he turned the horses loose to graze. Grass would be scarce in the days ahead, and he wanted the horses to be in the best possible condition before tackling the deep snows on top of Monida.

Taking his rifle, he trudged ahead for a ways. It was very cold now, his breath cloudy in the purpling light, the snow squeaking underfoot. Well away from the horses—the creak of saddle leather and the rip and chomp of grass—he stopped to listen to the night, but no sound drifted down the narrow channel of the road, banked on either side by knee-deep drifts.

Turning to make his way back, he came to an abrupt halt. In the north, he could make out the flicker of several campfires. Although too far away to tally, he estimated no less than four separate blazes, which would account for at least a dozen men, and perhaps as many as thirty.

Johnny swore under his breath. He was trapped now for sure, caught between an unknown element to the fore and a pack of killers at his back. It didn't require much consideration to decide he'd rather take his chances with a stranger than with Cutter's bunch, though, and he quickly returned to his horses.

He covered another mile before the last of the light drained out of the sky, forcing him to stop until the moon came up a couple of hours later. When it did, he pulled himself stiffly back into the saddle and forged ahead. It was almost 3:00 A.M. when the moon set, but by then the hills had retreated once more, and Johnny was able to continue on with just the stars to light his path. He reached the junction of the Beaverhead River and Red Rock Creek shortly after dawn, where the Utah road abandoned the former to follow up the latter. A pocket of aspens grew in the forks of the two waterways, and he splashed his horses across the creek toward it. He couldn't linger long, but he wanted a quick fire to thaw his feet and fix some rice and coffee for breakfast—a little inner warmth to keep himself going.

He was groggy from fatigue or he would have spotted the dead horse lying just inside the trees sooner. As it was, he didn't see it at all until a voice cut across the frosty air like a tomahawk, telling him to throw his hands skyward or be blown out of his saddle.

Chapter Twenty-One

"I mean it," the voice repeated. "Lift those hands or I'll shoot."

Irritated with himself for having been caught so flat-footed, Johnny reluctantly raised both hands.

"Throw your guns on the ground, then turn around and ride out of here."

It was a woman's voice, but Johnny took it as seriously as he would any Cut-throat. "I'd have to lower my hands to pitch my pistols," he said, scanning the trees until he spotted her crouched behind a pile of deadfall twenty yards away. His stomach tightened when he recognized the double-barreled shotgun pointed at him. "I mean you no harm," he added, cautiously lowering his hands partway. "I'm headed for Salt Lake City."

"You can't come this way," she replied firmly.

"Why not?"

"Because I said so. Don't argue with me, mister. I know who you are. You're one of Tucker's men."

"Ah," Johnny breathed, then carefully lowered his hands to his saddle horn. He ignored her when she told him to put them up again, saying instead: "I'm not a Cut-throat, ma'am, but they ain't far behind."

"I'll just bet they aren't," she answered. She eased out from behind the fallen tree, the twin muzzles of her scatter-gun never moving very far off Johnny's chest. "How do you know they're so close if you aren't one of them?"

He glanced at the dead horse—a mule, he corrected himself—flat on its side in the snow; its black hair was hoared with frost, almost invisible among the white-barked aspens. "Is that your only animal?" he asked.

"Don't you worry about my animals. I've got plenty of horses back here."

Johnny scanned the tiny grove. "I guess it's possible you've got a goat stashed in there somewhere, but you sure aren't hiding any horses nearby."

The woman trembled suddenly. Tears welled in her eyes. She brushed them away as if practiced at it. "Get out of here, mister," she said grittily. "Go tell Tucker that I'll kill him if he ever comes near me again. I swear to that."

"Ma'am, I reckon Tom Tucker would plug me before I got close enough to pass along that message. There's probably twenty or thirty Cut-throats following me. Tucker might be one of them. I figure Brett Cutter surely is. They're wanting my hide pretty bad."

She looked doubtful. "Why?"

"Because I killed Brett's little brother."

She lifted her face defiantly, and Johnny saw that she was young but haggard, with dark circles under her eyes. Her lips were dry from the cold, cracked almost to the point of bleeding, although she looked warm enough under a heavy wool blanket pinned cape-like over the shoulders of her coat. She was studying him intently, as if trying to gauge the honesty of his words. It was clear she didn't trust him, yet just as obvious that she would be in a bad fix if he was telling the truth and she sent him away.

"Ma'am," Johnny said gently, "I'm not going back. Cutter's sworn to have my head, plus the skin off my back for a quirt, and I won't let that happen if I can help it. But I can't just ride off and leave you here. I know the character of those men, and I think you do, too. I don't want to be crude, but you've got to know what they'd do to a young woman like yourself, stranded out here alone."

"Yes," she said harshly. "I know what kind of men they are. To call them animals would only insult the panther and the wolf. Tell me, mister, why shouldn't I just kill you and take your horses?"

For the first time, Johnny began to grasp the depth of the woman's desperation, the fear that toyed with her mind, and realized he was probably as close to death now as he'd been back at Dolsen's, when Bud Dixon first reached for his revolver.

"Ma'am, you've got your back against the wall right now, and I know that, but you can trust me if you'll let yourself. I'm not going to harm you."

She laughed without humor. "I trusted a man once. That's how I ended up out here. Tell me, why should I trust you when I couldn't trust my own husband?"

"Because I ain't pledging you anything. Right now, I've got a spare horse . . . that dun over there . . . and you're needing one. It's yours to ride if you want it."

It wasn't much of an answer, Johnny knew, but he wasn't sure there was anything he could say that would make a difference with her today. He eased his feet back in the stirrups, ready to dive off the Appaloosa's side and into the bushes if he had to.

Johnny could see the struggle in her face, could almost feel the delicate balance she hung in, just inches shy of pulling one of the shotgun's triggers. His stomach was knotted, his breath quick and shallow, but he didn't speak or make any gesture that might alarm her. Finally, exhaling loudly, she lowered the shotgun and moved the hammers to half cock.

"I need help, mister, I won't deny that. But I'll kill you if you try anything funny. I'm all out of forgiveness and God-fearing ways, and I swear I'll blow you apart if you give me cause."

Johnny nodded, but he couldn't help wondering if he was a fool to trust her. Under different circumstances, he might have wished her luck in finding some other means of transportation, but that wasn't an option here, halfway up this snowy mountain road. Without a horse, she would die.

"I'll honor your wishes as best I can, but you've got to understand that I don't intend to ride all the way to Salt Lake City worrying that you might get the wrong notion about what I'm up to and pull one of those triggers. If you've got to shoot something, you'll likely get plenty of chances soon enough. Just make sure it ain't me. Now, those are my rules, and you'll have to abide by them or, by damn, I will leave you behind. Understand?"

She nodded curtly. "Anytime you think I'm too much of a burden, let me know."

Johnny shook his head in exasperation. Stepping down, letting the Appaloosa's reins trail in the snow, he said: "I'll bring up the dun. Get what you want off your mule and we'll tie it behind the saddle."

She kept her shotgun with her as she retrieved her gear from the dead mule. There wasn't much—saddlebags, pommel bags, a skimpy bedroll. She strapped it to the dun's saddle while Johnny shortened the stirrups.

Moving around on foot, Johnny soon warmed up. The rising sun helped. He would have enjoyed a few minutes beside a fire, but decided they needed to make time now, with good light and a clear trail. To the northwest, the sky had turned blue-black overnight, with a towering bank of clouds looming over the Beaverhead country like a wrathful old man. Johnny eyed the slow-moving front apprehensively. He figured it would be on them before the day was out, with plummeting temperatures and, like as not, gale-force winds. By nightfall, the need for a fire would be a necessity rather than a luxury.

The woman was also watching the approaching storm, her brows knitted with concern. "Can we make it?" she asked.

"I reckon we'll have to. Cutter and his men will be pushing us hard all day. Brett wants me, but the rest of his crew will be more interested in getting out of Montana. They know they'll be strung up by vigilantes before spring if they don't."

They left the Beaverhead and started up Red Rock Creek, passing the huge cliff on their left that gave the stream its name. Johnny led, keeping the bay close on its lead. The woman followed at a distrustful distance. She was an enigma to Johnny, and about as far from what he'd expected to find out here as anything he could think of. But his bigger concern was still Cutter and his men, and how rapidly they were closing the gap between them. From here on, he'd have to think out his moves carefully if he wanted to make it to Salt Lake City in one piece.

Around mid-morning, when Johnny looked back, he discovered the woman had urged the dun up beside the bay. She was studying him intently, probably as confused by him as he was by her. Johnny nodded but didn't smile. "How are you doing?" he asked.

"What do I call you?"

"A lot of folks out here have been calling me Johnny Montana. My real name is John Owens."

"Why do they call you Johnny Montana?"

"A friend of mine tagged me with the name last spring on our way out here. I'd already been to Montana once before, hauling freight for an Army contract, and he knew about that. Then we had some Indian trouble last spring and I talked to them. The name kind of grew out of that."

"You talked a bunch of Indians out of attacking?"

"I don't rightly know if they were going to attack or not. They were mighty loud and acting mad, but I don't speak the language. I did pick up a little sign talk hauling freight in the Red River country, so I used that. We offered the Sioux some trinkets and tobacco, and they took it and rode off. For all I know, they'd just stopped to say howdy and some fool of a white man gave them a bunch of trade goods for the hell of it."

"That sounds brave," she said. "I think I know now why your friends call you Johnny Montana."

"What about you, ma'am? What should I call you?"

"My name is Allison Purcell. Allie for short. I was named after my father, who finally gave up hope for a boy after five daughters. His name was Allen."

"Allen, huh? Is your father still alive?"

She didn't reply, and, when he looked back, he saw that she'd slowed her horse and was staring at him with eyes as dark as a roiling sea.

"It was just a question," he said.

"You mind the road, mister, and don't be prying into what isn't any of your business."

Johnny turned back, his mouth set in a hard, straight line and, for the first time, wondered how big of a problem he'd created for himself by offering this woman a horse to ride.

Chapter Twenty-Two

The storm swept over them just before dusk, preceded by a gust of wind that shrieked past like something in agony. Johnny was still in the lead, the Appaloosa plodding low-headed through the knee-deep drifts. Although he'd been keeping an eye on the storm's progress all day, it had turned calm for the last hour or so, and he'd slipped into a kind of stupor, born out of weariness. Now, with the wind rocking him in the saddle, his drowsiness vanished.

Glancing back, he narrowed his eyes against the peppering grains of wind-driven snow. The storm's massive front had closed in swiftly, and he found himself staring almost in awe at the slowly writhing bank of clouds.

Allie kicked the dun close. "We can't possibly keep going in this!" she shouted above a second rattling blast of wind.

Johnny pulled his hat down tighter on his forehead. Ahead, through the thin veils of wind-tossed snow, he spotted a small pine forest, half hidden by the crest of the next hill.

"There!" he hollered, pointing. "There'll be shelter from the wind and wood for a fire in there."

"It's off the road," Allie pointed out.

By a good two hundred yards, Johnny thought, eyeing the deeper snow along the road. It was nearly even with his stirrups here, but it would be thinner on top where the autumn winds had swept it away. They could make it as far as the trees by letting the horses bull their way through.

"Stay behind me when we get on top!" he called. "I'll break trail with my Appy."

Allie nodded and drew her blanket tighter around her shoulders. Johnny gave the Appaloosa its head until they reached the bald crown of the mountain's shoulder. By then the small forest was barely visible through the shifting curtains of old, grainy snow. He reined the Appaloosa sideways to the wind, but had to pound the horse's ribs pretty hard with his heels to force it into the deeper drifts. The going was a lot tougher than he'd anticipated. The stocky gelding had to buck and jump to clear the crusted surface of earlier snows, snorting its displeasure every few yards while the wind whipped its breath away in tattered clouds. It took half an hour to cover the two hundred yards to the edge of the small forest, but the relief was immediate as soon as they entered the shelter of the trees. Here, the wind moaned rather than howled, and the snow barely reached the Appaloosa's pastern.

Johnny pushed deeper into the timber. After a few minutes, they came to a wide spot too small to be called a clearing, yet large enough to erect a shelter. Drawing rein, he waited for Allie to ride alongside.

"We barely made it in," she gasped, her voice shaded with panic. "How are we ever going to get out?"

"We'll get out," Johnny promised.

"How?"

"We'll get out if we have to snowshoe out."

She looked confused. "Where would we get snowshoes?"

"We'd make them," he replied bluntly. "Out of pine strips and rawhide."

She understood that, and glanced at the dun. "If we kill our horses, it won't matter if we reach the road again."

"We'll get out," Johnny repeated grimly, dropping from the saddle.

They took the extra gear off their horses and loosened the cinches, but left the saddles in place for the skimpy protection they would afford. Allie started collecting firewood while Johnny moved through the forest looking for dead stuff to frame a shelter. The light was fading rapidly by the time he'd rigged up a small but sturdy lean-to, shingled with pine boughs. They kicked and scraped as much of the snow out from under the shelter as they could, then brought in more boughs for carpeting, piling them nearly a foot deep as insulation against the frozen ground. When Johnny spread his bedroll canvas over the top for a floor, it was done.

After kindling a fire with her flint and steel, Allie built a backwall to help throw the heat inside the shelter. She had a little tin kettle for cooking, and filled it with snow that she brought in to melt over the fire.

"You'll have to fix your own supper," she informed Johnny curtly. "I only have enough food for myself."

The sharpness of her words caught him by surprise, but he recalled that she'd been like that all day—almost friendly one minute, hostile and distrusting the next. Although her fickleness was provoking, he reminded himself that she'd been through a lot recently, and faced perhaps even worse ahead.

Squatting beside his pack, he said: "I've got some jerky and rice in my saddlebags that you can fix for both of us." Digging out the tin billy from his own pack, he added: "I'll put some coffee on. How'd you like that?"

Allie stared quietly into the flames, then nodded. "That'd be good. I haven't had any coffee in almost three months."

Johnny whistled sympathetically. "That'd be rough," he said. "I haven't had any in just a few days, and I'd dang' near sell a tooth for a cup right now."

Allie smiled, the first one he'd seen from her, and it made him think that maybe she would come around, after all.

"I used to like tea," she said, after a pause. "My father would give us girls different blends every year at Christmas, usually from the Orient or Australia. We'd flavor it with orange peel or cinnamon. That's one of my favorite memories from childhood . . . the smell of spicy teas brewing on Christmas night."

Johnny smiled but didn't comment, remembering how quickly she'd clammed up earlier when he asked about her father.

"I suppose that sounds silly, sitting out here in a blizzard and not knowing whether we'll freeze or starve before it's all over, but it's been on my mind a lot recently."

"Sometimes a good memory can keep a body about as warm as wool," Johnny agreed. "At least on the inside."

She gave him a grateful look that made him wonder about her husband and how he would have responded to such a confession. Would he have shared the joy of her memory, or made small of it with a look or remark? She intrigued him suddenly, this gutsy woman with her vulnerabilities clinging to her like parasites. Yet he thought he'd be foolish to underestimate her. She had to be made of tough stuff; she wouldn't be out here if she wasn't.

"What about you?" Allie asked. "Do you ever pine for the past or wish you could go back to another place?"

"I don't have much of a past," Johnny said. "My parents died when I was young. I spent some time in an orphanage in Saint Paul, but I can't say those are fond memories."

"I'm sorry," Allie murmured. "I didn't mean to dredge up painful feelings."

"You didn't, and I ain't saying they're painful. I guess they just seem kind of meaningless compared to what I've done since then."

"Freighting?"

He smiled. "That about sums it up."

"Then you came to Montana to make your fortune?"

That made him chuckle. "I suppose that sums it up, too. I was driving for a guy out of Saint Cloud when the war broke out. He sold his business to the Union Army. Shipped all his wagons and mules south, then retired rich. It left his muleskinners out of work, though. Some of them went south with their outfits to haul freight for the Army, but I knew I'd never get rich that way."

"Is that important to you, to get rich?"

"Not rich so much as to just put together enough money to buy my own rig. I was thinking that with a couple of good, heavy wagons and a twelve- or fourteen-mule hitch, a man could do all right for himself. Especially if he picked his own contracts." He stared into the crackling flames. "I've been around freighting ever since I was fifteen years old. I know the business, and figure I could make a go of it with a little luck."

Allie smiled once more, a fleeting expression, although it made a world of difference in her looks. "My husband never had realistic goals," she said. "He wanted to be rich and own a mansion with servants. . . ." Her words trailed off and her expression abruptly hardened. Bending toward the fire, she pulled her kettle closer. "You said you had some rice, mister?"

"In my saddlebags."

"I don't muck around in another person's belongings," she said pointedly, "just as I won't tolerate anyone poking around in mine."

Johnny was quiet a moment, taken aback. Then he yanked a sack of rice from his gear and threw it to the canvas floor beside her. "Fair enough," he said brusquely, then pushed to his feet and disappeared into the darkness beyond the fire to check on the horses.

Chapter Twenty-Three

It was still blowing hard when they awoke the next morning. The treetops were whipping back and forth, and the snow that had blown in among the pines blanketed the back of their shelter.

Johnny and Allie barely spoke to one another as the gray light strengthened, even though the storm's fury obliged them to stay under their shelter. The sun never really made an appearance that morning, but, when Johnny figured it was as light as it was going to get, he trudged out to check on the horses. When he came back, his expression was somber.

"We'll bring them in one at a time if this doesn't stop before long," he said. "We can brush the snow off their hips and warm them by the fire."

"We're about out of wood," Allie said.

"Then we'll drag some more up."

Her face looked pale in the poor light, her lips thin with worry. "Did you see the road?"

"No, but it isn't snowing yet. What's blown in so far is old stuff. I've seen this before, a hard wind that doesn't seem like it'll ever stop. When it does, that's when it'll start snowing."

That was the way it happened, too. In the shadowless light of midday, the winds died without warning. Johnny and Allie were lying in their blankets, dozing, when the sudden quiet startled them awake. Pushing up on one elbow, Johnny peered out of the lean-to just as the first tentative flakes of new snow began drifting down among the pines. By the time he and Allie had their gear packed and the horses ready, it was coming down steadily, the flakes big but thankfully light; still, it was sticking immediately, an inch or more falling in the first twenty minutes. Watching it accumulate so quickly, Allie said: "Dare we even try to leave?"

"If we don't, I'm afraid we may never get out," he replied grimly.

"How far is it to the top of Monida Pass?"

"I don't know, but it'd better not be too far."

They mounted and wound back through the trees to the trail they'd broken coming in, hauling up when they reached the edge of the forest.

"It's drifted in," Allie said softly.

"It won't be as bad as it was yesterday. The surface isn't crusted like it was then."

Despite his words of encouragement, Johnny was relieved when they reached the road; that feeling increased tenfold when he saw that it wasn't drifted in, as he'd feared it might be.

They rode south without comment, the land itself quiet under the muffling fall of snow. Although still cold, without the wind it was no longer miserable. It was tough going, though. By noon, the soft powder in the road came up almost to the Appaloosa's knees, and all three horses were struggling. Johnny and Allie took turns breaking trail so that the burden wouldn't fall solely on one animal. Allie was up front when the sound of a rifle shot thumped heavily through the still air. She pulled up, twisting in the saddle to stare behind them as the shot's echo was swallowed by the clouds.

"What was that?" she asked.

Johnny had also stopped to look back. "Cut-throats, I reckon."

"Shooting at us?"

"No, it was too far away for that."

They were quiet for several minutes, listening, but no more shots breached the heavy silence. "Maybe it's someone's hunting," Allie ventured.

"There's no game this high," Johnny said, then swung back to face the cloud-curtained pass. "Keep riding," he ordered.

They pushed on even harder after that, pausing only once, when the road dipped close to the creek, to water their horses. Leaving the Appaloosa and the bay with Allie, Johnny walked back along their trail for almost two hundred yards, before stopping to listen. He stood there for several minutes, but nothing came to him out of the hazy distance. Still, his uneasiness persisted. The sense of something lurking out there, just out of sight, reminded him of his childhood fears of monsters hiding under beds.

Allie was mounted and ready to ride when Johnny came back. He paused beside his saddlebags to dig Andy's Colt from the near-side pouch.

"Have you got a belt?" he asked.

She drew a sharp breath. "Are they coming?"

"I didn't see anything, but I figure they're close. We wouldn't have heard that shot if they weren't. Sound doesn't carry well in this kind of weather."

She held her hand out for the pistol. "I don't have a belt, but I can carry it in my coat pocket."

He gave her the revolver, returning the plain leather sheath to his own saddlebag. "Do you know how to reload it?" he asked.

"Yes. I'm not fast, but I've done it before."

He gave her a small, pasteboard box containing a dozen linen cartridges and a small, tear-shaped capper. "All six chambers are loaded, but the nipple under the hammer isn't capped. Leave it that way until you have to shoot, and be careful you don't accidentally cock it on your coat when you pull it out."

"I know how to handle a firearm," she replied, annoyed.

Johnny nodded gravely. "Yeah, I reckon you do." Then he stepped into the Appaloosa's saddle and reined back onto the road.

They'd left Red Rock Creek some time before and were following a smaller stream now, although they occasionally lost sight of it when the road strayed onto higher ground. There was no sign of the sun through the heavy clouds, nor much perspective in the gray light that seemed to blur the lines between earth and sky. Visibility had clamped down to less than half a mile, and patches of damp fog crept over the hills around them like stalking hunters.

They stopped again in the middle of the afternoon to eat and rest the horses, sharing some of Johnny's jerky and dried plums, then wearily shoved on. The horses were starting to show the strain of the ever-deepening snow and lack of adequate graze and rest. Even the Appaloosa was looking gaunt in its flanks; its hips protruded sharply under Johnny's bedroll. In late afternoon the snow finally began to lessen, the clouds to pull back. Soon the faint, pearl orb of the sun appeared off their right shoulder, lifting Johnny's spirits. A light breeze picked up at the same time, and within minutes the dreary walls around them began to retreat. Raising his face to the clearing skies, Johnny breathed deeply, as if the air pouring in through the distant rift in the clouds was somehow fresher than what he'd been breathing since the storm closed around them yesterday. Then, lowering his gaze, Johnny cursed softly and Allie gasped.

"Is it them?" she asked.

"I reckon so."

They were still a couple of miles away—a short, stubby black line of men and horses against the fresh snow. Johnny counted five riders, each of them leading a spare mount.

"They've been switching horses," he said. "That way, they don't wear out either animal."

"Like you'd planned to do before you met me," Allie said guiltily.

Johnny shrugged. "It doesn't matter. I wouldn't have left you behind, no matter what I said yesterday." Then he looked at her and smiled. "Besides, you haven't been a burden. I was glad to have your help last night, tending the fire while I slept. I was mighty tired."

She flashed him a look of gratitude. "Thank you, Johnny."

It was the first time he'd heard her use his name, and he realized he liked the sound of it better than he would have thought. Gruffly he said: "Let's move out. It's gonna be a rough trail from here on, and no more breaks."

"We can't escape them," Allie said. "Not in these mountains, in this snow. There's no place to hide and no way to outrun them."

Johnny started to reach for the Henry, then changed his mind and slid the Hawken from its loop on his saddle horn. "I ain't shot that lever gun yet, and I'm not sure what kind of range it has, but I can drive a nail at fifty yards with this front-stuffer, and hit a bucket at two hundred yards nine shots out of ten. Unless they're armed with something better, their catching up isn't going to do them a lot of good."

"You can't hold them off forever."

"No, but if I can hold them off until dark, it might give us an edge. Let's just ride on for a while. We can worry about the rest when they catch up."

Chapter Twenty-Four

The clouds closed in again and the breeze died, but Johnny held no illusions about having been spotted by Cutter's men. Against these white hills, he and Allie must have stood out like banners.

By now, the snow was almost stirrup deep, and the horses' strength was waning. In frustration, Johnny dismounted to forge his own path for a while, but it was largely a wasted effort; within half an hour, he was back beside the Appaloosa, sweat dripping off the end of his nose.

"You'll kill yourself that way," Allie said.

"We'll both die if we don't start making better time."

"We've started downhill," she said quietly.

Looking around, he saw that she was right. The land was definitely sloping to the south, with pines in view on both sides of the road. Behind them, the rounded summit of Monida Pass reminded Johnny of the top of a huge bald head, seen from the rear.

"Sure enough," he said, grinning.

"If I remember correctly, it's shorter going down this side."

"Shorter, but rougher and steeper, is what I was told."

"Does that matter?"

"Not if it gets us out of this high country any quicker." He gathered his reins above the Appaloosa's neck, then stretched his toe for the stirrup. The back of his thigh cramped in protest, but he ignored it and heaved into the saddle.

Allie took the lead, and they finally began to make better time. Johnny kept the bay close, his focus more to the rear than forward. It was just coming onto dark when he caught his next sight of the trailing Cut-throats. It wasn't much more than a glimpse of a lone horseman appearing out of yet another thickening fog, but he called a warning to Allie. By the time she looked, the rider had vanished back into the low clouds.

"What did you see?" she demanded. "Was it Tucker?"

A shot whuffled past on their left, the sound of its report dull in the heavy air.

"Keep riding," Johnny said, bringing the Hawken to the cradle of his left arm. There was a shout from behind them, then several more shots pierced the twilight. Finally someone called out with authority to stop shooting at what they couldn't see. Johnny recognized the voice immediately, even though he'd only heard it once before, in Ruby City. It was Otis Call.

"Son-of-a-bitch," Johnny murmured, wheeling after Allie.

The tall pines continued to funnel in on either side, creating a narrow, serpentine corridor that seemed to suck up the remaining daylight. They'd gone no more than another hundred yards when the shooting started anew. Pulling the bay close, Johnny looped its lead rope around the saddle horn, then chased it ahead. "Keep moving!" he called to Allie. "I'll slow them down."

She glanced wildly over her shoulder. "I can help. Two guns would be better than one."

"No, keep riding. I want you breaking trail."

She nodded her understanding and kicked the dun into a swifter pace, the bay following hesitantly. Dismounting, Johnny draped the Appaloosa's reins over an alder poking out of the snow along the road, then walked into the middle of the wagon trace and sank down on one knee. It was like sitting in a pit, the snow shoulder high around him. In the rapidly fading light he could barely make out his pursuers, crowded five abreast across the road a couple of hundred yards away. He had to figure they'd already spotted him, and that was why they'd stopped. Realizing they were following at least two individuals, they were probably worried about a trap.

Johnny didn't know if they'd identified the person with him as a woman. He supposed it didn't matter. Sooner or later, Call's men would close in, either under cover or in a rush of superior numbers. When that time came, Allie's gender wouldn't matter. The only question would be how well she could shoot, and, right now, only she knew the answer to that.

"Montana!"

Johnny narrowed his eyes. He hadn't expected a conversation.

"Johnny Montana! This is Otis Call. There ain't no reason you have to die here, boy. All we want is your gold. Leave it there in the road and you can ride out of here unharmed."

Johnny didn't move. He knew he'd be hard to see in the deepening dusk. The Appaloosa, with its mottled markings, would be even more difficult to make out. That might give Call pause, but it wouldn't stop him for long.

"We know you're there, Montana. One of my men has a bead on your head right now. I'm persuading him not to pull the trigger to give you time to do the right thing. Don't make me look like a fool, boy. Your life is worth more than a pile of yellow dust."

Johnny shouldered the Hawken. The light was almost gone now, his targets little more than a distant smudge across the trail. "Go on back, Call!" he shouted. "Tell Cutter I got away. There's no point in any more men dying over this. I'm not going to give up my head and hide for a sick man's whim."

There was a moment's silence, then Call responded. "That's smart thinking, Montana. Cutter's a sick bastard, and no one here will argue that, but we've got to have that gold. We won't go back without it. What do you say? It's a fair deal I'm offering, and a lot more than you'll get from Brett when he catches up."

The darkness was almost complete now. Otis Call and his men were no longer visible. Lowering his rifle, Johnny quietly slipped over to the Appaloosa's side. He was gathering the reins when a chill trickled down his spine. At that same instant the Appaloosa threw its head up, its ears perked toward the trees flanking the road.

"Talk to me, Montana!" Call shouted.

Johnny let his breath out slowly. The Appaloosa was looking at a spot maybe thirty yards away, but all Johnny could make out was a black wall of towering pines. Soundlessly he slid the Hawken through its loop on his saddle horn, then palmed one of the ivory-handled Remingtons.

"What about some other kind of trade?" Otis called, desperate for a response, something to mark Johnny's location for his men. "You're not going to make it, otherwise. We've got too many men and horses. We'd run you down before you got halfway to Salt Lake City."

Sliding a toe into his stirrup, Johnny hauled himself carefully into the saddle, but there was no way he could mask the loud creak of cold leather shifting under his weight.

From the nearby trees, a voice shouted: "He's getting away!"

At the same time, a rifle barked close in, its ball whining above the Appaloosa's neck. Two more rifles cracked from above, and Johnny dug his heels into the Appaloosa's sides. He thrust the Remington behind him and fired twice, using the Cut-throats' muzzle flashes for targets. Then he holstered the pistol and bent low over the gelding's withers.

The sound of gunfire tapered off, and Johnny thought he'd made it. Then a giant hand seemed to reach out from nowhere and smack the back of his head. He slumped forward with a startled grunt, grabbing desperately for the saddle's tall, narrow horn. He wanted to slow the Appaloosa's reckless stride but his limbs refused to function properly. He couldn't control the reins or even find the rhythm of the running horse. All he could do was hang on, and he thought he was doing a good job of that until he heard the Appaloosa's hoofs retreating, felt the cold slap of snow in his face, then began a long slide into nothingness.

Chapter Twenty-Five

Allie reined to a stop, the pack horse crowding close as if afraid of being left behind. Her every instinct told her to keep running. In her mind, she could already see Tuck and his crew surrounding her—brazen-eyed, laughing with crude anticipation. She knew no one would blame her for fleeing. But she didn't. Whimpering low in her throat, she guided the dun off the road and dismounted.

The Colt Johnny had given her was still in her pocket, but it was the familiar shotgun she kept in her hands. She crept back into the road as if stalking a deer, crouching low and placing her feet with care, every sense keenly alert. The yells of Cutter's men had ceased, and their gunfire had quieted, but the silence wasn't complete. She cocked her head to one side until she recognized the muffled pounding of hoofs coming toward her. Resolutely she eared both hammers back. She felt like crying, but gritted her teeth instead, her pulse loud and jumping. But it wasn't a Cut-throat coming down the road. It was Johnny's Appaloosa, cantering roughly with its head to one side to avoid tripping over its reins. The horse snorted in fright and slid to a halt when it saw her, its head high, nostrils distended.

"Here," Allie said, stepping forward and holding out her hand. "It's me. You know me."

The spotted horse side-stepped into the deeper snow along the road and stopped. Its head was still up but it had her scent now, and was beginning to calm down. Allie held her hand out and the Appaloosa stretched out its neck to sniff her fingers, its soft lips fluttering.

"Good boy," Allie said, reaching a little farther and grasping the dangling reins. She led the horse out of the deep snow and secured it to a nearby sapling. Then she returned to the road to stare back the way she'd come, racked with doubt. The urge to run was stronger than ever now. Stronger even than on the night she'd fled Bannack. Johnny was dead. He had to be, or he never would have allowed the Appaloosa to escape. And she was alive. With three good horses and Monida Pass behind her, there was nothing to stop her, nothing between her and the safety of Salt Lake City. She could go on and never look back.

But she didn't, because she didn't know Johnny was dead. He was probably dead, and, if that was the case, then the Cutthroats would be between him and her, and closing fast.

Tuck would be closing fast!

A small, frustrated groan escaped her lips. "I don't owe you anything, mister," she whispered. "I didn't ask for your help, and I didn't promise you mine." Yet she remained rooted where she was, long enough that, when she did return to her horse, she didn't even question her sanity. "You idiot," she berated herself. "You stupid, starry-eyed fool."

It was the Appaloosa that led her to Johnny, sprawled in the snow beside the road. The spotted horse had acted spooky all the way back, dancing and tossing its head. Allie couldn't have predicted how far she would have gone before turning back, but she was immensely relieved when she came across Johnny's body less than two hundred yards up the mountain. He'd apparently hung on for quite a while before pitching from the saddle.

He lay face down in the snow, half buried as if he'd slid into it when he left the saddle. She prodded his shoulder, and he stirred and tried to speak, but he didn't make much sense. Allie peered upcañon. She couldn't see anything in the starless night, but couldn't shake the feeling that danger surrounded her. "Damn you, Johnny Montana," she hissed, punching his shoulder. "Get up."

But Johnny was beyond compliance. Muttering under her breath, Allie returned the shotgun to the dun's saddle, then led the Appaloosa forward. Kneeling at Johnny's side, she tried to pull him over on his back, but in the deep snow he was too heavy.

"Wake up," she said, panic rippling through her words. "You're too big for me to sling across the saddle, and I can't wait forever." She grabbed the hair at the back of his head and pulled his face out of the snow. "Johnny!"

He moaned, and one leg weakly churned at the snow.

"Easy," a voice warned from upcañon. "I heard something."

"Montana, is that you?" another voice rumbled.

"Stay back!" Allie shouted.

"Hell, that's a woman!" exclaimed yet another voice.

"I'll bet that's Tuck's woman," the first one replied, and Allie had to bite her lip to keep from crying out. Cutter's men were close, but shrouded in darkness.

"Come on, you dumb muleskinner," Allie breathed, pounding on Johnny's shoulder with her fist.

"Lady, we don't mean you any harm," the deep-voiced one said. "It's Montana we want. He killed some friends of ours."

Allie stalked to the dun's side and yanked the shotgun from her saddle. "Listen to me, mister!" she shouted. "I do mean you harm, and plenty of it if you come any closer. I've got a double-barreled shotgun and enough pistols to blow the whole bunch of you into raw meat."

"Easy, boys," the first voice cautioned. "Tuck said she was armed."

"Wha . . . what?" Johnny said, pushing clumsily to his hands and knees.

Allie returned to his side. "You've got to get up," she whispered fiercely, grabbing his arm with her free hand. "We have to get out of here."

He reached up blindly with one hand, as if feeling the air. A shot sounded, the bullet making a wet, fizzing sound as it passed through a nearby snowbank. Johnny got one knee up, then staggered to his feet. Allie guided him to the Appaloosa and helped him get his hands around the saddle horn. The Appaloosa had been acting like it wanted to bolt, but it must have scented Johnny, and stood quietly as she helped place his foot in the stirrup.

"Lady!"

Allie flinched. That one was close, too close, and she put her shoulder under Johnny's buttocks and straightened, leveraging him into the seat. Shoving the reins into his hands, she said: "If you fall again, mister, you're on your own." Then she returned to the dun and mounted.

"Hold it right there, girly. I got you covered!"

There, Allie thought, placing the location of the voice even as she lowered the shotgun's twin barrels.

"Dammit, woman . . . !" the man shouted, but whatever else he was going to say was drowned out by the roar of the shotgun's right-hand barrel, followed by a high, shrill scream.

"Look out!" someone even closer shouted, and Allie fired her second barrel.

Gunfire roared; muzzle flashes darted like yellow tongues. Allie sawed on the dun's reins, kicking the horse as hard as she could as she raced downcañon. She was aware of the bay in front of her, barely staying clear of the dun's hoofs. The Appaloosa was somewhere behind her. She didn't know if Johnny was still in the saddle, but remained firm in her resolve not to go back. She wouldn't risk capture a second time. Tears streaked her cheeks, mixing with the wetness of the falling snow as she fled into the night.

CHAPTER TWENTY-SIX

The snow quit falling two days later, but by then the tracks of Johnny Montana and the woman had vanished. Not even Shirt Jackson or Chico Sanchez had been able to pick them up.

Standing alone on an outcropping of broken shale, Otis Call stared out over the high, broad plain before him. The sky was pale blue and crowded with wispy, fast-moving clouds; under it, the land was as white as a new china mug, largely featureless, save to the east where the three knuckles of the Tetons squatted like knobs on the horizon. Other than a circling hawk exploring the foothills to the west, nothing stirred in all that vast expanse. Not even a deer or antelope.

A jingle of spurs intruded upon Otis's quiet reflections. Glancing around, he saw Tom Tucker climbing the rocky ledge toward him. Stopping several yards away, Tuck glared out over the empty landscape.

"They're out there," he growled. "I can feel 'em."

"Them, or her?" Otis asked, turning his back to the brooding killer.

Tuck chuckled low in his throat. "It ain't my fault you don't share my feelings for the fairer sex, Call."

"I've seen the results of some of those feelings," Otis replied, not bothering to mask his contempt. "They weren't pretty to look at."

"They asked for it," was Tuck's curt response. He started back to the outlaw camp, adding over his shoulder: "The old man wants to see us, *pronto.*"

Otis nodded but didn't immediately follow. He wasn't surprised that Brett wanted to see them. The last of the scouting parties had returned less than an hour ago, without having located Montana's trail. It was time to formulate another plan.

Their camp lay just below the southern entrance to Monida Pass. Brett had ordered a crude shelter to be hacked out of the timber east of the cañon's mouth. It had kept the worst of the snow off them, but it hadn't been nearly as snug as the lean-to Montana and the woman had built on the other side of the pass.

Thinking of that small, cozy lean-to brought an unexpected smile to Otis's face. His respect for Montana's cunning had grown steadily over the past week—although he still thought they might have surprised him and the girl if Charlie Ryder hadn't fired a shot that day on the other side of Monida, signaling Otis and his crew into the small forest where Montana had built his shelter.

Even though Montana's trail coming out of the trees had been obvious, Otis had sent Charlie and Dave Worthy in just to see what there was to see. They were supposed to give a shout if they found anything interesting, but Ryder, the damned fool, had fired his revolver into the air instead, announcing their presence to the whole mountain.

Otis supposed it didn't matter much now. Charlie had taken the brunt of the woman's first shot in the cañon two nights before, and lost most of his left arm as a result. It was amazing to Otis that Charlie was still alive. He and Ed Miles, who'd come in from guarding the Big Hole route just in time to take a bullet in the chest from Montana's revolver—probably one of the ivory-handled Remingtons taken off Brett's little brother, Lloyd, way the hell back on the Ruby River.

In his mind, Otis counted back along the trail of dead and

wounded—Lloyd and Little Tate Orr and Prairie Richards; Harley Lamont, killed by Brett but still another casualty on the tab; Joe Bill Hodson left wounded in Twin Bridges and probably hung by now; Cam Turner, Jim Peakes, Bud Dixon, and Dick Carter, all gunned down in Dolsen's trading post.

"Sweet Jesus," Otis whispered, adding up the numbers. Nine dead, and Montana no closer to being run down now than he had been the night he left Ruby City.

Otis's jaws clenched in frustration. He didn't share Brett's desire for revenge, but, by damn, that was a lot of good men killed needlessly, as far as he was concerned. All for one man's obsession to take his pound of flesh. Literally in this case. It was enough to make Otis feel half sick as he stepped down off the rocky ledge and made his way back to camp.

Brett was standing at the entrance of the main shelter when Otis approached. "Glad you could make it," he said sarcastically. "I kind of figured you'd come back with Tuck, since I sent him to fetch you ten minutes ago."

"I guess I don't fetch so easily any more," Otis replied. He glanced at the fire where Chico Sanchez and Jake Haws were squatting, eating elk wrapped in biscuits and drinking some of Poke Hardesty's good coffee. "You boys are the last ones in," he said, impressed. "How far'd you go?"

"Pretty far," Sanchez replied laconically.

"They went all the way to Camus Creek," Brett said, "then west to the Medicine Lodge and up that until they cut McGrew's trail and finally came on in. How far'd your boys go, Otis? I don't recall."

"They aren't my boys, Brett. They aren't yours, either."

"They are if they want their share of the gold."

"Like you said . . . it's their share. They've already earned it."

"Nobody's earned anything until Montana's been run down and skinned," Brett snarled.

"Let them go, Brett. We've lost enough men."

"Let 'em go?" Tuck echoed. He was looking at Otis as if he'd just spouted a mouthful of Mandarin. "Hell, we ain't lettin' nobody go. Are you loco? Montana's carryin' maybe forty, fifty thousand in dust, and no tellin' what the girl's got."

"Fifty thousand or a hundred thousand, it isn't worth dying for," Otis argued. "This ain't no green kid we're following, Tuck."

"Shirt disagrees," Brett reminded him.

"Shirt hasn't run him down yet, either."

Cutter's smile thinned condescendingly. "I seem to remember back at Lost Spring you couldn't speak highly enough of Jackson's mythical native abilities."

"Shirt's a good tracker, Brett. That isn't the point."

"That Shirt, he is a damn' good tracker," Chico said from the fire. "Is no his fault he don't find Montana or the girl."

"Nor yours, either?" Brett asked, scowling.

"By damn, is one hell lot of snow out there that we track through," Chico protested. "You cannot see tracks covered like that. Nobody sees those tracks."

"Nevertheless," Brett said dismissively, turning his back on the young Spaniard, "I'll not let him escape. Not after what he did to Lloyd." He gave Tuck a meaningful glance. "I won't let that girl get away, either, old friend."

Tuck's expression relaxed. Otis knew he would follow Brett to hell and back if that's what it took to get the woman.

Turning back to Otis, Brett said: "Montana's traveling light. He'll have to head for a trading post pretty soon or risk starving."

"You figure he'll head for Fort Hall?"

"It's his only choice, short of recrossing Monida Pass."

"He could go around Hall, live off the land. I saw the lean-to he made. He's got the savvy to survive out here."

"Savvy or not, living off the land in winter is a full-time occupation, and he won't want to do that. No, Montana wants to reach Salt Lake City and deposit his gold in a bank. He'll make a run for Utah Territory, but you may be right in speculating that he could by-pass Fort Hall. That's why I'm not going to concentrate all of our men there. It's the roads and trails leading south, and especially those that cross the Snake River, that we'll focus on."

"That's a lot of country," Otis said skeptically.

"*Ah,* but you'd be surprised at how few crossings there are over the Snake River, especially at this time of year. Come January, a man might cross on the ice, but, this early in the season, Montana's options are going to be limited to the ferry at Fort Hall, to White Horse Shoals east of there, or maybe, maybe, a flat stretch to the west of the fort, right before the lava fields."

Brett smiled at the puzzled look on the faces of his two lieutenants. "While you men were in the field last summer, I was doing my own work at Lost Spring. I spoke with a fair number of men familiar with that country. It was important that I knew the ways out, not just to cut off any thieving prospector, but for our own escape when the time came."

"Hell," Tuck snorted. "Here I thought you was sittin' up at Lost Spring scratchin' your ass the whole time, while me 'n' Otis and the others was doin' the dirty work. Maybe you earned your cut, after all."

Cutter's expression changed sharply, and Tuck's face paled.

"Shoot, I was just goorawin' ya, Brett," Tuck said quickly. "You know me. We've been together too long to take offense at something one or th' other of us says." After a pause, he added: "Ain't we?"

"Perhaps," Brett replied softly, so that only the three of them heard, "but for the sake of the men, and of my command, you won't let it happen again, will you . . . old friend?"

Tuck looked even more confused, but he nodded anyway.

"Good," Brett said, smiling with satisfaction. "I intend to split the men into smaller groups. Shirt Jackson and Dave Worthy will watch White Horse Shoals. Chico and Jake will cover the flats west of Fort Hall. I'll put Jack McGrew, Hank Bonner, and Chris Ewing right inside the fort, since I'm confident Montana will eventually have to make for that."

"And the rest of us?" Otis asked.

"You and Tuck will stay with me. I'll put Sam Hulse and Coffee Kearns somewhere in Portneuf Cañon, just below Fort Hall, and Poke Hardesty and Fred Dover at the O.C. Relay Station north of the Malad Mountains, just in case Montana does by-pass Hall."

"And the three of us?" Otis asked.

"We'll find a cabin in Malad City where we can hole up until this is finished," Brett said with finality. "Once Montana's dead, we'll split the gold and go our separate ways."

"We'll split the gold with the men," Otis amended.

Brett flashed him an irritated look. "Of course, with the men."

Otis nodded without any real satisfaction and walked over to where the men were gathered among the rocks, out of the wind sweeping off the flat plain. Shirt Jackson and Sam Hulse looked up as he approached, and Sam kicked the sole of Dave Worthy's boot to awaken him. Otis made a motion for the three men to follow him out of earshot, then briefly outlined the details of Cutter's plan. None seemed particularly thrilled with their new assignments, but no one complained too much.

"I'll tell you, if it wasn't for the gold Montana's totin', I'd let him run," Sam remarked.

"I would, too," Otis said. He didn't add that he was tempted to do it anyway, take what they had now and make a dash for San Diego before the law or a vigilante committee showed up, and the hell with Brett.

Shirt, though, was of a different notion. "I want that bastard. It ain't right that some dirt-grubbing tin-pan is making us look like a bunch of monkeys."

"I don't much care about that," Dave said. "It's Charlie I'm thinkin' about. What's gonna happen to him?"

Sam laughed. "By damn, Davey, I didn't hear Ryder's name mentioned. Sounds like your ol' buddy ain't a part of the plan no more."

Otis looked at Dave curiously. "This is no different than what happened to Joe Bill up at Twin Bridges," he said.

"The hell it ain't. Charlie's one of us, Otis. Like Little Tate was. Like me 'n' Sam 'n' Shirt is."

"We can't stay, and Charlie wouldn't survive an hour in the saddle," Otis replied patiently. "You've got no choice, Dave, unless you want to give up your share of the gold."

"Do that," Sam taunted, his lips peeling back in a cold grin. "Stay here and nurse that little dumb ass."

"He ain't a dumb ass," Dave retorted.

"He's wolf bait," Shirt said bluntly.

"Charlie didn't duck when he should've," Sam added. "He got hisself shot for his own stupidity. I'd call that a dumb ass."

"It's finished," Otis said abruptly, making a slashing gesture with his hand. He glowered at Dave. "You stay if you want, but you'll kiss your share of the gold good bye. Cutter'll see to that, and there's not a man here who won't back him up."

"That ain't fair, Call," Dave said, his hand rising ever so slightly toward his revolver. Then he let it fall away, gritting his teeth in defeat. "God dammit, it ain't fair."

"No, it isn't," Otis agreed solemnly. "But it's the way it is, so the next time the shooting starts, don't forget to duck."

Sam laughed and walked away. Shirt followed him. They went out to where the horses were picketed. Others were already there, bringing in their mounts, preparing to pull out. Otis watched stonily for a moment, then walked out to catch his own mount.

Chapter Twenty-Seven

Johnny's eyelids fluttered open to the bright blue of a midday sky. He lay unmoving for several minutes, then cautiously sat up and looked around. He was in his bedroll under a cedar tree, using a litter of dead needles and scaly bark for a mattress. Peering through the green boughs revealed a sparse forest of widely scattered trees identical to the one that was sheltering him. Pushing his blankets back, he crawled out from under the low cedar and stood up.

Allie sat on a rock a few yards away, eyeing him with a look of detached skepticism, as if she doubted he would be able to keep his feet much longer. Beyond the fringe of the trees he could see the horses grazing on the tall, autumn-cured grass that pushed up through the fresh snow. There was a fire pit in front of him, but no flame, and the ashes looked cold, lifeless.

"Where are we?" he asked in a dry, scratchy voice.

"I wouldn't know."

"Where's the road?"

She stabbed a thumb over her shoulder. "Out there somewhere. It was snowing hard when I left the main road. All I had to guide me were those mountains behind you, but they could've bent and twisted in any direction."

"No, that makes sense," Johnny said, turning a slow circle. "Those mountains are to the north, part of the range we came over. And those"—he nodded toward a trio of jutting crags to the southeast—"should be the western slopes of the Tetons."

"They're the Tetons, all right," Allie agreed. "I saw them when I came north last spring. But I still don't know how far east we came in that storm. Not that it'll matter. The Utah road is west of here. I guess we'll find it when you're ready to leave."

"I'm ready right now," he said. "Just give me a minute to collect my thoughts."

Allie's laughter was low and mocking. "You barely know which end is up, otherwise you wouldn't be standing in the snow in just your socks. Besides, the horses need rest, even if you don't. They're about done in."

Johnny stared at his feet, only now realizing how cold they had become since leaving his blankets, but, at Allie's remark about the horses, he looked up in alarm. "What's wrong with the horses?"

"We nearly killed them coming over Monida, that's what's wrong with them. We're lucky we didn't cripple the whole lot. Livestock can't take that kind of punishment."

Squinting into the sunshine, Johnny was startled by the horses' gauntness, the washboard appearance of their ribs through their heavy winter coats. He started to walk in that direction, but a wave of dizziness stopped him. Returning to his bedroll, he lowered himself gently and stripped off his wet socks, then pushed his feet under the blankets.

"You feeling all right, mister?" Allie asked without rising.

"It's mister again, is it?"

"It's a simple question," she replied curtly.

Johnny lay back and closed his eyes. "I feel light, kind of. Like I could float off if I wasn't careful."

"That's probably because of your head. You took a pretty hard lump to the back of it. I finally decided a bullet did it, but it must have been a hang-fire or a long way off, otherwise it would've busted your skull open like a pumpkin." She pushed to her feet. "Something solid on your stomach would probably help. You haven't had more than a few swallows of broth since we've been here."

"How long's that been?"

"We were two days getting this far, and two more since then."

His eyes opened wide, and he raised his head. "Four days?"

"I've been waiting for you to die, since it didn't seem proper to take your horses while you were still breathing."

"That was kind of you," Johnny replied dryly, exploring the hard lump on the back of his head with gentle fingers.

"I guess it was too far from your heart to kill you," Allie stated matter-of-factly, then looked off to the southwest. "I won't start a fire just yet, though. Some Cut-throats were poking around in that direction a couple of days ago. I'm not convinced they've taken off for good yet."

"You sure they were Cut-throats?"

"I'm sure," she replied flatly. "I'll kindle a fire at sundown, when the light's too poor to see the smoke, then put it out before it gets dark enough to see the flames. I'll only need enough to warm up some broth and fix some meat. I've been setting snares for rabbits and having good luck at it." She was quiet for a moment, then added: "You ought to get some rest, mister. You're pale enough now that I'm having trouble seeing you against all that snow."

"Where are my guns?"

"One of your revolvers is beside your saddle, where you've been laying. You must've lost the other one when you fell off your horse, because I haven't seen it. I've been keeping that shiny yellow rifle of yours with me, but I'll bring it over if you're worried about it."

"No, keep it," he said, pulling the blankets up to his chin. "I feel so cross-eyed now I probably couldn't hit the ground in three tries."

At least that's what he tried to say, but the words seemed to tumble toward the end, his thoughts falling back and down into the warmth of sleep.

It was dusk when he awoke next, but he felt better. Allie was hovering over a small fire, stirring the contents of her little tin kettle while a rabbit, skewered on a peeled willow limb, browned over the flames. The aroma of the sizzling meat brought a long rumble to his stomach, catching Allie's attention.

"You figure you can crawl over here and feed yourself, or do you expect me to serve you?"

"I can walk," Johnny said, taking note of the hard edge in her words. He rummaged through his saddlebags for a pair of dry socks, then threw his blankets back and pulled them and his boots on. He stood with care, but there was no light-headedness this time, just a weakness in his limbs that he knew food and rest would cure. His greatcoat lay atop his bedroll and he put it on, but left his hat where it was. He knew it would take a few more days before he felt like tolerating any pressure around his head.

At the fire, he said: "It's too bad you didn't snare an elk. I'm hungry enough to eat one for supper."

She gave him a wry look. "I doubt if you'll finish that bunny."

He sat down on a log Allie had apparently dragged up for that purpose and held his hands toward the warmth of the fire. Allie came over to sit beside him, although careful to keep some space between them. "That meat's still pink close to the bone, but you can start on the broth. It's rabbit, too."

"What I could use is a cup of hot coffee," he said, which earned him a disdainful glance.

"I reckon broth'll have to do until you get to a fancier restaurant than this," she said.

"Damn, woman, you've been sitting on fight ever since I woke up. Are you mad because I didn't die?"

"I'm mad because I had to take care of you like you were a

little baby, which isn't my job. At least if you'd died, I'd have your horses for my trouble."

"If money's your concern, I'll gladly pay you for your efforts."

"It ain't your money I want, mister. I want to get out of these horrible mountains alive, which I figure isn't likely now. You know Cutter's not going to let us reach Salt Lake City. Not when they've got us cornered like they do."

"Brett Cutter and his men have been trying to corner me ever since I left Ruby City," Johnny replied. "They haven't done it yet. I don't intend to make it any easier for them tomorrow."

"Sure," Allie snorted. "I've been watching how tough you've been these last few days."

He turned back to the fire, swallowing the angry retort perched on the tip of his tongue. "Maybe I do owe you an apology. You could've kept running. . . ."

"You don't owe me anything," she said, cutting him off. "Just like I don't owe you anything. Not any more. My debt to you for that dun horse is paid in full."

"You've never owed me anything, Allie."

She stood and wiped her hands on her skirt. "I guess it's a matter of perception. Personally I don't care what you think, as long as you understand that I don't owe you anything any more." She nodded toward the fire. "Don't let that burn too long. I don't want any Cut-throats seeing it and getting nosey. As soon as that rabbit's browned all the way through, put it out."

Johnny watched her stalk off into the gloaming, her spine so rigid she could have used it for a pry bar. He wondered what was really bothering her. Was it the husband she'd mentioned in their mountaintop lean-to? Tucker? Maybe it was all men. Or perhaps only him.

Sighing, he tugged the willow skewer from the ground, then

kicked snow over the fire, plunging the camp into a dusky gloom. Likely he'd never know what chafed her, but, as he tore a hind leg off the rabbit, he had to admit it worried him. Her distrust and animosity could become a liability down the road, and, if it got bad enough, it could even get one of them killed.

Chapter Twenty-Eight

Although Johnny's strength returned quickly, the horses' didn't. Allie had been right when she said they were lucky they hadn't crippled any of them coming over Monida Pass. That long, arduous climb and descent—the lack of adequate graze and decent water, the lashing winds and freezing temperatures, coupled with the hard days before they'd even reached the mountain range—had taken its toll on all three animals. The bay had suffered worst, having been hard-used long before the wagon party's attempted escape, but the Appaloosa and dun were also weakened.

With the horses worn down, Johnny and Allie elected to stay where they were for a few more days. They wanted to give the stock time to rebuild their stamina for the final push to the Mormon settlements along the Great Salt Lake. Although they hadn't seen any sign of Cutter's men since Allie watched two of them pass to the southwest several days before, neither of them believed the outlaws had given up.

"Tuck won't," Allie stated with a conviction Johnny found chilling. Thinking of the gold in his own packs, he knew the others wouldn't, either.

Although Johnny stayed close to camp that first full day on his feet, by the second, he was starting to grow restless. He wandered the cedars with his Hawken, and haunted the rim of the bluff where Allie had spotted the two Cut-throats. From it, he had a clear view of the Snake River Plain that separated them from the rushing waters of the Snake. The vista would have been awe-inspiring under different circumstances—long empty spaces, stubby buttes, far-off mountain ranges—but Johnny's thoughts were generally elsewhere. Like Allie, he figured that, sooner or later, Cutter would send some men back for a second look. This time, he feared they wouldn't be turned away by the bluffs.

He also kept close tabs on the horses, although there wasn't much he could do beyond currying them down every evening with a brush fashioned from wads of grass. The spur marks on the Appaloosa were healing nicely, with new hair already coming in, and the small cuts on their legs, made while bucking through the crusted snow on top of Monida, were barely noticeable.

Allie increased the number of snares she set and was soon bringing in two and three rabbits every day. What they didn't eat immediately, she roasted and hung in trees to take with them when they left—fresh meat to supplement their dwindling supply of jerky, rice, and dried fruit.

They got along, although not well. Allie's aloofness remained. She would respond to his comments and even occasionally ask a question regarding the long journey that still lay before them, but, otherwise, she kept up a solid wall of defensiveness.

It was because of her coolness that Johnny was surprised four days later—their sixth in camp—when he returned from a lengthy survey of the Snake River Plain to find her rearranging her rabbits in a tree and singing softly to herself. He stopped to listen, half hidden behind the cedar that sheltered his bedroll. Allie was stringing up new carcasses with a line made of woven grass, passing it through the tendons of the rabbits' rear legs. Johnny didn't recognize the song, but the tune struck a chord that reminded him of a time from his own past, another woman who had once sung quietly to herself as she went about her chores. There was a small boy in that picture as well, not yet an orphan, playing on a hook rug with wooden blocks painted in gay colors. Johnny cast deeper into his memory for details—the color of her eyes or the tilt of her smile—but found nothing beyond the music of her voice and the happiness it contained.

Although he didn't move or speak, Allie must have sensed his presence. She whirled; the quiet contentment of her expression vanished behind a mask of indignation. "What are you looking at?" she demanded.

"I wasn't looking at anything. I was just listening." He came around the cedar and leaned the Hawken inside the tree, against a bough.

"You were looking," she accused, her eyes sparking with anger. "I've been looked at enough these last few months. I don't intend to tolerate it from you."

"I didn't mean to insult you. I just enjoyed hearing you sing. You've got a pleasant voice. A lot better than what I listened to all last summer, sharing a dug-out with three men."

"If you want to listen to someone singing, I'd suggest you take it up yourself."

He grinned. "I tried it once. The results were disappointing."

But Allie wouldn't be distracted. "I figure I killed a man the other night, dragging your sorry hide off that mountain, but I haven't felt any regret for it. I'll shoot you, too, if you get any randy notions."

"Lady, I've got no notions about you whatsoever. Besides, you made that threat to me once before, back on the Beaverhead. I believed you then, and I still do."

Allie calmed down after that, but her voice remained edgy. "It's time we left here," she said abruptly. "Those horses aren't going to get any fatter until spring, and winter's barely begun."

"I've been thinking the same thing," Johnny admitted. "Truth is, I'm getting tired of being chased around these mountains. It ain't setting well, and I've made up my mind, Allie. I'm not going to do it any more. When I leave here, I'm heading for Salt Lake City. I intend to be there before the week's out."

There was relief in her eyes. "I've been waiting for you to say that."

"It'll be rough going. Cutter runs a tough bunch, but I figure they put their boots on the same as any other man."

"I'm not afraid to die. Not any more. I've made up my mind about that. But I don't want to be caught."

"We'll need supplies," he said gently. "We can pick up what we'll need at Fort Hall."

Allie nodded. "I'm low on powder and shot for my double-barrel."

"They'll have it."

She smiled bleakly. "It'll be good to see a trading post again, maybe some friendly faces for a change."

Johnny didn't reply. He already had an idea of what they'd find at Fort Hall, and he didn't think it was going to be very friendly.

Chapter Twenty-Nine

They rode down out of the cedars and onto the Snake River Plain. Here, there were precious few trees, but lots of sage and rabbitbrush. Although the wind continued sharp out of the northwest, the snow wasn't deep and they made good time.

Johnny kept the Henry booted under his right leg, preferring the Hawken balanced across his saddlebows for such an open country. He'd lost one of Lloyd's ivory-handled revolvers in his tumble from the Appaloosa's saddle coming off Monida, but he'd replaced it with his old Remington-Beals model. Allie still had her shotgun and Andy's Colt, and Johnny no longer had any doubts regarding her willingness to use them. He thought they were both relieved to be on the move again. The waiting had gnawed at them, while the desire to have this journey finished, one way or the other, had grown stronger with each passing day.

They followed Camas Creek part of the way, then turned more directly south toward the Snake. Frank McCarty had outlined what he knew of the route with a rough map, traced in the dirt outside the Redhawk Gulch dug-out. He'd said then that, with the rivers running low at this time of year, there would probably be more than one place to cross the treacherous Snake, but he'd recommended a ford the Indians called White Horse Shoals.

"It's about half a day's ride upstream from the trading post," Frank had said. "Just something you might want to keep in mind, in case things don't pan out the way we hope they will."

The old hostler's words had turned out to be prophetic, Johnny mused as he guided the Appaloosa up the steep slope above Camas Creek and topped out on the high desert plain. Back at the dug-out, none of them had really expected Cutter's men to follow him over Monida Pass. But, of course, none of them had foreseen Johnny's being discovered so quickly, or that, in the course of his escape, he'd have to kill Brett Cutter's brother.

Jogging her horse alongside the Appaloosa, Allie said: "Do you know where you're going?"

"More or less. We should reach the Snake by nightfall, then follow that downstream to White Horse Shoals, where we'll cross to the south side of the river. Barring bad luck, we ought to reach Fort Hall by tomorrow night."

"Do you think they'll be waiting for us there?"

"I reckon so, Allie."

"Maybe we should go around it."

He'd already considered that, weighing the risks of finding Cutter's gang lying in wait at the old Hudson's Bay trading post versus the uncertainties of the long trek south without adequate supplies. "We'll scout the place before we ride in," he said. "If it looks too chancy, we can push on, but we'll need supplies soon. We can't make it to Salt Lake without them."

Allie didn't respond, and, after a couple of minutes, she eased back on the dun's reins, dropping into line behind the bay.

They reached the Snake by sundown, but Johnny hadn't foreseen the sheerness of the bluffs above the river. From here and in this waning light, the water looked dark and forbidding, the shelves of ice jutting out into the still pools along the banks like saw blades.

They rode downstream until the light faded completely, then made a cold camp. By dawn they were back in their saddles, but shivering and miserable. They continued downstream with their shoulders hunched to the wind, bandannas pulled up over their faces to protect them from the blowing snow. By midday, Johnny realized he'd underestimated the distance to White Horse Shoals, and it was closer to late afternoon when they finally came in sight of the crossing, rippling below them like a ruffled shirt front. A well-worn trail led down to the river's edge. They reined onto it gratefully. The relief from the wind when they passed below the rim of the bluff was immediate, and Johnny yanked the bandanna off his mouth. He'd felt like he'd been suffocating all afternoon.

They'd been without water for almost two days, having taken their last drink from Camas Creek early yesterday morning, and the horses lengthened their strides eagerly when the trail leveled out. There was a wide flat on this side of the river, and sandbars covered with slim, red-barked alders. Small pools of clear water stood among the alders, and it was to one of these, well back from the Snake's exposed southern bank, that Johnny led them. He dismounted with his eyes on the far shore.

"What is it?" Allie asked, following his gaze across the broad river. There was a flat on the other side too, although not as wide as this one. A narrow fissure, opening about twenty yards above the crossing, ran back into the hills to the south, while a stone cliff with a flat, rocky top towered above the narrow flat some fifty yards below the shoals. A solitary, wind-screwed piñon rose from the cliff's crown like a bushy green bow, and a knee-high stone cairn—the kind Indians used to build for look-outs—had been constructed beneath its scraggly branches. From here, it was impossible to tell whether the cairn had been built a hundred years ago, or that morning.

"What do you see?" Allie asked.

"Nothing. Just a feeling."

Dismounting, she moved behind her horse. "I know that feeling," she said in a tiny voice. "It's Tucker, isn't it?"

"Not necessarily." He moved up to where the Appaloosa was drinking. "Come get some water," he said. "I'm just jumpy."

"We should've known they'd be waiting for us. They've probably got men all up and down this river."

She could be right, Johnny thought, but he didn't say it. Bellying down between the Appaloosa and the bay, he lowered his lips to the pool's icy surface. The water slid smoothly over his wind-chapped lips, soothing the rawness of his throat. He could have drunk a lot more, but he didn't want to risk making himself sick.

When Allie had slaked her own thirst, they forced their horses away from the water. He didn't want them water-logged, in case they had to make a run for it.

Eyeing the rippling currents from over the seat of his saddle, Johnny said: "That crossing doesn't look too bad. Maybe knee-deep and rocky, but not overly dangerous. I'll go first and take the bay with me. You stay close and keep low. Sink down behind that saddle horn all you can."

He studied the ford silently for another minute, then returned the Hawken to its loop and pulled the Henry. "If it comes to a fight, I'm thinking it'll be close-up work, near the other bank. This lever gun will be a lot better for that than the Hawken." He glanced at Allie. "Your shotgun won't be much use, either. Not past fifty or seventy-five yards, and the Colt won't be any better. If we have to lay into 'em, hold your fire as long as you can. When you get up close, let 'em have it. Your shotgun first, then the pistol."

"All right."

He grinned. "Just give 'em hell, Allie. Like you did that night on Monida."

"I'm not afraid," she replied. "Not much, anyway."

"Let's go." He stepped into his saddle.

Allie swung onto the dun and arranged her skirts, the heavy outer skirt and the lighter summer dress she wore under it, modestly over her ankles. Settling the shotgun across her lap, she said: "I'm ready."

"We'll go in fast," he said, then pulled his horse around and slammed his heels into its ribs. The Appaloosa surged into a run, the bay leaping after it like a deer. Leaning forward, Allie popped the ends of her long reins against the dun's hip, and was less than twenty paces behind when Johnny hit the edge of the river.

The Appaloosa was forced to slow down when it reached the deeper, swifter currents toward mid-channel, picking its footing over the rocky bed with care. They were about halfway across when the first shot rang out. The bullet zipped past Johnny's ear with a quick, thumping whine, and he glanced almost resentfully at the stone cairn on top of the bluff, where a tattered cloud of powder smoke drifted among the pinon's branches. A second shot followed as they neared the southern shore, but Johnny held his fire until he was on dry land. There, he yanked the Appaloosa to a stop and whipped the lever gun to his shoulder, firing twice in quick succession while shouting for Allie to make a run for the fissure to their left. She didn't waste time. Snatching the bay's lead rope as she cantered past, she hauled the smaller horse after her.

A third shot buzzed the air close to Johnny's shoulder, and he swore, cranked another round into the Henry's chamber, and fired again. He was almost starting to feel in control of the situation when a second man appeared unexpectedly at the base of the cliff with a long-barreled caplock rifle. He stopped when he saw Johnny and threw the rifle to his shoulder, but Johnny managed to drive him back with several quick rounds from the Henry.

While he was doing that, the first man rose from behind the

stone cairn and shouldered a stubby carbine. Johnny's heart sank as he yanked the Henry back up to snap off a shot that should have gone wild for being so rushed. Instead, the man on the cliff jerked under the bullet's impact, then stumbled sideways. His carbine fell, one knee buckled, and suddenly he was spinning outward, arms and legs spread wide as he dropped down the cliff's face.

Figuring he'd given Allie all the time he could afford, Johnny leaned forward and yelled in the Appaloosa's ear. He kept the Henry ready just in case, but reached the mouth of the fissure without any more shots being fired. Although he continued to watch over his shoulder for pursuit, only the echo of the Appaloosa's hoofs accompanied him through the narrow, stone-walled chasm.

He caught up with Allie about a quarter of a mile up the gorge, where it finally widened into a more typical draw. Her progress had been slowed by the bay and her own fears of what was happening behind her, but, when she saw Johnny, she wrapped the lead rope around the smaller horse's saddle horn and gave it a stinging slap with her reins. The bay leaped forward and Allie cut in behind it, pounding the dun's ribs with the sides of her stirrups. They didn't stop until the draw petered out about three-quarters of the way up the ridge. Allie pulled the dun around to keep an eye on the fissure, and Johnny drew up at her side.

"Who was it?" Allie demanded. "How many were there? Was Tucker one of them? Did you see Tucker?"

"There were just two that I saw. Tucker wasn't one of them." He let out a long breath, recalling the bushwhacker he'd sent tumbling off the cliff's face, the long black hair fanned against the bright blue of the afternoon sky. "I saw Warshirt Jackson, though. I recognized the other one, too. Dave Worthy. Both of them were a part of Otis Call's bunch from Ruby City."

Allie noticed the subtle change in his demeanor. "What's wrong?"

"I think I killed Jackson."

A peculiar hardness began to creep into her eyes, a look Johnny had noticed before when they spoke of Cutter and his men. "Does that bother you?" she asked. "Killing one of those bastards?"

"No, but it's not something I feel like cheering about."

"I'd cheer," she said flatly. "I'd cheer for every damn' one of them who doesn't live to rape or rob or murder ever again. Jesus, mister, what's the matter with you? They've been trying to run you down for two weeks, and you're feeling bad because you killed one?"

"I've killed more than one," he reminded her, "and I know what they're trying to do. That doesn't mean I have to feel good about it."

Allie didn't reply to that, but Johnny could read her feelings in her expression. Yanking the dun around, she rode off at a brisk trot, the bay following dutifully. Johnny watched as he had so many times before, noting the rigid set of her shoulders, the tight rein she kept on the dun even as she forced it into a stiff lope. He knew she didn't understand his feelings about Shirt's death. He didn't fully understand them himself, other than that the Chickasaw half-breed had been a little more personal than the others. He'd been a party to Russ's death outside The Bucket Saloon, and a part of the crowd that had come up the hill after him and Andy and Frank, back at the dug-out.

But there was more to it than that. Johnny had known who Warshirt Jackson was long before this journey south had begun, and he'd feared the man for his deadly reputation. But Jackson was dead by Johnny's own hand. In the end, the infamous Chickasaw killer had been nothing more than a man.

Johnny glanced once more at the narrow gorge winding up

from the Snake River, but it remained empty, the snowy trail through its center marred only by the prints of their own horses.

Chapter Thirty

They stayed on the ridges where the wind-blown snow was thinnest, and made travel easier. Just before dusk, they passed the old, abandoned military post of Fort Hall, sitting on the near bank of the river like the ruins of an ancient city. They didn't stop or go down. Johnny knew from Frank McCarty that the trading post of the same name—the old Hudson's Bay Company fort—lay only a few miles beyond the deserted barracks. What commerce still took place in that part of Idaho Territory occurred there.

Darkness caught them on the trail, forcing them into another cheerless camp under open skies. They spent the night shivering in their blankets, slapping down gaps in the heavy wool whenever a tongue of frigid air slipped inside. By morning, a solid film of ice covered the shallow slough where they'd stopped, and the cold seemed to penetrate deep into their bones. They were in bad need of a fire, Johnny knew, and a warm meal dripping with fat to restore heat to their bodies from the inside out, but he refused to let Allie kindle one this close to the trading post. He worried that Dave Worthy might have beaten them to the fort yesterday by staying close to the river and taking advantage of established trails, while he and Allie approached the post through the hills.

"If Worthy's there, they'll be expecting us," Johnny predicted over Allie's chattering teeth. "There's no point in letting them know where we're at until we're ready."

"I hope death is warm," Allie said dully. "It might be worth it, if it is."

"Don't let your hopes of dying get too high. They don't have us yet."

The sun was just coming up when they crested a final ridge and spied the old post, once a major stop along the Oregon Trail, squatting in the middle of a large flat on the banks of the Snake. Independent traders still used the place, but it was no longer owned by a single company, and its influence had waned in recent years. There was a small herd of horses grazing in the river bottoms to the north, and teepees were scattered along the post's south wall where they could take advantage of the adobe's reflective warmth. A pair of massive wooden gates hung open on sagging hinges, and the path inside was hard and gray with snow packed into ice. Johnny's gaze lingered on the horses, but he didn't recognize any of them.

"There aren't very many, are there?" Allie ventured faintly.

"Not as many as I'd expected." He counted eighteen head, and figured most of them had to belong to the men of the post, its hunters, trappers, and traders, not to mention the inhabitants of the teepees. Hope stretched slowly, like a spring vine reaching for the sun. Had Cutter changed his mind and taken the bulk of his gang south? Or was this just a ruse, bait to lure them inside the fort's thick, earthen walls?

"Are we going in?" Allie asked.

"Yeah. We've got to have supplies. We couldn't last two more days with the little we have left."

"So what do we do?" She was watching him closely, as if to gauge their chances through his reply.

"We have to figure there are Cut-throats down there, but it's still early and the sun's at our backs. That'll be to my advantage. They shouldn't be able to make out who's coming in until I'm almost to the gates. I'll just mosey on in like I was passing through. You stay up here and. . . ."

"No!"

He glanced at her with a gentle smile. "They won't be looking for just one person, Allie."

"Don't do this," she pleaded. "Not after everything we've been through."

He was quiet a moment, wondering if he would ever understand her. A couple of days ago, he would have sworn she'd sacrifice his life for her own without hesitation or remorse; today she was practically begging that they stay together to face whatever challenge awaited them. It made about as much sense to him as trying to juggle water, but he finally shrugged and said: "All right, if that's what you want. We'll go down together, win or lose, live or die."

Her expression softened. "Thank you."

"I'm not sure I want your thanks," he admitted. "We'll ride straight in. If Cutter's got men down there, they'll find us quick enough."

Allie nodded and checked the caps on her shotgun. Johnny returned the Hawken to its saddle horn loop, then slid the Henry from its scabbard. "I'll lead," he said.

Reaching for the bay's lead rope, Allie said: "I'll be right behind you."

There was a well-worn path leading down off the ridge, easily discernible under the snow. Johnny reined onto it and gave the Appaloosa its head. No one greeted them as they rode through the main gates, although a few dogs, looking more like hungry wolves than pets, raised their heads curiously. Several independent traders used the post communally, but only one had his door open at this early hour. Johnny stopped in front of it and dismounted, and Allie stepped down at his side. "I'll go in first and see what there is to see," he said. "I'll whistle if it's safe."

Allie nodded and he gave her a smile and a wink, neither of

which matched what he was feeling inside. Then he stepped through the door and to one side, out of the light. He wouldn't have been surprised to have been met with a hail of bullets, but only the pop and crackle of the blaze in the fireplace greeted him. There was a candle burning on the counter, where a man in his early thirties was bent over a ledger. He looked up when Johnny entered.

"Howdy, friend. You're up early."

"You alone?" Johnny asked.

The merchant's gaze turned wary. "I am, but, if it's robbery you've got in mind, I ought to warn you. . . ."

"It ain't," Johnny interrupted. Allie must have overheard the exchange, for she ducked inside, then quickly stepped into the shadows behind the door, as fleeting as a ghost.

The storekeeper's expression crumbled. "*Aw,* hell, I know who you are."

Johnny moved to the far end of the counter, where he could keep an eye on the front door as well as the entrance to the back room. "Is that right?"

"You're Johnny Montana, and that gal is Tom Tucker's woman."

Allie moved out of the shadows, her shotgun leveled threateningly. "I'm not Tucker's woman, mister, and I never have been! I'd rather be dead!"

Taken aback, the trader hurriedly raised both hands. "I didn't mean to insult you, ma'am. That's just what a couple of the boys have been saying, but they're probably liars."

Tears welled in Allie's eyes. "They are if they say I ever gave Tucker a minute's worth of attention. I won't have my name degraded like that."

The trader nodded his agreement. "I got no argument with that, and I won't let it happen again. You got my word on it."

"My name is Allison Purcell, but you call me Missus Purcell."

"I will, and believe me. . . ." His words trailed off as Allie glided back into the shadows behind the door. Exchanging a glance with Johnny, he let out a large sigh of relief. "Feisty, ain't she?"

"Shut up," commanded her voice from behind the door.

"We need some supplies," Johnny said, drawing the trader's attention away from Allie. "I wouldn't turn down a hot breakfast, either, if the price was right, but, first, tell me who's here. How many men does Cutter have waiting for us?"

"There were several here a few days ago, but most of them have scattered. Some went to different crossings up and down the river, and the rest went south." There was no emotion on his face at all when he added: "They're wanting you pretty bad, friend. They say you bushwhacked some of their pards up in Montana, then stole a man's. . . ." He glanced at the door where Allie was hidden and didn't finish his sentence.

"And you believed them?" Johnny asked.

The storekeeper was silent a moment, then shook his head. "I guess not. I sure as Hades don't trust 'em. Fact is, I'll be glad when the whole bunch of you ride out."

"Those men are killers," Allie said from the shadows.

Studying the open door, Johnny asked quietly: "Is Tom Tucker one of the men here?"

"Nope, he rode south with Cutter and them. They'll be waiting for you down the trail, I expect. Assuming you get out of here alive."

"Who's here?"

"There's three. A big guy called Jack McGrew, then Hank Bonner and Chris Ewing. They're all tough nuts, but I'd rather go up against Bonner and Ewing together than McGrew by himself."

Johnny nodded, figuring that was good information to have. He crossed the room to the front window to peer out through the wavy glass. On the second floor balcony across the quadrangle, a lanky man in a black and white steer-hide vest was speaking over his shoulder into an open doorway. Moments later, a second man appeared, strapping a gun belt around his waist. Johnny recognized both of them from his wild ride through Twin Bridges.

"They've got a room over there," the storekeep explained, "although they ain't paid no one for it yet."

"I see a man in a cowhide vest, and another with a blond beard."

"That'd be Ewing and Bonner. Ewing's the one with the vest. Listen, friend, I'm not wanting my place shot up. Why don't you take this outside?"

"I like the odds better in here," Johnny replied. "We'll let them come to me for a change." He glanced around the room. Now that his eyes had adjusted to the dim interior, he could make out Allie behind the door, her shotgun already cocked in readiness. "They'll be coming any minute," he said quietly. "Stay where you are and don't make a peep until they're all inside."

She nodded, and the trader murmured: "*Aw,* hell."

Johnny glanced at the door to the rear room. "Where does that lead?"

"The storeroom. I've got a bunk back there, too."

"Is there another door?"

"Nope, just a window that opens into the empty lot between my place and Phillips's, but it's shuttered for the winter. Nobody'll come through there without making a hell of a racket."

Johnny turned to the window. A third man had appeared on the balcony with Ewing and Bonner. "This McGrew, has he got a big gut and carries his pistols butt forward on his belt?"

"That's him," the storekeeper said morosely.

Johnny's muscles tightened as the three men headed for the stairs at the west end of the balcony. "You got a gun back there, storekeep?"

The merchant nodded cautiously. "Sure."

"Get it up here where I can see it."

"Why?"

"So I can turn my back on you, and so you don't have to worry about getting your head blown off in the next couple of minutes."

The storekeeper's face blanched, but he quickly reached under the counter and brought out a pair of big, single-shot horse pistols.

"Pull the caps and toss 'em to Missus Purcell."

The storekeeper quickly did as he was instructed, the pistols clattering loudly across the wooden floor to come to rest at Allie's feet. She kicked them into the corner, then met Johnny's gaze with an uncompromising smile that said she was ready.

"Here they come," he said softly. He was staring out the window to where the three Cut-throats were crossing the frozen quadrangle with their hands on their pistols. None of them wore coats, despite the freezing temperatures, and Johnny knew they were expecting a fight. Making a swift decision, he leaned the Henry against the wall, then turned to face the door just as the shadow of the killers fell across the threshold. He moved his hand to the ivory-handled revolver on his right hip, but didn't draw it.

CHAPTER THIRTY-ONE

Chris Ewing was the first man through the door. He hesitated with his spurs hanging outside the threshold, watching Johnny, who stood just beyond the shaft of morning sunlight slanting in through the window. Then he eased another couple of feet into the room and backed up until his shoulder was pressed lightly against the door's edge. He had no idea Allie was behind him with a shotgun.

Hank Bonner entered next. He also hesitated briefly at the door before walking stiffly to the counter, where he stood facing Johnny with both thumbs hooked behind the buckle of his gun belt.

Jack McGrew brought up the rear. He paused at the door as the others had done, his gaze darting between Johnny and the storekeeper. Then, with a voice like a bear's growl, he demanded: "Where's the girl, Kendrick?"

For a moment, the storekeeper acted like he was going to reply. Then his mouth snapped shut and he shook his head. Sliding his considerable bulk inside, McGrew eyed the door to the storeroom suspiciously. A slow smile crept across his face. "She's in there, ain't she?"

"Come on in, McGrew," Johnny said with forced cheerfulness. "I'll buy you a drink."

McGrew laughed and crossed to the counter, placing himself several feet from Bonner. "I'll buy my own drink in a minute, Montana, to celebrate the money I'm about to collect on your lousy head."

On a hunch, Johnny said: "That's what Dave Worthy and Shirt Jackson thought, too. We left them at White Horse Shoals yesterday."

McGrew frowned and Bonner stood up straighter, his hands falling away from his buckle. "You saying you've already tangled with Jackson?" he asked Johnny.

"Hush, Hank," McGrew scolded, as if speaking to a child. "It doesn't matter what happened to Worthy and the 'breed. If they let a pilgrim and a woman. . . ."

"Oh, Christ," Ewing said suddenly, his hands coming partway up, his eyes widening. "It's the woman, Jack. She's behind me."

With everyone's attention fixed on Ewing, Johnny eased the ivory-handed Remington from its holster, so that, when McGrew turned back, he found the six-gun pointed squarely at his gut. "Drop your pistols, Ewing," Johnny said easily.

"By God, if you do, I'll shoot you myself," McGrew threatened.

"Go ahead and let 'em fall," Johnny urged. "It ain't worth dying over. You, too, Bonner."

"Don't neither of you tramps even think about it," McGrew snarled.

"*Aw,* hell, Jack, they've got the drop on us," Ewing breathed in defeat.

"God damn you," McGrew growled.

"Allie!" Johnny called. "When the shooting starts, you kill Ewing first, then Bonner."

"That won't be hard to do at this range," she promised, and Ewing took a half step forward, as if poked in the spine from behind. "There's not going to be much left of you if this twelve-gauge goes off, is there?" she asked the gunman in front of her.

"Dammit, Jack, she'll do it," Ewing said tightly. "You know she will."

"Hush your trap, Ewing," McGrew said, glaring at Johnny. "Montana, even with that pistol pointed at me, I'm gonna shoot you down like a dog, and it won't matter if I've already got a bullet in my heart when I do it. You're as good as dead if you and the girl don't drop your guns right now."

"I don't think so, Jack," Johnny replied. "Fact is, I think you're bluffing. I also think you're too smart to die for bounty money you'd never spend. That goes for you, too, Bonner."

Hank Bonner licked nervously at his lips. He'd been staring at Allie and Chris, but now he turned to McGrew and shook his head. "It's over, Jack. We underestimated 'em."

"We didn't underestimate anyone!" McGrew shouted, spittle flying from his mouth, but Johnny could hear the uncertainty in his voice, and knew the stocky gunman was approaching a divide. Soon now, he would either surrender his guns or start shooting.

Johnny curled his thumb over the Remington's hammer. His finger was already tight against the trigger. "Throw 'em down, McGrew," he barked.

"Do what he says, Jack," Ewing added earnestly.

"God dammit!" McGrew bellowed. "God damn it all to hell." His eyes burned with cold fury. "All right, I'm gonna pull my pistols and set 'em on the counter."

"Uhn-uh," Johnny returned, his heart thumping loudly. "You pull 'em one at a time and real slow, then toss 'em over here."

McGrew's face was livid, but he did as he was told. Bonner was next, then Ewing. Johnny gathered the pistols around him with the side of his boot, then motioned for the three men to face the bar. While Allie covered them with her shotgun, Johnny checked them for hide-out weapons. He found a sawed-off Kerr sidehammer revolver on McGrew, plus the usual assortment of knives, including a wicked-looking Arkansas toothpick tucked inside one of Ewing's boots.

With the three disarmed, Johnny marched them to a table beside the fireplace at the far end of the room and told them to sit down, then instructed the storekeeper to start breakfast for all five of them. "Make it a big one," he added. "We've all got a long day ahead of us."

Kendrick didn't let them down. He served up venison and thick slices of bread with gravy, plus fried potatoes seasoned with onions, and coffee strong as a Missouri mule. Johnny and Allie ate while standing at the counter, their guns ready. McGrew barely touched his food, but Ewing and Bonner dug in with hearty appetites and undeniable relief. When they finished, Johnny ordered enough supplies to last him and Allie another five days. Then, leaving Allie with the prisoners, he and Kendrick took the provisions outside and packed them on the horses. When they went back inside, no one was eating and a tense silence hung over the room.

"Trouble?" Johnny asked, but Allie only smiled, a tight little upward curl of her lips that told him she had everything under control. "All right, boys," he said, palming a revolver. "On your feet. We're going on a hike."

McGrew scowled. "We ain't goin' nowhere, Montana."

"What did I tell you about sassing back?" Allie asked, and McGrew's face darkened.

"You ain't no lady, I'll tell you that," he said, then looked at Johnny. "You're a fool to ride with her, Montana. You're lucky she ain't slit your throat in the middle of the night."

"I believe you," Johnny replied pleasantly. "Come on now, on your feet."

They trooped outside in single file. Johnny booted the Henry, then swung into the Appaloosa's saddle. Allie fastened the bay's lead rope to its pack, then climbed onto the dun. Motioning with the Remington, Johnny said: "Let's go."

They left Fort Hall as they'd entered, silently and without

fanfare, although Johnny knew at least a dozen pairs of eyes followed them through the gates. Outside, they turned onto the river road and headed downstream.

The sun was well up as they left the fort's shadows, the sky a pale winter's blue, more the color of a robin's egg than the deep sapphire of summer. It was still bitterly cold, though, especially along the river, where the breaths of man and beast fogged the damp air.

Johnny put the outlaws out front and kept them moving steadily along the frozen, rutted track. Within a mile, they left the river to continue its westward journey while they turned south with the road. By now, all three Cut-throats were puffing heavily, with first Ewing, then Bonner, lamenting the icy winds.

"For God's sake, man," Bonner uttered after an hour of steady tramping through the snow. "Are you trying to kill us?"

"Keep moving," Johnny replied in a distracted tone, his thoughts forging ahead, grappling with the uncertainties that still lay before them—the whereabouts of Dave Worthy, Brett Cutter and his lieutenants, Tom Tucker and Otis Call; not to mention those as yet unaccounted for. Kendrick had named Chico Sanchez, Sam Hulse, Jake Haws, Coffee Kearns, Poke Hardesty, and Fred Dover, although he'd insisted he didn't know who had gone where.

"Cutter doesn't want you slipping past him," Kendrick had explained while he and Johnny stowed supplies inside the Appaloosa's saddlebags. "That's why he's got his men scattered from here to Sunday like he does."

Cutter's logic was easy to understand, Johnny thought, yet flawed in a way as old as war itself. By dividing his men so thinly, the outlaw leader had created not so much a barrier to Salt Lake City, but a wall riddled with gaping holes. With a little luck, Johnny figured he and Allie stood a fair chance of punching through it somewhere.

It was almost noon when they came to a stream out of the south, making its way toward the Snake. Johnny called a halt and the three outlaws stumbled to the side of the road and collapsed. Their breathing was labored, their faces sheened with sweat, and McGrew's hair, under his hat, had dripped perspiration that was already freezing, clattering like dull chimes whenever he turned his head.

Staring at Johnny, McGrew spoke for the first time since leaving Fort Hall. "You plannin' to walk us all the way to Salt Lake City, Montana?"

Johnny didn't reply. He was peering south to where the road disappeared into the broad mouth of a cañon. "Do you recognize this place?" he asked Allie.

"I think so. That's Portneuf Cañon. The road follows the creek through it to higher ground. It'll bend east for a ways, then back south into a wide valley. There's a low mountain range between here and Malad City, but I don't think it'll be too hard to cross. Not like Monida was." She gave him a meaningful look. "Utah will be on the other side of Malad."

"How far?"

"There's a big Oliver and Company relay station just this side of the mountains that we should reach by tomorrow afternoon. We can cross the Malad mountains to Malad City the next day, and be in Utah in another couple of days." She shrugged apologetically. "It was last spring when Alton and I came through on our way to Bannack. I may not be remembering it correctly."

"You've done all right so far," Johnny said, then looked at McGrew. "Why, no, Jack," he replied to the man's earlier question. "I don't intend to walk you all the way to Salt Lake City. As a matter of fact, I think this'll be far enough." Aware of Allie's startled glance, he added: "By the time they hike back to

Fort Hall, they won't be in any condition to trouble us any more."

"You don't know that," she argued. "I say we kill them now, and let the buzzards feast."

"I've killed enough men," Johnny replied. "I won't do it without cause."

"How much cause do you need?" she demanded. "They've hunted us like dogs ever since the Beaverhead. Do you think they'll stop now?"

"These three will."

McGrew was watching Johnny thoughtfully. "Do you always let a woman do your talking for you, Montana?"

"Oh, she's not talking for me," Johnny said calmly. "She's talking for herself. If you don't like what she's saying, deal with her."

"I ain't dealing with no woman," McGrew said. "Tuck won't, either, once he gets his hands on her."

"Shut up, McGrew," Johnny said, swinging the muzzle of his revolver around to face the larger man. "And while you're at it, shuck those boots." He glanced at Ewing and Bonner. "You, too, gents."

"Our boots?" Bonner echoed in disbelief. "Go to hell."

"Get 'em off," Johnny repeated curtly. "Otherwise, I might be tempted to go along with Allie's suggestion."

"You might as well kill us now, Montana," McGrew said. "I'd rather die from a bullet than freeze to death."

"You won't freeze," Johnny said. He leaned back to fumble under the flap of his near-side saddlebag, bringing out a small pasteboard box that he tossed to the bandit. "Those are matches," he said. "I bought 'em off of Kendrick just for you."

"What the hell are we supposed to do with these?" McGrew asked suspiciously, turning the tiny box over in his hands as if he'd never seen one before. *That was possible,* Johnny thought.

Matches were new on the frontier, and not many people were willing to spend money for what a piece of flint and steel could do for free.

"If you're smart, you'll go down to the river and gather enough wood to build a fire," Johnny said. "That way, you can dry your feet and warm your noses. Then, when you're feeling all nice and comfortable, you can start walking back to Fort Hall. If I were you, I'd stay with the Portneuf to the Snake, then follow that upstream to Fort Hall. There's more wood along the rivers. You'll make a mile or so before you have to stop and build another fire. Then you can start all over again."

"Dammit, Montana, it'll take us two days to reach the fort that way," Bonner said. "We won't survive the night without warm clothing."

"You will if you don't doze off and let your fire go out. Work hard, boys, and by tomorrow night you'll be snug in your beds again. With luck, you won't lose more than a few toes between you."

"Son-of-a-bitch," Bonner breathed.

"I'll kill you," McGrew growled. "I'll track you down wherever you go and skin you for my own quirt."

Johnny smiled easily. "Maybe, but I'm betting once you're on your feet again, you'll be happy to leave these mountains forever. Go back to California, Jack. I hear the sun always shines in San Diego."

"Let's go," Allie said. "We're wasting time."

Johnny motioned once more with the Remington. "The lady's growing impatient, boys. Shuck those boots."

The three outlaws exchanged glances, then, slowly, Ewing, followed by Bonner, pried the wet leather from their feet. McGrew watched for a moment, then swore and heeled off his own footwear. Johnny strung all six boots through a saddle string and knotted it off, then kicked the Appaloosa into a walk, following the road. Allie lowered the shotgun's hammers and jogged alongside on the dun. Neither looked back.

Chapter Thirty-Two

Johnny had been down on one knee. Now he stood and let his gaze run east along the narrow trace of road bordering the Portneuf River. The tracks of Cutter's men, made more than a week before, were clearly visible in the sun-pocked snow. It was the three distinct sets of tracks that overlaid them that worried him.

Sitting her horse a few yards away, Allie eyed the dark cañon wall that towered above their left shoulders in sheer cliffs and broken parapets. Johnny knew she also feared an ambush, similar to what Dave Worthy and Shirt Jackson had sprung on them back at White Horse Shoals. But there was something about the openness of these prints, out here plain as day for anyone to see, that defied the logic of a trap. To Johnny, they spoke more of flight and abandonment than they did of treachery.

"What if they're just trying to make us think they left?" Allie asked. "For all we know, they could be watching us right now."

"Maybe, but we can't scout out every nook and cranny before we pass it." He glanced at the western sky. The sun would set early tonight, down here in the bottom of Portneuf Cañon, but they still had a few hours of light remaining, and he wanted to make the most of them. "We've got no choice, Allie. Not unless we turn back or go around and, with the mountains surrounding us, trying to go around might be a bigger risk than facing Cutter."

He stepped into his saddle. "We'll keep our eyes peeled and our ears open," he promised.

Allie nodded, but made no effort to hide her misgivings.

They rode on in silence, watching sharply as the day progressed. Within an hour, Johnny began to notice that the cañon walls seemed lower, the grade under their horses' hoofs steeper. Soon, the road swung south again, its pitch rising noticeably. As dusk settled over the cañon's floor, softening the harshest edges of the precipice, Johnny spied a mule deer raising its head from a swale along the Portneuf. It was the first large game animal he'd seen in weeks, and it heartened him to watch her watching him, her big ears flapping inquisitively.

"Hungry?" Allie asked.

"Not that hungry," he returned quietly.

A break in the sheer stone cliff where the sun, reflecting off the gray-black rocks, had melted the snow in a shallow pocket caught Johnny's eye. There would be good grass up there, he knew, and shelter from the wind. He pulled the Appaloosa to a stop.

"What is it?" Allie asked.

"We'll camp up there."

"There's still some light left," she reminded him.

"Some, but not much. Let's go down to the river and water our horses and fix something warm for supper. Then we can move up there. It'll put a wall at our backs, plus give us the high ground in case someone tries to sneak up on us overnight."

His gaze returned to the mule deer just as it slipped into the dense brush along the river. Seeing the doe had awakened something within him that he realized had been growing steadily for some time—a need for normalcy again, a routine that didn't involve living like a rabbit always under the shadow of the hawk. He was tired of the long chase. And, surprisingly, he was growing weary of his conversations with Allie, always centered around

Brett Cutter and Tom Tucker and what the Cut-throats would do next. He'd been riding with the woman for almost two weeks, yet knew little more about her now than he had when he first saw her on the Beaverhead. So that night, after settling into their bedrolls where they could keep an eye on the slope below them, he said: "Where will you go after this, Allie? Assuming we make it to Salt Lake City in one piece."

For a moment, he didn't think she was going to reply. Even in the shadows under the cliff, he could sense the familiar tenseness of her body. Then, abruptly, she seemed to relax. "Davenport," she said.

"Iowa?"

"Yes."

"Is that where your family is?"

"Uhn-huh. My father and mother, my sisters and their husbands." After a pause, she added: "Alton is . . . was . . . my husband. He left me some months ago."

"Is that why you're out here on your own?"

"Yes," she replied in a whisper. There was another pause, longer this time. "I suppose at first I was waiting for him to come back, hoping that he would. I was terrified of being alone, yet even more terrified of leaving what I knew on Grasshopper Creek. But the funny thing is, after a while, I began to realize that I wasn't as helpless as I'd thought I was, that I didn't really need someone else to survive. I decided I wanted to make it on my own and not run back to Daddy like some little girl, a failure."

Her comment caught him off guard. "What do you mean? That going home is a failure?"

"No, not that, but . . . I wouldn't be here without your help."

He smiled, reminding her: "I'd be dead, too, Allie, back there on Monida. It was you who saved my hide that night, but I don't see myself as a failure."

She gave him a grateful look but shook her head. "You got into trouble only because you loaned your second riding horse to a helpless woman."

"Helpless?" He laughed. Not just the usual quick chuckle, but loudly and with feeling; the sound of it echoed distantly off the far walls of the cañon. "You are a number of things, Allie," he told her sincerely, "but helpless sure as hell ain't one of them. You're one of the most capable women I've ever known."

A look almost like hope came into her eyes, then just as quickly vanished. She followed it with a question Johnny knew was meant to change the subject.

"Tell me about the Indians you stopped from attacking your friends last spring."

"There's not much to that story."

"It earned you the name everyone out here seems to know you by."

He was quiet a moment, reflecting on the incident. Coming West seemed like another lifetime now, a journey he'd heard about from someone else.

They'd left Minnesota in April—twenty-seven men and a dozen women accompanying their husbands. There'd been a pack of dirty-faced youngsters, too, flocking around their mother's skirts at night like fuzzy chicks. The families and some of the single men had driven wagons pulled by oxen or mules, but maybe a dozen of the men, Johnny among them, had been on horseback, leading pack animals that carried their supplies.

Russ Bailey and Del Kirkham had been with the outfit. Johnny had met Russ in a St. Paul mercantile, where he'd been purchasing goods to take with him. Russ and Del were already on their way West from lost jobs in Milwaukee. They didn't meet Andy Tabor until later, in Montana. Johnny had been plain old John Owens then, although Russ had started calling him Johnny soon after the small wagon train stretched out along the Dakota Trail.

It had been late in the day when the outfit rolled into the broad, grassy valley of the James River. Everyone had been cold and tired after having been caught in the open by an icy rain earlier that day. They were looking forward to a real fire fueled with wood rather than buffalo dung. But a party of Yankton Sioux were already there, holed up in the trees along the river. And who knew, Johnny thought, maybe they had been there deliberately, like Del and some of the others believed, lying in wait for the train.

The Sioux had numbered close to fifty warriors, almost two to one odds over the men of the wagon train, but the whites had been well-armed—every man carrying a rifle and at least one pistol apiece—and several had been mounted on swift horses. Despite their weaker numbers, they would have presented a formidable defense. Johnny figured the Yanktons had to know that, so maybe that was why they'd come out of hiding when they did, with the whites still a couple of hundred yards away. There'd been a few tense moments until a lone Sioux—a chief, judging by the eagle-feathered war bonnet he was wearing—came forward on a flashy pinto and signaled that he wanted to parley.

Of the men with the train, only Johnny had any experience dealing with the wild tribes, freighting along the fringes of the plains. He didn't speak Sioux, but he'd picked up enough sign language to get along, so it was he the wagon train volunteered to ride out and speak with the chief. Although the conversation had been hard to follow for both of them, in the end, Johnny had been able to purchase safe passage across Sioux lands for five new butcher knives, several twists of tobacco, a tin of coffee, and ten pounds of sugar. Both sides had been satisfied with the deal.

Johnny's accomplishment had impressed the members of the train, although he knew fate had played the larger hand. Without understanding the language, he figured he'd been lucky not to have started a fresh Indian war.

He related the incident briefly to Allie, saying only that he'd talked to the Sioux and offered them some trinkets to let the train pass.

"There really wasn't all that much to it," he added. "Russ was just trying to be funny when he started calling me Johnny Montana. I don't think he meant for the name to stick."

"But it did."

"Yeah, but I doubt if it'll last. When I leave these mountains, I figure the name Montana will stay behind."

"Where will you go?" A small smile played across her dry, cracked lips. "Assuming we make it to Salt Lake City in one piece?"

"Back to Minnesota, I guess."

"To start your shipping company?"

He grinned in spite of himself, and it occurred to him that he missed the freighting business—working with mules and handling the big, double-hitched rigs. It took a special skill to thread an outfit like that through a crowded city street or across a swift-flowing ford, but he was a good driver, and, with his own rig and negotiating his own contracts, he figured he could become a good businessman, too. "Yeah," he said. "I guess that's what I'd like to do. Start my own company."

"Have you ever thought about going into business somewhere else?"

"Where?"

"Davenport."

He looked at her, not sure he'd heard correctly. "Iowa?" he asked, after a moment.

She nodded and Johnny turned away, uncertain of his reply. His eyes dropped to the distant road, barely visible in the darkness at the bottom of the cañon, and he heard Allie catch her breath.

"Yeah," she echoed, following the direction of his gaze.

Chapter Thirty-Three

They rode into the district headquarters of the Oliver and Company Stage Line late the next day. The prints of the three riders they'd discovered yesterday in the snows of Portneuf Cañon were still in front of them, making good time. *Damned good time,* Johnny thought, puzzled by the pace the Cut-throats had set for themselves. When he and Allie first crossed their sign, the tracks had been less than a day old. Now their lead was closer to twenty-four hours—a day and a night.

The O.C. station was a small but tidy complex of corrals and sheds, with a bunkhouse for summer employees and a blacksmith and harness shop for repairs. A fair-size house for the district manager stood across the yard, gray wood smoke unraveling above its chimney. A sign on the verandah roof proclaimed: *Rooms for Rent,* and below that: *Meals.*

A dog came trotting out from behind the house as they drew near, barking loudly to announce their arrival. A few seconds later, a stout man with a steel-gray beard stepped onto the verandah and shushed the dog. He held a cocked rifle in his hands and carried a pistol in the waistband of his trousers, but, even heavily armed, he looked more resolute than intimidating. He watched them warily until they pulled up about thirty feet away, then said: "Are you Montana and the Tucker woman, or some more of Cutter's bunch?"

Eyeing the cocked rifle deliberately, Johnny replied: "I'm the one they call Montana. This is Allie Purcell, but she doesn't belong to Tucker. She doesn't belong to anyone."

The man's gaze softened when he looked at Allie, and he lowered the rifle's hammer to half cock. "I kind of figured as much, but, after this past week, I wanted to be sure."

"They still around?" Johnny asked.

"No, they pulled out at sunup this morning."

A plump, round-faced woman in a clean but faded dress appeared at the door. Shorter than the man, her hair a softer shade of gray.

"Don't you go frightening these poor folks, Linus Mattingly," she scolded, wedging past him onto the verandah. "They've had a spell of it, I'd say. They look half froze and half starved, at best."

The man called Linus smiled obligingly and set his rifle aside. "You're right, Dee. I forgot my manners. Step down, friends, and forgive my absent-mindedness. I'll take care of your horses while you go inside and warm up."

"I've got a stew on the stove," Dee added, "made with peas and carrots and good old turnips, and there'll be biscuits and butter and cold milk for supper, if you'll stay."

Johnny whistled appreciatively. "It's been a spell since I've had anything that sounded half that good," he confessed.

"Then get down, young man, and I'll get the biscuits started."

But as Linus moved toward the dun, Allie suddenly jerked the horse sideways, out of his reach. The Mattinglys' dog, a big shepherd, growled threateningly.

"We can take care of our own horses, Mister Mattingly," Allie said stiffly.

Johnny had already loosened his right foot from the offside stirrup to dismount. He paused, then settled back in his seat. "The man means us no harm," he said. "Take your pommel bags with you, if you're worried about them."

"Why should I be worried about my pommel bags?" she fired back.

Grinning, Johnny went ahead and stepped down. "Because you've been watching them like a hawk ever since you first hung them over that saddle. I don't know what you've got in them, but I can guess."

Lowering her voice, Allie hissed: "What I've got in these bags is none of your business, mister."

"I didn't say it was," he said, frowning. "Dang it, Allie, don't you trust me yet?"

Her jaws worked back and forth in agitation, before she grudgingly dismounted. "All right, take the horse. It's yours, anyway. But I will keep my pommel bags and shotgun."

Allie shoved the dun's reins into Johnny's hands, then unlaced the twin bags hanging from her saddle horn and slung them over her shoulder. He handed her the Henry to take inside with the shotgun, and she accepted it as if it were a chore. When she stepped out of the way, the two men led the horses to the barn.

"She's feisty," Linus ventured, once they were inside.

"She's had a rough go of it lately," Johnny said, making an effort to hide his irritation with her from the older man. Yet as he watched Linus move back along the bay to loosen the cinch, he wondered if she didn't have a point. There was an awful lot of gold in those panniers.

"What's going on up there?" Linus asked, tugging on the latigo. "In Montana, I mean."

"About what you've heard, I'd reckon. Was Brett Cutter here?"

"Cutter was here about a week ago, just long enough to drop off a couple of lug-heads called Poke Hardesty and Fred Dover. He rode off almost immediately, and I haven't heard of him since. Then early last night, three more toughs showed up." He glanced at Johnny. "They called themselves Dave, Coffee, and

Sam. Know them?"

"Wouldn't have been Dave Worthy and Sam Hulse, would it?"

"I didn't catch any last names, but the one called Dave didn't stay. He looked worked up to me. Scared, maybe. Sam spent the night, but kept to himself. He was a short, skinny fella with a dark beard, if that tells you anything. Had a mean look about him, too."

Johnny sucked in a slow breath, recalling the man who'd gunned down Russ Bailey in front of The Bucket Saloon. Linus's description fit Hulse, although Johnny knew it could've fit others, too. "A mean look ain't much of an identifying characteristic with that bunch," he said. "Do you know where they went when they left here?"

"They didn't say, but they all pulled out. Sam left alone at dawn. The others took off maybe half an hour later, acting mysterious. They took their bedrolls, so I don't expect them back." He nodded toward a draft horse in a stall near the front of the barn. "I got on ol' Molly there and rode out a ways this afternoon, to look around. From their tracks, I'd say two of them stayed with the Utah road. The other three veered off to the east. There's a longer route to Salt Lake City going that way. It's rougher than riding straight south with the main road, but it can be done if a man's determined enough. Maybe they intend to watch that trail and keep you from escaping the back way. Or maybe they decided to call it quits and slip out without Cutter knowing about it. Hardesty and Dover talked about it more than once."

"You said Hardesty and Dover stayed with you?"

"Dee rents a couple of rooms to travelers during the summer, so it was a natural place for them to bunk. Plus, they paid for them up front." He glanced at Johnny. "I wouldn't have tried to kick them out even if they hadn't paid. Dover and Hardesty aren't cut from the same bolt of cloth as men like Cutter or Sam Hulse, if that's who he was, but they're ornery enough to be dangerous, and I've got Dee to think about."

"I wasn't judging you, Mister Mattingly."

"I know you weren't, son. I'm just stating the facts."

When they finished unsaddling the horses, Johnny checked their shoes, tightening those on the bay and rasping off a little excess growth from the Appaloosa's front hoofs. Linus handled the halters, and, when they were done, they put the animals in separate stalls, then fed and watered them. It was dark in the barn when they finished, but Johnny hesitated. As if reading his thoughts, Linus said: "No one'll bother your tack, but, if you're worried about it, you can take your gold inside with you."

It was more or less the same thing Johnny had said to Allie earlier, and he wasn't unaware of the smile that played across the older man's face. Shrugging, Johnny said: "No, if you say it's safe, I'll leave it."

The two men walked outside, latching the door firmly behind them. In the west, the sky was a pale reddish-orange, streaked with wisps of turquoise and gold. It was a beautiful sunset, but cold in appearance, and Johnny was grateful they wouldn't have to sleep outside tonight. He was looking forward to four solid walls and a tight roof, a decent meal served on real china, eaten with forks—even if it did seem a little like a condemned man's last request.

There was a woodpile on the north side of the house, and Johnny and Linus both grabbed an armful on their way inside. The Mattinglys had a nice home. The kitchen was large but comfortable, with a harvest table capable of seating upward of twenty diners on benches along either side. The stove featured two ovens, with a warmer affixed to the overhead pipe. The front room was smaller. It had a sofa and a pair of upholstered chairs arranged in front of a fireplace centered on the rear wall, where it could provide warmth to the rooms behind it as well.

Allie was seated in one of the chairs, holding a cup of what looked like warm cider in her lap. Dee sat across from her, her own drink within easy reach on a small table at her side. She was working on some embroidery when the men entered, but set it aside when she heard the clatter of firewood dumped in a box beside the stove.

"They'll be hungry," she said, pushing out of her chair.

Allie followed the older woman into the kitchen, shooting Johnny a dark look as she passed him. He glanced after her with a puzzled expression, but she kept her back to him, her shoulders straight under the worn fabric of her dress.

Watching her, it occurred to him that he'd never seen her without her outer garments before—the blanket cape she wore over an old wool coat several sizes too large, with a lighter canvas jacket under that. She'd shed her beat-up old hat, too, and loosened her hair from its ponytail to cascade down over her shoulders, more gold than brown in the yellow light of the kitchen. She was slimmer than he would have guessed, her breasts small, her hips rounded. She moved with a willowy grace that gave him a suddenly disquieting feeling, as if he'd accidentally seen her naked, and he turned away abruptly to follow Linus into the front room.

"An attractive lass," Linus observed mildly, moving to the fireplace where he pulled a small green tobacco tin and a briarwood pipe off the mantle. "Have you known her long?"

"Not quite two weeks. Hectic ones, though."

"I would suppose so," Linus replied, thumbing the lid off the tobacco can and dipping his pipe inside. "Do you smoke?"

"No."

"Feel free to remove your revolvers if you'd like. The dog will warn us if someone comes snooping around."

Johnny hesitated only a moment, then unbuckled his gun belt

and laid it on the floor next to the front door, where the Henry leaned against the jamb. He sank into the chair closest to the fireplace but couldn't seem to relax. Linus remained standing in front of the pulsating flame, smoking his pipe. The two men had conversed easily in the barn, but now an awkward silence grew between them. Johnny half expected more questions about his and Allie's flight from Montana, but the older man remained blessedly mute until they were called to supper twenty minutes later.

The meal was as good as Dee Mattingly had promised, the milk and butter a special treat to Johnny, who hadn't savored such luxuries since leaving Minnesota in the spring. They ate in the kitchen, clustered around the end of the table nearest the stove, and afterward retired to the main room with coffee and cider. Allie and Dee shouldered the bulk of the conversation, with Linus throwing in short comments from time to time.

Johnny continued his silence, his eyes straying more and more often to Allie as the evening wore on. He remembered the way she'd looked at him when he'd come inside after caring for the horses, and pondered on the way she refused to look at him now. For a long time now, he had regarded her as a partner—competent, hard-working, intelligent, sometimes aggravating, occasionally dangerous—but always a partner. Locked in the same desperate struggle as he was, driven by the same goals of self-preservation. Not even while recuperating among the cedars west of the Tetons had he found the time to contemplate anything more. Certainly he'd never viewed her like this, with her hair down, her figure conspicuous under the thin material of an old blue summer dress.

Her beauty surprised him, as did the awakening urges it stirred within him. Where there had been confidence before, he now felt doubt—about himself, about his relationship with Allie. Thinking back, he suddenly regretted the things he'd foisted upon her, the hard and uncompromising support he'd come to expect from her. He'd treated her as if she were a man, another Russ or Andy, and he understood now that their interdependence would have to change. Here, in the relative safety of the Mattinglys' cozy home, Johnny knew that what he and Allie had forged together on their long ride south could be no more.

Chapter Thirty-Four

Once there had been twenty-six, all of them tough, proud, and efficient. Men who were afraid of no one. Now there were three, and those numbers were weighing heavily upon Otis Call's mind as he pulled the cabin door shut behind him and headed for the corral. Although he hadn't seen it at the time, he thought now that they'd made a mistake in scattering their men up and down the Snake River, then stationing the rest of them south along the Utah road, creating a thinly drawn T with a thousand gaps.

If there was strength in numbers, and especially against an enemy as wily as Johnny Montana had proved to be, they'd weakened themselves considerably by splitting their forces, and Otis feared they would soon come to regret that decision.

Although the sun had already set on this lonely outpost of mud and log huts the locals insisted on calling a city, the higher elevations to the east were still bathed in a soft, amber light. Pausing with his hands thrust deep into the pockets of his bear-hide coat, Otis stared wistfully at those far-off crags; for a moment, he wished he was among them, free of the worries Brett and Tuck had brought onto the gang with their single-minded obsessions over Montana and the Bannack woman.

Sighing, he turned toward the ramshackle collection of homes and businesses that was Malad City. With the advent of winter, there weren't many residents left. A general store with a saloon in one corner had remained open to accommodate those hardy souls who remained, but most of the population, including the business owners, had trekked south with the closing of Monida Pass to wheeled traffic. They would return in the spring, once again to fleece the northbound gold-seekers with their exorbitant prices for food, lodging, and supplies.

Putting his back to one of the corral's sturdy corner posts and hooking a heel over the lower rail, Otis pulled a crumpled cigar from the cartridge pouch on his belt, idly straightening it with his fingers. His thoughts shifted to the men who'd ridden with him that fall. At least those who were left, Shirt and Sam and Dave. He wondered if they were still at their posts, or if they'd given up and slipped away.

At one time, he would have considered such an act akin to treason. Lately he'd come to believe that they were all fools to stay, risking everything for something as perverse as a man's hide to braid into a quirt, his skull to bleach and mount on a saddle horn like some kind of macabre Christmas ornament. But Otis knew Brett would never leave without those two pieces of Johnny Montana, just as Tuck would never give up on the woman he waited for with an opium addict's twisted craving.

Otis wasn't sure why he stayed. He figured if he pushed it, Brett would cut him his share of the gold already on hand—for old time's sake if nothing else. Yet he remained silent, as if compelled to stay, to see how it all played out, and, in the end, to discover what his part was in the overall scheme.

A thin smile tugged at the corners of Otis's mouth. It wasn't lost on him that the three men here in Malad were the original three—Brett and Tuck and Otis. Was it a coincidence, he wondered, that this trio of partners from California had ended up here together, while to the north, a lone renegade and a desperate woman were whittling down the gang's size one by one, even as the individual shares of gold increased with every man killed or left behind? Or had Brett planned it that way, an elaborate double-cross that not even the most suspicious among them would be able to pin on him with certainty?

Brett was smart enough to pull such a ruse, Otis knew, and ruthless enough. There was damned little decency in Brett Cutter, and none at all in Tom Tucker.

Movement along the road from the north caught Otis's eye, and his fingers slowed on the cigar. A rider came into sight, galloping hard. With a sense of dread growing in his breast, Otis returned the cigar to his cartridge pouch.

The horse slowed to a lope as it entered town, then a trot. Otis winced as the animal came closer. Sweat darkened the reddish hairs across the sorrel's chest, and its flanks heaved with a deep, angry rattling that could be heard a block away. Stepping away from the corral post, Otis raised a hand to signal the rider. He'd already decided this wasn't going to be good news. Otherwise, Dave Worthy would still be up on the Snake River with Warshirt Jackson.

"Call!" Dave shouted, urging his lathered horse forward.

"What are you doing here?" Otis demanded as Dave rode up.

"Saving my hide, by God."

Otis took note of the panic in Dave's eyes. "Where's Shirt?"

"Shirt's dead. Probably the boys Brett left at Fort Hall are dead, too."

"Montana?"

"He's on his way. Ain't nothin' gonna stop him."

Otis's fingers unconsciously brushed the Colt holstered at his waist. "Did you try?"

"Hell yeah, I tried. So did Shirt. That's what got him killed. Nearly got me killed, too. Montana was fair smokin' the air around my head with that lever gun used to belong to Lloyd."

The door to the cabin swung open and Brett and Tuck came out. "What are you doing here?" Brett snapped when he recognized Worthy. "You're supposed to be at White Horse Shoals with Jackson."

"I was at White Horse Shoals. Shirt still is. He had a bullet in his heart and a broken neck the last time I saw him."

Brett's eyes narrowed. "Who killed him, Worthy? Was it you?"

"Who the hell do you think killed him? It was Johnny Montana. He's gonna kill you, too, before he's through, but I don't aim to be around to see it. I'm cuttin' my pin, Brett. I just want my share of the gold first . . . what we took off them Ruby River tin-pans."

"You don't get a single nugget until I get Montana's hide," Cutter returned flatly.

Dave glanced at Otis as if seeking his help, but Otis already knew Brett wouldn't budge. Shrugging, Otis said: "You're on your own, Davey."

Dave curled forward over his saddle horn. "God dammit, Brett, don't you get it? Johnny Montana's coming, and you ain't. . . ."

There was a roar and a flash of muzzle blast, and Dave was cut off in mid-sentence. He straightened in his saddle, then glanced over his shoulder at Tuck. The muzzle of Tuck's revolver was dribbling smoke, and Dave breathed: "*Aw,* hell." Then his horse stepped nervously to the side and Dave Worthy tumbled to the ground, dead.

Brett was watching Otis cautiously, a hand on his Colt, and, when he spoke, his voice was harsh with condemnation. "He was your man, Call, your responsibility. Either bury him, or haul his body into the sage where no one has to look at it."

Chapter Thirty-Five

Linus Mattingly was waiting for him outside, smoking his pipe in the light of a quarter moon and a sky full of stars. He didn't turn around when Johnny eased quietly out the front door, but he didn't seem surprised, either. Taking the briarwood from his mouth, he said: "So you're leaving us?"

"It's time," Johnny replied quietly.

"Midnight?" Linus half turned, cocking his brow questioningly under the rim of a knitted wool cap pulled down over his ears. "I assume Allie's still asleep."

"As far as I know."

Johnny had taken a small room at the rear of the house, but he'd already decided he wouldn't stay the night. Removing only his boots, he'd laid down to rest, listening for the distant chime of the mantle clock in the living room to toll off the midnight hour. When it did, he gathered his gear and slipped outside, careful not to disturb the others in their rooms. He hadn't expected to find Linus waiting for him.

"Will you take the long way around," Mattingly asked, "or do you intend to continue to tempt fate with your life?"

"It was you who said they had men guarding both routes."

"There are other trails you can take. I could draw you a map if you're interested."

Johnny considered the proposal for only a moment, then shook his head. "I appreciate the offer, though. When I left Ruby City a couple of weeks ago, it was my plan to ghost through Cutter's men and be out of the territory before they knew I was gone, but that didn't pan out. I guess somewhere along the line, I got tired of running."

Linus's voice softened. "Pride is hardly worth dying for, young man."

"To tell you the truth, I'm not sure I believe that any more. I used to, but a fella can change his mind if he's pushed hard enough."

"What about Allie? Don't you think you owe her something?"

Johnny smiled. "No, and she wouldn't, either. Me and Allie met by chance, then threw in together because of Cutter and his men, but I always knew that, when we reached Salt Lake City, we'd go our separate ways. In the meantime, maybe I can clear the way a little, get rid of some of the riff-raff blocking the road to Utah."

"Risking your own life in the process?"

"I ain't trying to be noble. I'm just not going to run any more. I'm tired of it." Linus's disapproval was obvious, but Johnny didn't give him a chance to argue. "Allie's a good woman, Mister Mattingly, but she's made it plain what she thinks of me . . . what she thinks of all men."

"Allie's scared, Johnny. She's terrified. I spent less than a full evening with her and I saw that much. I don't know what or who created that distrust, but your slipping away like this won't help it any."

"You know as well as I do that a woman doesn't have any business getting involved in what I'm about to get involved with. Allie couldn't help it before, and she did a hell of a job for all the trouble she found herself in. Ain't a man alive could've done any better. But she's safe now, and that's what it all boils down to. What kind of a man would I be if I took her away from that, threw her right back into the pot?" After a pause, he added: "You can take better care of her than I can, Mister Mattingly.

You can see to it that she reaches Salt Lake City next spring without harm."

"Ah," Linus said softly. After a moment's silence, he changed the subject. "Did you kill Warshirt Jackson at White Horse Shoals?"

The question brought Johnny up short. "Yeah," he replied suspiciously.

"And Cam Turner and Bud Dixon at Van Dolsen's trading post?"

"They had me cornered there, Mister Mattingly, so I fought them as best I could, but I would've lost that fight if Van hadn't thrown down on my side with a ten-gauge."

"Then it's true," Linus said, almost to himself. "Listening in on Hardesty and Dover, I didn't really think it was possible. Not of some pick and shovel man from the Montana gold fields."

"I've been lucky," Johnny admitted.

"I don't know if any man is ever that lucky. Once, maybe even twice, but not time after time, and especially not against men like Jackson, Turner, Dixon, and them. I know their reputations. So do Hardesty and Dover. That's why they're afraid of you. Those still with Cutter might brace you because they're more afraid of him, but I suspect, given the opportunity, most of them will avoid you if they can."

Johnny was silent a moment. It was a point he hadn't considered, and one he didn't quite know whether or not to believe. But there were a few facts that hadn't changed, and one of them was that, no matter how many men Johnny Montana might have killed in the last couple of weeks, Brett Cutter and Tom Tucker hadn't changed their minds. They never would.

Lifting the Henry to the crook of his left arm, Johnny said: "I guess it doesn't matter, Mister Mattingly. I'm through running."

There was disappointment in Linus Mattingly's face, but acceptance, too. "I don't guarantee this, Johnny. No one said anything outright, but I think Cutter will be waiting for you in Malad City. He'll have all the supplies and liquor he wants there, but still be far enough away from the Utah settlements that he won't have to worry about the law for a while. If it was me, that's where I'd go."

"How many men does he have with him?"

"He had two when he left here. If those two who rode out this morning join him, that'll make four. Five with him, but that's just a guess. He could have a dozen men with him by now."

"I guess that's a chance I'll have to take." He turned to the older man and smiled. "Thanks for your advice, Mister Mattingly, and for the food and the warm bed, and especially for the help I know you'll give to Allie."

"You're welcome, Johnny. More than welcome." He pulled a blunt-fingered hand from his coat pocket and thrust it forward. Johnny accepted it with gratitude. "Good luck, son, and watch your back out there. You've bested some tough men so far, but the worst are still in front of you."

Chapter Thirty-Six

Tuck swore at the jug-headed roan he'd bought last spring in San Diego. The horse had just dodged behind Otis Call's big buckskin, and the loop that had been about to drop over its neck plopped harmlessly into the half-frozen mud of the corral, instead.

Lowering his voice while maintaining a steady string of profanities, Tuck reeled in the muck-stained lariat. The roan was on the other side of the corral now, kicking at the rails and making enough racket that Tuck feared it might bring Brett or Otis outside to investigate the noise.

Fighting to control his expanding rage, Tuck forced himself to remain where he was and give the horses a minute to calm down. He'd made up his mind last night that he was going back to find the Bannack woman, rather than risk having her escape through the bungling of one of Cutter's half-wits, and he didn't want anyone trying to stop him.

Tuck knew what Brett and Otis thought of him. The expressions on their faces whenever he brought up the subject of the woman were unmistakable, as was the way they'd started to treat him—like some kind of diseased animal they didn't want to get too close to. They thought he was sick, but Tuck knew who the real deviant was. His only regret now was that he'd given up the chase too soon. Time had allowed the memory of the Bannack woman to pick away at his will, like a fingernail worrying a scab. He wished he'd never allowed himself to become sidetracked by Brett's obsession for revenge.

Now there, Tuck thought, was a true example of perversion. What kind of man wanted another human being skinned for a quirt, his skull bleached for a saddle ornament? To Tuck's way of thinking, Brett Cutter had a hell of a lot of gall implying that he was crazy.

His impatience finally winning out, Tuck shook out a fresh loop as he eased toward the center of the corral. The roan stood rock still at the far side of the enclosure, head high, ears perked forward. "Hold still, you jackass son-of-a-bitch," Tuck muttered in as pleasant a voice as he could muster. "Just let me get this noose around your god-damn' neck, then we'll see who's boss."

But the roan had endured more than one of Tom Tucker's fits of rage, and wouldn't be fooled by an engaging tone. It broke to the left while Tuck was still thirty feet away. Anticipating the move, he quickly darted in the same direction. His loop curled over the roan's head just as the horse surged into a run. Cursing, Tuck braced his legs for the socket-tearing jolt of the horse hitting the end of the lariat. But the roan surprised him. With the noose snugly in place, it stopped docilely.

And a damn' good thing, too, Tuck thought savagely. He'd have beaten the horse senseless if it hadn't.

He led the roan to the barn and quickly cinched his saddle in place. His bedroll, saddlebags, and rifle were stacked against an inside wall. It took only moments to stow it all on the horse. As he guided his mount away from the barn, Tuck gave the small log cabin he shared with Otis and Brett a resentful glance. Although his intention had been to slip away undetected, it angered him that no one had come outside to see what all the commotion at the corral had been about. He knew they had to have heard it, but he didn't think either of them had so much as peeked out the window.

Well, the hell with them, Tuck thought as he wheeled his horse toward Malad City's single, broad street, part of the main road between Utah and the northern mining communities. An expression of grim satisfaction touched his face as he jogged past Dave Worthy's grave, half hidden in the sage behind the corral. At least he'd done that much, he told himself. One less leech clamoring for his share of the gold. One less Samaritan interfering with his plans for the Bannack woman.

Tuck's jaw knotted as thoughts of the Bannack woman flamed up in his mind, and he kicked the jug-headed roan into an eager lope. She'd escaped from him once. She wouldn't do it again.

Chapter Thirty-Seven

Allie knew something was wrong as soon as she entered the kitchen the next morning. Dee was at the stove, scrambling eggs while bacon sizzled in a smaller skillet on one of the back burners. Linus stood out of the way, holding a cup of coffee to his face so that the aromatic steam could caress his cheeks. From his hunched shoulders and bright red nose, Allie knew he'd just come in from morning chores.

Their silence was a warning she didn't understand until her eyes went to the front door and the empty spot beside it where Johnny's rifle had leaned last night. Although the corners of her mouth pulled down in disappointment, she didn't rush to the door like some love-struck teenager. Looking at Linus, she said: "When did he leave?"

"About midnight."

Allie felt a small lurch in her chest. "Well, it's no more than I expected," she said, struggling to keep her feelings contained.

Dee, though, held a different opinion. "I'd say it's a lot more than you should have to expect."

"Now, Dee," Linus chimed in. "You know there's more to it than that."

"No, it's fair," Allie insisted, before the older woman could respond. "Johnny didn't owe me anything. In fact, I owe him. He saved my life by bringing me along, and nearly lost his own more than once because he did. It's just good sense on his part to . . . to leave me behind. Now he'll have two riding horses to. . . ."

"He didn't take the dun," Linus interrupted. "Just the Appaloosa and bay."

Allie nodded, but she felt vaguely confused. *Why would Johnny leave behind a second mount?*

"Guilt," Dee avowed, as if in answer to Allie's unspoken question. "Pure and simple and all male." She planted both fists on her hips and glowered at Linus as if daring him to challenge her. "It's the coward's way out and you know it, Linus Mattingly."

"Johnny's not a coward," Allie said quietly.

"There are all kinds of cowards, dear," Dee replied. "You don't have to defend him."

Allie looked at Linus, her brows furrowing. "I don't understand why he left the dun. It's his horse."

"Guilt," Dee said stubbornly. "Pure and simple."

"I don't think it was guilt," Linus said. "I think he meant for you to have it, Allie. He asked me to help you get to Salt Lake City when the time was right."

"When the time is right? What does that mean?"

"Johnny's gone to settle some matters, and he wants you to wait here until Brett Cutter and his men have cleared out."

Allie's thoughts flashed immediately to Tom Tucker. She knew he would never clear out. Not while one or the other of them was still alive. "Johnny went after Tuck, didn't he?" she whispered.

Linus nodded. "Yes, miss, I expect he did. I guess he went after all of them."

"My God," Allie whispered. She went to the window above the sink to peer out through a wreath of sunlit frost. A patchy fog clung to the low places among the crinkled hills, but she knew it would burn off before midday. The sky above the hills was already a bright, cloudless blue. If Johnny left the station at midnight, he was already too far ahead for her to catch up.

"Don't think about it, dear," Dee urged. "Just don't think about it at all. Keep your thoughts on next spring and going home to see your mother and father."

Allie tried to recall the route between here and Salt Lake City, but it had been so long ago, the country so uninspiring, that only bits and pieces remained—the low, cedar-covered mountain range that separated the Mattinglys' home from Malad City; the ferry at Bear River Crossing in Utah Territory that had cost them the princely sum of two whole dollars just to cross twenty yards of muddy water; the long road south along the front range of the Wasatch Mountains, sprinkled with farms and small, tidy communities. On a good horse and riding hard, Allie figured Salt Lake City couldn't be more than three days away.

She turned away from the window to discover the Mattinglys watching her as if they already suspected her response.

"My plans haven't changed," she told them calmly. "I'll be on my way after breakfast."

"You can't do that, miss," Linus protested. "A young lady has no business traveling alone in this country."

"I've been on my own for most of the summer, Mister Mattingly. I don't suppose a few more days will destroy me."

A few more days could be the end of her, if she ran into Tom Tucker, Allie realized, but she wouldn't back down now. Tuck was a risk she was prepared to take, not so much for Johnny's sake as for her own.

She forced herself to eat a hearty breakfast, knowing it would probably be her last decent meal in a while. Then she retrieved her outer garments from her room—her coat and jacket and hat and mittens, and the heavy wool blanket that used to cover her bed on the coldest winter nights back in Davenport. Dee had offered her better clothing last night, but Allie had refused, accepting only a sturdy blanket pin to keep her makeshift cape more securely around her shoulders.

The Colt revolver that Johnny had loaned her was still in the pocket of her coat, along with some extra ammunition. With the shotgun in her left hand and the pommel bags dangling from her right, she went to the front door, where Dee waited to wish her a safe journey. Linus's reluctance at having a part in any of this was obvious as he pulled on his coat and hat to accompany her to the barn.

"Be careful, dear," Dee admonished, giving Allie a quick, firm hug. "Don't trust anyone."

The remark brought a taut smile to Allie's lips. She had no intention of trusting anyone again.

She and Linus saddled the dun together. Allie laced the pommel bags to the horn of her saddle, then slid the double-barreled shotgun through its loop as Linus tied her bedroll behind the cantle. There was an awkward pause when they finished, then Linus went to the big front door and swung it open. Allie led the dun outside and stepped into the saddle before Linus could offer assistance. She adjusted her skirts, then raised her head to stare down the lane to the main road. For a minute, she almost didn't believe her eyes.

"I'll be damned," Linus said, coming up beside her. "He came back."

Allie's lips thinned, the brief flash of happiness that had exploded within her fizzling like a damp fuse. "So it would seem," she replied coolly, then glanced at Linus and forced a smile. "Thank you for all you've done, Mister Mattingly, and especially for all you offered to do."

"I'm just glad you've got a man to take care of you now," Linus said obliviously.

"Yeah, ain't I lucky," Allie replied sardonically, then heeled the dun toward the road.

To his credit, Johnny didn't ride in to meet her. He waited where he was, holding the bay's lead rope in his free hand. Allie kept the dun to a walk, her emotions swirling in confusion. She considered riding past him without acknowledgment, but decided she didn't want to play that game. When she was about ten feet away, she lightly twitched the reins and the dun immediately stopped. She let Johnny speak first; he owed her that much.

Placing both hands atop the flat horn of his saddle, Johnny said: "I decided since we've come this far together, we ought to finish together, too."

"That's big of you. I noticed you felt different last night, though."

"I won't argue with you, Allie. I was wrong to sneak out, and well down the road before I finally realized it. I came back to say I was sorry, and to tell you I'm taking the Utah road to Salt Lake City. Cutter will be waiting for me somewhere down the line. Probably Tuck will, too. You'd be a damn' fool to come along, but . . . hell, I couldn't think of anyone I'd rather have by my side."

Allie felt her breath catch in her throat, but, before she could examine her feelings too closely, something hard and angry slammed up inside of her, as solid as a brick wall. "You ran last night," she accused, cursing herself for the quaver in her voice. "How do I know you won't do it again?"

"I came back."

"But you ran first!"

"I can't change that, and I can't promise I won't make any more mistakes in the future." He dropped his eyes to the backs of his gloved hands; when he lifted them again, there was no doubt on his face. "A lot of folks will say I'm a fool and a coward to take a woman along on something like this, and maybe they're right. But I came back to give you that choice. It's not theirs to make, Allie, and it's not mine, either."

"You're not a coward," she said, then smiled in spite of her anger. "Maybe a fool, but definitely not a coward. All right, Johnny Montana, let's go to Salt Lake City. Together."

Chapter Thirty-Eight

They reached the lower slopes of the Malad Mountains by late morning and started the long, gentle climb toward the pass. It was a clear, beautiful day, and by noon the temperature was pushing forty degrees, the first time it had climbed that high since those long-ago days in Montana.

There was no warning to announce the bullet that slammed Johnny from his saddle. Not even a puff of gunsmoke, spied from the corner of his eye. One minute, he and Allie were riding along at a brisk trot. The next, he was tumbling from his saddle, the blast of the shot coalescing perfectly with the metallic *thunk* of lead striking steel.

He heard Allie's remote cry, echoing more rage than fear. Then his head and left shoulder struck the hard ground with a solid *whump,* and all he could do was lie there with his eyes shut, his limbs distant and unresponsive. After what seemed like hours but couldn't have been more than a few seconds, he heard the deep-throated bellow of Allie's shotgun, followed by the pounding of hoofs as their horses raced away. When he opened his eyes to call her back, he found himself alone, the road empty in both directions.

He was lying on his left side, his face half buried in a snowdrift. It took more effort than he would have expected to push himself onto his back. He felt better that way, with the full sky above and the sun warm on his face, but the silence was troubling. Cautiously he sat up and looked around. He was sitting, splay-legged, at the side of the road, surrounded by a thin forest of short, gnarled cedars. There was no sign of his ambusher, nor of Allie and the horses, save for their tracks heading south at a breakneck pace.

He ran his fingers tentatively over his face. They came away wet but clean, covered with snow rather than blood. A glance down across his body revealed nothing alarming, but as he sought an explanation for his spill, he gradually became aware of a steady throbbing above his right hip. Unbuttoning the greatcoat, he brushed it back to reveal a small, bloody spot just above the waistband of his trousers. Tugging the shirt tail out of the way, he muttered a low curse. The bullet had struck the handle of his Bowie knife a glancing blow, shattering the wood but deflecting harmlessly off the steel tang. There were several shallow cuts within the immediate vicinity, not to mention a sore spot the size of a cantaloupe that was already starting to discolor into a bruise, but he seemed otherwise unharmed.

Getting to his feet, Johnny shoved the shirt tail back into his trousers, then pulled the greatcoat over it. Although a couple of the deeper cuts continued to ooze some blood, his greater concern now was for Allie.

His rifles were still on the Appaloosa, but he had his revolvers—Lloyd's fancy, ivory-handled Remington and his own, older-model Beals. He carried the spare cylinders for the newer Remington in a pouch on his belt, but that was all the extra ammunition he had.

He found his hat and put it on. All around him, the land appeared empty, chillingly silent. It was as if he'd been dropped there by a giant eagle, a discarded morsel too tough to chew, too heavy to carry. Without a rifle he felt vulnerable, but he knew he couldn't stand there forever, waiting for someone to come along with an extra horse. Nor could he afford the time it would take to hike back to the Mattinglys for a fresh mount—

assuming they even had anything other than the chunky draft horse, Molly, that Linus kept in the barn.

With no other choice before him, Johnny pushed on. At this point, all he could do was hope that whoever had taken a shot at him had been alone, and that Allie was somewhere up ahead, safe and waiting for him to catch up. Because if not, the alternative would be too frightening to consider.

Chapter Thirty-Nine

With the dun's gait growing steadily rougher, Allie knew her run was about finished. Reluctantly she pulled the exhausted animal to a walk. The tawny-colored horse was stout-hearted, but it had been pushed too hard over the last few weeks, and no longer had the stamina to maintain the pace Allie had set for it. Meanwhile, the wiry grulla of her pursuer continued to narrow the gap between them. Less than five hundred yards back now, while the low mountain pass to the south looked as far away as ever.

With fresh tears coming to her eyes, Allie reined off the narrow road and into the trees. Distantly she heard the man on the grulla—a short, slim figure under a wide-brimmed black hat—shouting for her to stop, but she had no intention of giving up so easily. The dun may have reached the end of its rope, but she hadn't.

The trees were taller here than they'd been down below, where Johnny had been shot—pines rather than stubby cedars, growing close enough together to offer some cover. Maybe not enough to throw off pursuit, but enough, she hoped, to slow down her stalker, and give herself some time to figure a way out of this mess.

Allie hadn't intended to abandon Johnny, although she reasoned now that doing so had probably been for the best. She could still see the look of surprise on his face as he'd spun out of the saddle, but she had no way of knowing if the wound had been fatal.

She'd seen the puff of gunsmoke blossom from the cedars above them a split second before Johnny was hit, but her return fire had been a waste of powder and shot. Johnny's ambusher had been concealed atop a rocky ledge at least two hundred yards away, while Allie's return shot had barely disturbed some cedar boughs about half that distance up the side of the mountain.

Making matters worse was that the shotgun's blast, coming on top of Johnny's unexpected and unusual dismount, had spooked the Appaloosa into bolting, taking with it the firearms Allie needed if she was to stand her ground—the Hawken and Henry rifles. Although she'd taken off in immediate pursuit, the dun was no match for the spotted gelding. The Appaloosa had quickly outdistanced her, refusing even to slow down for the first mile. By then, Johnny's ambusher—now her pursuer—had retrieved his horse and was closing in from behind.

Allie hadn't dared take time to try to capture the panicky Appaloosa. With the darkly bearded Cut-throat already within rifle range, she'd slapped her heels to the dun's sides. Galloping past, she'd been oddly relieved when she glanced over her shoulder to see that she'd frightened both the Appaloosa and the hard-blowing bay into the timber along the road, out of the Cut-throat's path. That meant the rifles strapped to the Appaloosa's saddle were still available, if she could figure out a way to reach them.

Right now, doubling back through the trees seemed like her best bet. Yet as she guided her mount deeper into the pines, another problem reared its head. If the man on the grulla couldn't see her, she couldn't see him, either. Had she thrown him off by dodging back to the north, or had he heard or caught sight of her through the trees and adjusted his own course accordingly? If he was following her tracks, Allie figured she stood a good chance of finding the Appaloosa and retrieving one of the rifles. But if he tried to head her off in the forest, then it would be anyone's guess.

Keeping the dun to a walk, Allie wedged the shotgun's checkered steel butt plate between her foot and the side of her stirrup and hurriedly reloaded the right-hand barrel, the one she'd emptied at the ledge when Johnny was shot. The Colt was still in her pocket, all six chambers capped and ready to fire.

She flinched when a mountain jay burst through the trees in front of her, then forced herself to relax, looking behind her for some sign of the man on the grulla. It was only at the last instant that the unexpectedness of the startled bird's flight rang a warning in her mind. She whirled in the saddle just as a club-sized chunk of dead pine spun out of the trees toward her. Although she raised an arm defensively, she couldn't avoid the blow entirely. The wood cracked sharply against her elbow, and the shotgun slid out of her nerveless fingers. It fell into the snow, sliding several yards downhill before coming to rest against a lichen-covered boulder.

With a startled cry, Allie threw herself from the horse's back and scooted after it. She could hear the Cut-throat's swift approach through the trees—the snap of dead branches, the crunch of trampled the snow—but dared not take time to look around. She scooped the long gun into her hands, cocking both hammers even as she spun around to face her attacker. But as her finger sought a trigger, a second blow crashed into the side of her head, and she was flung into darkness.

Chapter Forty

A sense of heaviness settled over Johnny as he knelt beside the tracks coming out of the cedars—a single set of hoof prints, turning so abruptly onto the path of Allie's fleeing dun that the horse's rear legs had nearly slid out from under it in the snow. Now the rider, whoever he was, was obviously in pursuit, matching the dun's reckless gait with his own.

"One horse," Johnny murmured, raising his eyes to the shallow notch of the Malad summit, still many miles away. "One horse, one rider."

That was heartening to an extent, but not completely reassuring. He was glad they hadn't stumbled onto the whole gang, but he also knew it would take only one determined individual to bring down their plans. It all depended upon the identity of the unknown horseman, and how badly he wanted them.

How badly he wanted Allie.

Johnny's expression was grim as he pushed to his feet. The road stretched before him in a long, uphill grade for maybe a mile before it dipped over a shoulder of the mountain and disappeared. Doggedly he bent to the task. It was tough going in the deeper snows of the low mountain range, and he had to stop more than once just to catch his breath.

It was a couple of hours later when Johnny came to a break in the trail and stopped. Two sets of prints turned off here, while two more continued south along the road at the same perilous gait they'd maintained ever since he'd been shot out of his saddle.

The tracks leading into the trees intrigued him. Stepping off the road with one hand cautiously gripping a holstered revolver, Johnny eyed the snowy trail closely. It led up the middle of a shallow gully that came off the mountain above him. In the spring, the gully would run full tilt with melt, but at this time of year it was little more than a broad, dry trace under its blanket of snow.

Johnny followed the path uphill for several yards, then stopped and whistled loudly. An answering nicker came back almost immediately. Johnny whistled again, then called for the Appaloosa to show itself. A couple of minutes later, the spotted gelding's head poked out from behind a cedar tree eighty yards away, its small ears pricked forward curiously.

Grinning, Johnny said: "Come on down here. I've been looking for you."

The Appaloosa pushed past the small cedar and picked its way down the gully, stopping only when it was close enough to push its head gently against Johnny's chest. Johnny scratched the trimmed bridle path behind the gelding's ears affectionately. Then a branch snapped above him and his hand dropped to the ivory-handled Remington, but it was only the bay, stepping out of the trees like a small cow elk, its nose high to test the wind. The smaller horse stopped to whicker its own tentative greeting.

Johnny's relief was immeasurable. "Come on!" he called. "I've been looking for you, too."

The bay was a little more timid than the Appaloosa, but by the time Johnny had returned to the road and straightened the saddle, the smaller horse had come around. He straightened the bay's rigging, too, but didn't take time to check the panniers. Those sacks of yellow dust seemed suddenly trivial now, with

Allie in so much danger. Two minutes later, Johnny was mounted and riding hard for the Malad summit.

Chapter Forty-One

Gingerly Allie explored the small abrasion inside her lower lip with the tip of her tongue. Although brassy with the taste of blood, it seemed minor, and was barely swollen. Her arm hurt worse, but even that was more of an inconvenience than a handicap. Leaning from her saddle, she spat out a mouthful of pink saliva, then looked up with crooked grin. "Maybe he's hiding under that rock over there," she taunted her captor, jutting her chin toward a bucket-size stone sitting just off the road. "You know Johnny's part Indian? He could hide under a walnut shell if he wanted to."

Sam Hulse gave her baleful look. "I ain't tellin' you again to shut that trap. You don't, I'll shut it for you."

Allie forced herself to laugh spiritedly. "Gag me and you'll never find your way out of these mountains. This road forks up ahead more times than you can count. More times than I can count, in case you're no smarter than you look."

"I've been over that road before, gal, and there ain't no fork in it. Not that I'd need you tellin' me how to find my way out even if it did." Sam was scanning the broken country to the south, no doubt looking for some clue to Johnny's location. "I won't need a gag, either," he added menacingly. "I'll cut your damn' tongue out and feed it to the crows. Then we'll see how much you have to say."

"You wouldn't do that," she goaded the skinny killer. "Tuck would take a strap to your backside like you were a little boy."

"Shut up," Sam growled. "I'm tryin' to listen."

"Maybe the reason you can't hear anything is because your heart's beating too loud." Allie knew her own had been, when she'd awakened to find herself lashed snugly to the dun's saddle, her hands bound behind her back, her ankles strapped to the stirrups.

Hulse had told her his name right off, and Allie remembered Johnny saying he was a member of Otis Call's crew from Ruby City, the one who'd killed Johnny's friend, Russ Bailey. But it had been Hulse's next words that froze Allie to her core—his promise that Tuck was waiting for her in Malad City, and that he, Hulse, intended to deliver her into his hands before the moon set that night.

"It'll give you something to look forward to," Sam had jeered, slicing the rope around her shoulders with a clasp knife and pushing her upright in the saddle. He made the threat to intimidate her, but, instead, it had given her a goal. To drive Sam Hulse into enough of a rage to murder her before they reached Malad.

Retying her wrists to the saddle horn, Hulse had added: "You can ride like a man if you can stay awake, or I can put the ropes back on and let the saddle horn punch you in the guts until you puke."

"You can do what you want, mister. Just remember that I intend to spit on your corpse before this is over."

"We'll see," Hulse had replied curtly as he replaced the dun's bridle with a makeshift halter and lead rope. That had been several hours ago. Since then, the sun had dropped behind the mountains to the west, plunging the Malad's east-facing slopes into rapidly cooling shadows.

Allie had been thoroughly confused as they wound their way through the trees, following game trails so faint she barely recognized them as such. It wasn't until they came out on the road and she recognized her old tracks in the snow that she finally realized where they were—back just above where Sam had ambushed Johnny. He'd completed an almost full circle to avoid the more sinuous wagon route. It was the tracks of two additional horses on the road, overlapping hers and Sam's, that brought the outlaw to an abrupt halt.

"Johnny," Allie breathed. She looked at Hulse, her eyes bright with new-found hope. "He's coming after you, Sammy. What are you going to do when he catches up?"

"He ain't caught up yet," Hulse replied, studying the tracks. "He ain't likely to, either, but maybe I ought to go ahead and put a gag in your mouth. That way, I can concentrate on slipping up behind him without your constant yapping."

"That ain't likely," she said, then continued the lie she'd begun earlier. "Johnny's part Indian. You couldn't get within a hundred yards of him without him smelling you." She wrinkled her nose and made a face. "Maybe not even that close. You stink pretty bad."

"Christ, lady, don't you ever shut up?" He tugged the dun up beside his grulla, then leaned close. "Listen to me, gal, I ain't gonna cut your throat, no matter how much you want me to or how much you push me. But I ain't gonna put up with this constant yammering, either. By God, you cork that mouth if you want to be able to scream when Tuck lays his hands on you."

Allie's face paled in spite of her resolve not to show weakness. "You don't know what Tucker's like, do you?" she said in a low voice.

Hulse leaned back, his expression almost sympathetic. "That's the sad part, lady. I do know what that son-of-a-bitch is like. That's why I won't turn you loose or kill you. If Tuck ever found out I did, he'd do worse to me than he plans to do to you." His expression softened. "I will say I'm sorry I caught you. If I'd known Montana wasn't dead or bad wounded, I'd have stayed behind to finish the job and let you go. At least then I'd have the gold, not to mention a legitimate excuse for your escape. Tuck wouldn't have liked it, but Brett would've backed me up. He wouldn't if I turned you loose now."

"He doesn't have to know."

"Likely he wouldn't, but I ain't gonna take that chance."

It took all the will Allie possessed to straighten her shoulders and pull herself together. It angered her that she'd momentarily lost control of her composure in front of Hulse, and she vowed not to let it happen again. Forcing a smile, she said: "Well, it doesn't matter. Johnny's still between us and Tucker, and he won't. . . ."

"You might as well forget that notion, too," Hulse interrupted. "Johnny Montana ain't no more a Indian than I am, but I don't plan to ride into a ambush the way he did." He jerked the dun's head up. "Let's get to ridin', gal. We can still make Malad before the moon sets if we hurry."

Allie had no more words left and, for the moment, precious little fight. They rode through what remained of the afternoon in silence and, close to the top, passed the point where Johnny had turned off the road to follow their tracks into the trees, where Allie had attempted to double back. She stared bitterly at the Appaloosa's prints in the snow. She knew that if Johnny stayed with their trail all the way, it would be hours before he exited the forested slopes and discovered himself back on the road near where he'd been shot—a broad and useless circle. Meanwhile, Sam was leading her south at a steady jog, the miles ticking off rapidly now that he'd decided to go on into Malad City for help.

"Me 'n' Brett and whoever else is down there can come back up here tomorrow and flush him out," Sam said, eyeing Johnny's tracks. He gave Allie an inscrutable look. "I reckon that'll give Tuck all the time he'll need with you."

Earlier that afternoon she would have told him to go to hell, but she lacked the energy for it now. Her hands, still bound to the saddle horn, ached and her toes tingled painfully from the cold and restricted circulation. Even if she could free herself, she didn't know how much good she would be able to do with her fingers swollen like tiny sausages.

It was full dark by the time they reached the summit, the sky so alive with twinkling stars it almost seemed to have its own pulse. The crisp night air needled her lungs, but she didn't complain and Hulse didn't stop. Far to the south, she caught sight of a cluster of lights in the middle of a broad valley, and knew she was looking at Malad City. Sam had promised that they would make the small community before moonset, and, as they started down the southern grade, Allie thought he was probably right. But instead of discouraging her further, that brief glimpse of isolated humanity renewed her determination, if not to survive, then at least to choose her own method of execution.

Allie studied Sam's narrow shoulders in the diffused light. In the last hour, he hadn't looked back more than three or four times. He was tired, and, with the end in sight, he seemed to be growing careless. The odds that he would remain that way were slim, but Allie reasoned slim was a lot better than none at all.

Quietly she bent forward until she could reach the rope around her wrists with her teeth. She didn't know how much good it would do. Even if she did manage to gnaw through those bindings, her ankles would still be tied to the stirrups. But she wouldn't give up. Not as long as even a flicker of life remained in her body.

The first strand of rope parted silently after less than twenty minutes of gnawing, and Allie reared back in surprise. Hulse glanced suspiciously over his shoulder, but she met his eyes with anger and kept her mouth shut. He turned back to face the southbound trail without speaking, rolling his shoulders as if to loosen his muscles. Allie's back was knotted from bending forward at such an unnatural angle, and her jaws were cramping, but her hopes had grown significantly with that first severed strand, and she was soon back at it.

Two more strands parted within the next half hour, but by then the agony in her cheeks had spread throughout her face, the muscles lumping up painfully along the narrow line of her jaw. Up ahead, Sam's head was bobbing sleepily; once, she even heard him snoring lightly as he rode along in a doze, allowing the grulla to pick its own path, set its own pace. Allie worked her chin back and forth, but she was too impatient to wait for the soreness to dissipate. Soon, she was back at it, her teeth sawing desperately at the rope's final strand. Just as it started to give, a snore caught in Sam's throat and he jerked awake.

Allie sat up quickly, ignoring the spasms of pain that lanced through her back. She kept her expression blank when he glanced back at her, but her spirits fell when he jerked his horse to a stop. "What the hell are you doing here?" he demanded.

For a moment, Allie didn't know what he was talking about. Then she heard a rough bark of laughter from behind her and twisted in the saddle to see a lanky form riding out of the ink-like shadows close to the pines.

"I've been waiting for you," Tuck said, kicking his horse forward. But as he drew near, Allie realized it wasn't Sam Hulse he was talking to. Coming alongside, he reached out to touch her wrists, half raw from her struggles with the rope.

"So close," he taunted hoarsely, his eyes searing into hers. Then he gave her wrists a hard, upward yank, testing the strength of the rope's remaining strand. Allie cried out involuntarily, her head snapping back in pain, and Tuck chuckled, breathing into her ear: "So wonderfully close, and, in the end, so horribly far."

Chapter Forty-Two

Otis threw his blankets back when he heard the town dogs start barking at the north end of the street. Although he knew anything could have set them off—a pack of wolves in the hills, a cougar prowling the tiny community's back lots—something inside of him rejected those simpler explanations. He rolled smoothly out of his bunk to strap on his gun belt and pull on his boots and hat. He was just thumbing his suspenders over his shoulders when the door to the cabin's single back room swung open and Brett stepped out, dressed and armed.

"What's the ruckus about?" Brett asked, pausing at the table where a coal-oil lamp sat unlit, a box of matches beside it. Although the cabin's interior was shadowy, several embers, gleaming like dusty rubies in the fireplace, illuminated the small front room clearly enough to see by. Outside, the clopping of hoofs entered the front yard, and they heard Tuck whoop loudly from the corral. Seconds later, the front door banged open and he tramped inside, dragging a smaller creature behind him on the end of a rope.

Otis's heart sank. He didn't know much about the Purcell woman, for all that Tuck had dwelled on her almost exclusively for the past couple of weeks. He wouldn't have even known her name if he hadn't overheard Jake Haws and Chico Sanchez talking about her. It was Chico who had once referred to her as a rabbit. Otis saw the resemblance immediately. In the dim light just before Brett lit the table lamp, she looked small and vulnerable, a rail-thin husk of a woman, already conquered. But as the light flared, Otis saw something in her eyes that Chico hadn't mentioned, and it brought a smile to his lips. It could be, he mused, that Allie Purcell wasn't the rabbit some of the boys thought she was.

Then Tuck grabbed her by the arm and jerked her to his side. "Whatcha lookin' at, boy?" he snarled at Otis.

Otis tried to force his smile away, but it wouldn't go, and suddenly he didn't care if it did or didn't.

"God dammit, you keep them black buck eyes off her, Call," Tuck warned, then darted a look to Cutter. "She's mine, Brett. You said I could have her."

"She's yours, Tuck," Brett replied mildly, then exchanged a look with Otis.

Otis had never seen Tuck fall this far before, his lust so perversely exposed for everyone to see. Perhaps it was the long wait, coupled with the fear that she might escape the broad loop they'd set for her. Or maybe it was just, as time went by, Tuck's illness was getting worse. Although neither of them had mentioned it when they heard Tuck in the corral earlier, sneaking a saddle onto his horse, Otis knew he and Brett had both hoped Tuck wouldn't come back, that perhaps Johnny Montana would do what neither of them had the gumption to do.

A second figure appeared at the door. Sam Hulse glanced once around the cabin, then said: "Howdy, Otis. Howdy, Brett."

Brett's eyes widened when he saw Hulse. "What are you doing here, and where's Montana?"

"Montana ain't far behind," Sam assured him, then nodded toward Allie. "I figure we can use her for bait."

"Bait!" Brett's chin jutted forward dangerously. "What the hell were you thinking . . . ?"

"What happened?" Otis asked, cutting in.

Sam stepped warily inside and closed the door. Keeping Brett in front of him, he quickly related the events of the previous afternoon. When he finished, Brett turned to Otis and Tuck. "It's up to us now, boys. Montana's outfoxed the others, but we can still run him down."

"Uhn-uhn," Tuck said, wrapping his arm around the woman's shoulders in a grotesque imitation of a lover's embrace. "You go after Montana yourselves, if that's what you want. Me 'n' the gal's stayin' here."

A look of contempt crossed Brett's face, but he didn't push it. Either he'd already recognized the futility of argument, or he just didn't want Tuck around any more. "All right, Tuck stays, but everyone else goes."

"Suits me," Otis said, pulling on his heavy bear-hide coat even as he headed for the door. Sam followed, both men eager to get away as quickly as possible—before the screaming started.

Chapter Forty-Three

Leaving the Hawken on his saddle, Johnny levered a stubby copper cartridge into the Henry's chamber, then made his way to the north wall of the Malad City Livery. It was a clear night, alive with stars, and he appreciated the deeper shadows next to the stable's thick log walls.

Out front, the deserted street seemed to echo with the clamorous baying of dogs. Johnny figured it had to be Tucker and Hulse who had set off the barking. The two men and Allie had been about twenty minutes ahead of him all night, so the timing would be right, although it surprised him that no one had come out to investigate, or yell for the dogs to shut up. Apparently Brett Cutter and his men had made the same impression on Malad as they had on southwestern Montana. As he'd ridden into town, Johnny hadn't spotted a single person on the street.

He paused at the livery's corner, his thumb resting atop the iron spur of the Henry's hammer. Hearing the low thud of approaching hoof beats, he cautiously peeked around the corner. Three men were coming down the middle of the street, heading north. Although it was too dark to make out their faces in the shadows under their hats, Johnny knew who they were. The man on the near side, wearing a shaggy coat that made him look as big as a bear, would be Otis Call. The one on the far end was Sam Hulse. And the man in the center, leading a leggy pack horse with a sturdy chest strapped to its back, was Brett Cutter.

Taking a deep breath, Johnny thumbed the Henry's hammer back to full cock. The three horsemen were less than fifty yards away when he stepped into the street. Otis cursed and jerked his horse to a stop. Cutter and Hulse followed suit.

"Who's there?" Cutter demanded, keeping a tight rein on his nervously dancing horse. "Identify yourself."

"I reckon you know who it is," Johnny replied. He walked forward deliberately, the Henry held ready in his hands.

Chapter Forty-Four

Allie thought her scream surprised her more than it did Tucker. She hadn't intended for it to slip out, even though she knew it had been building up inside of her ever since Tuck jerked the dun's lead rope out of Sam's hand on top of Malad summit. She'd held it in all the way down the mountain, and had considered herself still in control of her emotions when Brett Cutter left the cabin with the trunk of stolen gold. It wasn't until the door swung shut behind him that something inside her began to tear loose. Like pieces of a riverbank giving way to spring floods.

Even then, she'd resisted, swallowing back her fear, keeping her lips clamped tightly shut. The scream didn't break completely free until Tucker turned away from the door and started toward her, giving Allie her first clear view of his face in the lamplight.

She'd known all along that Tuck was evil, but she'd never seen it this evident before, his lust as ugly as a festering wound. This wasn't the Tom Tucker she'd known in Bannack. This was her worst nightmare come to life.

Allie's scream, short and startled though it was, brought a malevolent grin to the outlaw's face. He threw off his coat and hat and vest, tossed his gun belt after them, then shrugged out of his suspenders. He was tugging his shirt tail free when Allie started to sidle off. Laughing, Tuck pulled her back with the noose he'd put over her neck when he lifted her from the saddle.

He'd redone the knots on her wrists, too, loosening them so that circulation could return to her fingers, although he'd been quick to reassure her that kindness wasn't his motive.

"I don't want anything to be numb," he'd told her, rubbing her fingers gently, his breath warm on her cheeks, tinged with a stench that reminded her of death.

At the time, all Allie could do was stare straight ahead, sick with the knowledge that all her efforts had failed. She would die now. Not quick, from an angry man's gun, as she'd hoped—Hulse's fear of Tucker had proved too strong for that—but slowly, in pain and humiliation.

Her thoughts flitted briefly to Johnny but she knew he was too far away, that he would never find her in time. Despite his promises, he had failed her, too.

Tuck wouldn't, though. It was kind of ironic, Allie thought, that in the end, the only man she'd really been able to count on was the one who was about to kill her.

Sliding the blade of his knife between her wrists, Tuck severed the single remaining strand of hemp holding them together. Allie didn't try to flee. She knew that was what Tuck wanted. Instead, she let hands fall limply to her sides, while Tuck raised the blade to her cheek, drawing its tip gently down over the soft, sun-tanned flesh.

"God, I've been waiting for you," he breathed. "I thought I'd go crazy if you didn't come to me soon."

"I didn't come to you," Allie reminded him. "You came after me, remember?"

"It doesn't matter. I've been waiting for you for weeks, and now I have you. You reckon that'll make tonight any sweeter?" He turned her around almost gently, pulling off her makeshift cape and the heavy wool coat, then tossed them carelessly onto a rawhide-bottomed chair. Allie's gaze followed the coat enviously. Within its pockets resided what was probably her last chance—the Colt revolver Johnny had given her, and which Sam Hulse had failed to look for. The revolver had been bumping against her hip all day, a constant reminder of what might be possible if she could only free her hands for a few minutes. And assuming she could handle it. After having been bound for the last twelve hours, her fingers felt stiff and cumbersome.

"This'll take a while," Tuck informed her confidentially, nodding toward her hands. "I see by the way you're holding them that they still hurt. I want 'em limber again, able to feel."

"To feel what?"

"Everything." Allie's blood chilled; Tuck laughed. "Your face just turned pale, and you don't even know what I'm gonna do yet. Do you want to?"

"No." She edged ever so slightly toward her coat and cape. "Why don't you surprise me?"

His eyes brightened with joy. "You were so quiet on the way in that I thought you'd given up, but you haven't." Then his expression changed subtly. "The same old Ellen, so damn' cocky and smug. You always did think you were better than me, didn't you?"

Allie froze. "You've got the wrong woman, mister," she said tonelessly. "My name's Allie, not Ellen."

"Don't," he said, shaking his head warningly. "Don't fight me."

"Jesus, you know, don't you?" Allie whispered with new understanding. "You know I'm not Ellen."

But there was another force involved now. Something that had been there all along. A piece from his past, all withered and charred, but clamoring to be free, given control. Then Tuck shook his head and stepped back, almost staggering. He looked at Allie and took a deep, ragged breath. "It won't be so bad," he promised softly. "Hell, with luck, you'll be dead by morning."

Allie darted for her coat, the revolver pocketed there, but

Tuck was quicker. She figured he might be, so, as he lunged to head her off, she veered unexpectedly toward the table. Tuck yelped in surprise as his arms swept through the empty air. He whirled and his eyes widened as she caught the lamp on the table with the back of her hand and sent it crashing to the floor at his feet.

"You bitch!" he yelled as the fragile glass exploded, splattering his legs with coal oil. Yellow flames skittered quickly across the floor on one side of the room. He jumped back, slapping at the flames already crawling up his legs, and Allie, knowing he had latched the front door, scurried into the back room and slammed the door.

There was no light save for what crept in under the door. She could hear Tuck cursing hysterically as she crossed the room to a small, shuttered window above the rumpled bed. Her fingers clawed at the latch even as the crackling flames in the front room grew louder. Smoke began to seep under the door. She palmed the latch back and jerked the shutter open. The window was small, but she thought she could wiggle through. She was running her fingers along the top of the frame in search of a handhold when the door crashed open and Tuck stumbled inside.

Flames were swirling up the outlaw's legs, illuminating his face with an unearthly glow. Allie moaned in terror as he lumbered toward her. She tried to dive headfirst through the window, but the footing on the bed was spongy and she lost her balance. Before she could make a second attempt, Tuck wrapped his hands around her waist and yanked her back.

Allie grunted as she bounced off the grass-filled mattress and onto the floor. Tuck fell on top of her. She could feel the heat of his burning clothes through her own heavy skirt, but couldn't tell if he did. Tom Tucker had become a man possessed.

In the front room, coal oil-fueled tongues of fire chewed

hungrily at the cabin's log wall, and columns of smoke whirled and dipped like mutant dancers. Tuck's fingers circled her throat. Allie batted them away. "Hold still, you little whore!" he shouted.

"Get off me. We're burning."

"We'll burn in hell together for what we did." Tuck's eyes blazed with renewed fury. "You didn't think I'd find you, Ellen, but I did. A dozen times I've found you, but this time, you won't get away."

"Off . . . me . . . you sick . . . bastard," Allie gasped. She curled her hand into a fist and struck him in the cheek. Tuck barely blinked. His fingers fumbled at her throat, thumbs pressing inward. She tried to twist free but his grip was too powerful.

"Never again," he grated. "Never again."

Darkness fluttered at the edges of Allie's vision. Blindly she jabbed at Tuck's face with her fingers, clawed at it with her nails. He screamed when they found his eyes, then screamed again as she raked at them with desperate viciousness. Through the smoke, she saw him grab his face, saw blood seeping between his fingers, and, with everything she had left, she hit him flush on the chin. Tuck's head rocked back and, quick as a cat, Allie scrambled free.

Roaring hoarsely Tuck grabbed for her. Still on her hands and knees, she kicked back savagely, the heel of her shoe connecting forcefully with Tuck's elbow. He howled as his arm gave out from under him with a sickening crunch. Dropping to her belly where the smoke wasn't quite so suffocating close to the floor, she crawled awkwardly into the front room. Her head bumped into something heavy and solid and she looked up to see her coat draped across the chair where Tuck had thrown it. She reached for it just as Tuck's fingers closed around her ankle.

"God damn you!" Allie shrieked, yanking the coat off the chair. She could make out the hazy features of his face, the bloody, mushy socket where his left eye had been, the dripping ball of his right eye.

"Bitch," he rasped.

"Bastard," she choked, frantically searching for the pocket that held her revolver even as Tuck dragged her closer. His hand locked on her knee, then her thigh. Allie's fingers raced over the coarse material. She could feel the Colt through the fabric but couldn't find the pocket's opening. Then Tuck's hand locked on her waist and he jerked her under him. Flames from his clothing ignited Allie's heavy outer skirt. His remaining eye glared into hers. He tried to brush the coat aside, but Allie held it tight, keeping its protection between her and the flames devouring Tuck's clothing, blistering his flesh.

"I was gonna kill you," he croaked. "Gonna make it easy for you, but not now. Now we'll burn together, and it'll finally be over. You and me, and nobody will ever know what we did."

He tried to laugh, didn't have enough air. Smoke was everywhere; flaming embers fell from the rafters like brimstone. Allie's hand found the pocket of her coat and dipped inside, but something was wrong. Her fingers skidded lightly over the revolver's grips but were unable to grasp them. "I hate you," she whispered, her strength fading.

"That's funny," Tuck replied, his fingers suddenly loosening, "because I've always loved you. Always."

She pushed him away. He sprawled limply across the floor at her side, his breath rasping like a file drawn across seasoned oak. Allie squirmed free of her burning outer skirt before the flames could eat through to the light summer dress she wore under it. She rolled onto her stomach, but had lost all sense of direction and had no idea where the front door was. Then her arms gave out and her face struck the floor. She heard Tuck behind her. "Ellen!" he called, but she'd already left him.

Chapter Forty-Five

Johnny stepped into the street, the Henry cocked and ready to fire.

"Who's there?" Brett Cutter demanded. "Identify yourself."

"I figure you know who it is," Johnny replied.

"Montana?"

"Owens. John Owens."

Cutter was silent as he digested this new piece of information. Then he nodded sagely. "Of course, but they call you Johnny Montana."

"I wanted you to know the real name of the man who's going to kill you tonight," Johnny replied.

"Bold words, Montana, but a sucker's bet if you believe them." A scowl creased the bandit's face. "Who are you, Montana? What are you? A lawman? A bounty hunter?"

"I'm a prospector, Cutter. You know that."

"I don't believe you. I turned nearly two dozen men loose on you, Montana, every one of them a professional. Yet here you stand. No ordinary man could do that."

"You're wrong about that, Cutter," Johnny said. "I'm just a tin-pan wanting to hang onto what's mine. When I got tired of being run all over the country, I stopped. That's when I discovered that Cutter's Cut-throats were just men, too, though not one of them fit to wipe the muck off Russ Bailey's shoes. Your man Hulse killed Russ up in Ruby City a few weeks ago. Russ was my friend."

"You murdered my brother," Cutter charged. "Gunned him down like a stray dog."

"I haven't killed anyone who wasn't trying to kill me first. That includes your brother."

"You think you're the equal of me, Montana, but you're not. You're not even close." He turned to the black man at his side. "Kill him," he said bluntly.

"I reckon not," Otis Call replied mildly. He was watching Johnny closely, but there was no animosity in his posture, and his wrists remained folded casually over his saddle horn. "That was you up there in Ruby City that night, wasn't it?" he asked. "Standing in the shadows beside McCarty's Livery."

"How'd you know?" Johnny said.

Otis shrugged. "I couldn't rightly say, but I've known it for a long time. Knew it that night when I saw you standing in front of The Bucket Saloon." He glanced at Cutter and, after a pause, shook his head. "Naw, I ain't gonna buck him for you, Brett. It was your brother he killed, not mine."

"By God, you'll kill him, Otis, or I'll. . . ."

"You'll what?" Call demanded sharply, and Brett had no answer to that. Otis gathered his reins. "I don't want any part of this, Montana. Let me ride out of here and our fight will be finished."

"The gold stays," Johnny said.

Call glanced at the pack horse standing behind Cutter, the trunk strapped atop its sawbuck, and suddenly laughed. "I reckon so," he said, then he reined his buckskin around and rode off without even an *adiós*.

Johnny turned to Russ's killer. "What about you, Hulse? You want to ride out of here under those conditions, or do you intend to stand with Cutter?"

"The hell with you, Montana." Hulse looked at Cutter. "The hell with you, too. We could've been in San Diego by now if not for you and Tucker, all of us rich and warm."

"We can still be rich and warm," Cutter said, his voice edgy, tinged with worry. "Stand with me, Sam, and we'll split the gold between us. Run, and I swear I'll hunt you down. You and Otis both."

Hulse only laughed. "Don't worry, Cutter, I ain't goin' nowhere without my gold." Then his hand dived for his revolver, and Johnny snapped off a round from the hip.

Johnny's bullet struck Hulse in the shoulder, spilling him from his saddle. With a startled shout, Cutter palmed his Colt, hurrying off a round that zinged past Johnny's elbow just as Johnny ducked behind the shelter of a nearby anvil stump. Dropping the Henry as he scrambled behind the massive, waist-high stump, Johnny drew the ivory-handled Remington. One of Cutter's bullets struck the anvil above his head, spraying him with a fine mist of hot lead. Johnny cursed and rolled onto his side, pushing the Remington far enough past the edge of the stump to fire three times in rapid succession.

On the street, Cutter's horse was crow-hopping wildly, while Brett shouted threats at his mount and tried to keep his revolver fixed on the anvil. Hulse had staggered to his feet and was holding his pistol in his left hand. Johnny fired once at the weaving outlaw, then lunged clear of the stump, firing twice more as he raced for the livery.

Hulse's bullets followed Johnny like angry hornets, shearing off flakes of wood from the stable's wall, hissing past his shoulders. But Hulse was encumbered by the wound in his shoulder, forced to use his weak-side hand, and his shots went wide, allowing Johnny to duck past the livery's corner.

With his back to the wall, Johnny fished a loaded and capped cylinder from thc pouch on his belt. He dropped the ivory-handled revolver's rammer part way down, then pulled the base pin half out and rolled the spent cylinder free of the frame, letting it fall to the ground. He replaced it with the fresh cylinder, snapped the pin and rammer back into place, then pulled his old Remington-Beals from its holster. With both pistols cocked and ready to rip, he eased back to the livery's corner.

Cutter was nowhere in sight, but Hulse was still standing in the middle of the street. Johnny's right eye had barely cleared the edge of the wall when the wounded gunman opened up, his bullets peppering the thick logs in front of Johnny's nose.

Johnny swore and stepped back. Then, taking a deep breath, he spun past the livery's corner with both Remingtons raised shoulder high, firing methodically one after the other as he advanced toward the street.

Hulse yelled as a slug tore into the flesh of his upper arm, then stumbled backward when a third bullet struck him in the chest. "Cutter!" Hulse cried weakly. "Damn you, Brett."

Johnny stopped and slid his right foot forward a half step. He sighted down the long, octagon barrel of the ivory-handled Remington.

"You son-of-a-bitch," Hulse wheezed to Johnny. He raised his revolver, but never got another chance to fire it. Johnny squeezed the Remington's trigger, and Hulse grunted loudly as the bullet slammed into his heart. He dropped to his knees, then toppled to the side, his revolver slipping harmlessly from his fingers.

Johnny immediately began backing toward the shelter of the livery, his eyes searching desperately for Cutter. He'd almost reached the corner when he heard the Appaloosa nicker from the trees behind the stable. He whirled and fired, so fast he was breathing powder smoke almost before he knew he'd pulled the trigger.

In the deeper shadows near the rear of the stable, Brett Cutter took three small steps forward, into the pale light of the stars. His revolver tumbled from his fingers but he paid it no heed.

"Who . . . who are you?" he asked a final time. Then his knees buckled and he pitched face-first to the snowy ground.

Chapter Forty-Six

Johnny was guided to the cabin at the south edge of town by the flames licking at the belly of the night sky. Smoke curled thickly into the darkness, and glowing embers darted like fireflies in the updrafts. Dismounting at the corral, he hitched the Appaloosa, the bay, and Cutter's pack horse carrying the trunk of gold beside Allie's dun, then walked over to where Allie was sitting in the snow. Tears streaked her cheeks, and her heavy outer skirt was gone. The summer dress she'd worn under it was scorched near the ankles, the flesh above her shoes red and painful-looking. Small burn marks spotted the backs of her hands, and a deeper one puckered the flesh under her right eye. She looked up when Johnny approached, her voice raw and skillet-hard.

"Where have you been, Johnny Montana?"

"Owens," he said quietly, staring toward the burning cabin's open door to where a man lay blistered and blackened almost beyond recognition. "Tucker?" he asked.

"I don't know." She looked around. "Where is everyone . . . the townspeople?"

"I figure they're still staying low. I can't say as I blame them. Cutter's bunch wasn't an easy crowd to live with."

"No, they weren't." With his assistance, she struggled to her feet. "Was it you?" she asked in a croaking voice.

"Was what me?"

"Was it you who pulled me out of the fire?"

He shook his head. "Are you sure you didn't crawl out on your own?"

She said—"No."—but Johnny thought she still looked kind of dazed. "I remember. . . ." She frowned, glancing around. "I remember . . . a black man."

Johnny started to reach for his revolver, then let his hand fall away. "Was it Otis Call?"

"I guess it could've been anybody," she admitted. A cough racked her body, nearly bending her double. Johnny put a hand on her back to steady her until she stopped. He left it there when she straightened up.

"I saw a sign down the street that claims they rent rooms," he said gently. "We'll stay here a few days, until you're feeling better."

"We can't forget the others," she reminded him. "Chico Sanchez, Jake Haws . . . no telling how many more."

"I haven't forgotten them," he assured her, but he was remembering what Linus Mattingly had said to him on the night he left the relay station.

They're afraid of you, Johnny. They'll avoid you if they can.

And who knew, maybe Mattingly was right.

"Let's worry about the others when they show up," he told Allie. "Right now, you need to take care of those burns." His hand moved on her back, rubbing it gently. "We need to take care of them . . . together."

Allie didn't immediately answer. Then, slipping an arm around his waist, she leaned close so that he could help support her. "I think that might be a good idea, Johnny Owens," she agreed.

ABOUT THE AUTHOR

Michael Zimmer grew up on a small Colorado horse ranch, and began to break and train horses for spending money while still in high school. An American history enthusiast from a very early age, he has done extensive research on the Old West. His personal library contains over 2,000 volumes covering that area west of the Mississippi from the late 1700s to the early decades of the 20th Century. In addition to perusing first-hand accounts from the period, Zimmer is also a firm believer in field interpretation. He's made it a point to master many of the skills used by our forefathers, and can start a campfire with flint and steel, gather, prepare, and survive on natural foods found in the wilderness, and has built and slept in shelters as diverse as bark lodges and snow caves. He owns and shoots a number of Old West firearms, and has done horseback treks using 19th Century tack, gear, and guidelines. Zimmer is the author of five Western novels, and his work has been praised by *Library Journal* and *Booklist,* as well as other Western writers. Jory Sherman, author of *Grass Kingdom,* writes: "He [Zimmer] takes you back in time to an exciting era in U.S. history so vividly that the reader will feel as if he has been over the old trails, trapped the shining streams, and gazed in wonder at the awesome grandeur of the Rocky Mountains. Here is a writer to welcome into the ranks of the very best novelists of today or anytime in the history of literature." And Richard Wheeler, author of *Goldfield,* has said of Zimmer's fourth novel, *Fandango* (1996): "One of the best mountain man novels ever written." Zimmer lives in Utah with his wife, Vanessa, and two dogs. His website is www.michael-zimmer.com. His next Five Star Western will be *Wild Side of the River.*